THE KEEPER

DARRAGH MARTIN

Little Island

The Keeper

First published by Little Island 2013
This edition published 2015

Little Island
7 Kenilworth Park
Dublin 6W
Ireland

www.littleisland.ie

Cover design by Pony and Trap
Typesetting by Robert Mirolo
Printed in Poland by Drukarnia Skleniarz

Little Island receives financial assistance from
The Arts Council (An Chomhairle Ealaíon), Dublin, Ireland.

10 9 8 7 6 5 4 3 2 1

To Ita and Gerard

About the author

Darragh grew up in Dublin, where he often daydreamed about the DART train going somewhere more magical than Howth Junction.He was given a Fulbright Scholarship to develop his writing in 2006 and has been living in New York City since, where he teaches literature at Columbia University, writes plays and admires trees. Darragh is represented by the Lisa Richards Agency and has a website at www.darraghmartin.com. This is his first novel for children.

In case you're not Irish

Just in case you find some of our names and words unusual, there is a list at the back of the book that gives you the meanings of Irish words used in this book and tells you how to pronounce them.

THE ISLAND OF T

NORTH WEST VOLCANOS

DROICHEAD AN C

FIRE F

FOREST OF SHADO

DRAGON'S COVE

THE DESOLATE DESERT

SLIABH NA GAOITHE

THE HOULI

TO DUBLIN

Chapter 1
The Strange Book

Ordinary books don't move. Ordinary books are quite happy waiting to be picked up. You could leave an ordinary book somewhere uncomfortable – at the bottom of a dark schoolbag or in the middle of a shop window and it wouldn't dare budge, even if it had to sneeze. Nobody had told the Book of Magic this, though, so it jumped into Oisín's hands without so much as a flap of its pages.

Oisín stared at the dusty little book in his hands. It fitted snugly in the cup of his palms like a bird that had found just the right size of nest. It seemed too tattered to be opened, let alone to jump. Oisín looked around Granny Keane's spare room, hoping to find a clue about where it had come from. It wasn't easy. Granny Keane's idea of a spare room was more a place to keep all her extra stuff and less a room to house her grandchildren while their parents were away on business. The small room was filled with clutter: an old sewing machine, boxes full of hats, stacks and stacks of books towering from the floor to the ceiling. Stephen, Oisín's older brother, was sprawled on one of the two camp beds, looking grumpy even while he slept.

Oisín loved staying at his granny's house because there were so many strange books to read. Some of them had yellow pages and more wrinkles than she had. Some of the encyclopedias were as heavy as boulders. Others had peculiar titles, like *The Terrible Sheep Vampires of Clonmacnoise*, which Oisín had been planning to read until the other, little book had jumped into his hands. *Not jumped*, Oisín thought, as he searched for a gap in the stack. Fallen, it must have fallen. It couldn't be that special there wasn't even a title on its dusty green cover. Oisín placed it on top of the stack and picked up *The Lives of Great Inventors* instead.

'Dogbreath! Stop making noise, I'm trying to sleep.'

Stephen had woken up. Stephen was fifteen and far too old to be spending time at Granny Keane's, in his opinion.

'I'm not doing anything,' Oisín protested.

'You're reading.'

Oisín tried to read very quietly. Sometimes older brothers weren't worth annoying, especially when they had stronger punching arms than you.

'I can hear the pages turning!' Stephen shouted as he threw his pillow across the room.

Oisín closed his book. Sometimes older brothers were just asking to be annoyed.

'Yeah, well, I can't sleep with you snoring. Just because you look like a walrus doesn't mean you have to sound like one.'

This time it was one of Stephen's smelly runners that came flying across the room. Oisín was safely behind a stack of books when it whacked against the wall. After twelve years of being Stephen's brother, Oisín was very good at ducking.

Oisín flicked through the book he had picked up. He could have had an older brother like Wilbur Wright, who could have helped him invent airplanes. Or an older brother like Jacob Grimm, with whom he could have written fairy tales. Instead, he had Stephen.

'Nerdling, stop making noise.'

'I'm not doing anything.'

'You're breathing!'

Oisín turned his page as loudly as he could. Stephen's other runner flew across the room.

Then a funny thing happened. Just as the runner was about to hit Oisín in the head, there was the little book again, up off the stack and batting the runner back towards Stephen. Oisín caught his breath. Somehow *The Lives of Great Inventors* had fallen to the floor and the little book was sitting back in his hands as if nothing had happened.

A breeze from Dublin Bay drifted through the open window. That was all it was, Oisín thought, both relieved and disappointed. A regular old book had just been picked up by the wind and bumped into Stephen's shoe. Oisín turned back to the pile of books, about to return it to the top.

And then the book shifted slightly in his hands, like a cat turning into the sun.

Until that June morning, Oisín Keane's world had been pretty normal, for a twelve-year-old. He slouched his way to school most mornings and squabbled with his brother and sister most evenings. Often he wished for things to be a bit more exciting. But the ghost he heard in the attic usually turned out to be his mother looking for Christmas decorations. Or the new teacher he was sure was a zombie ate egg salad sandwiches rather than brains for lunch. This was the first time that anything exciting had actually happened to him. Something that could only be magic. Oisín felt his body prickle like it was waking up, as if magic was the missing limb he never knew he had.

'What are you looking at, Wordworm?'

Stephen was out of bed and standing over his shoulder.

'Nothing,' Oisín said quickly, jamming the book into his hoodie pocket. Whatever it was, he was pretty sure he didn't want to share it with Stephen.

Stephen squinted at him suspiciously.

'I hope you're not using this,' he said, reaching for his deodorant.

Oisín almost laughed. As if he could be bothered with deodorant when there was the chance of magic in the world!

'What are you smiling at? You're not to read any more of Geriatric Barbie's books. You're already enough of a freak.'

'Don't call Gran that,' Oisín responded.

'I'm the eldest, so I can call her what I want, Shortsquirt.'

'You mean you're the stupidest, you lily-livered loon.'

Granny Keane had a copy of William Shakespeare's *Collected Works* and Oisín liked hurling random insults from it at Stephen, who hated things he didn't understand. The truth was that Oisín didn't understand most of the insults either, but Stephen didn't need to know that.

'I've told you to stop reading that book,' Stephen fumed. 'And I am not a lily-whatever –'

'Livered loon!' Granny Keane said, entering just as Stephen was about to strangle Oisín. 'Oh, I did some Shakespeare in my day, yes: 'Lord, what fools these mortals be!' I did like that one. A Midsummer Night's Dream, wasn't that the one?'

It wasn't surprising that Granny Keane would like a play about dreaming. She wasn't like the other grannies that lived in Clontarf. She didn't have any old lady coats or smell like hospital and she never made soup out of chicken bones like Granny Keogh did. She didn't even watch *The Late Late Show*, because it clashed with her Bollywood dance lessons. In fact, she *did look a bit* like an older Barbie doll. She wore brightly coloured beads and scarves and her long white hair fell down to her waist. Though he couldn't be sure, Oisín thought he felt the book shift in his pocket as she entered. If Granny Keane noticed anything unusual, she didn't let on.

'I always wanted to play Othello or Hamlet instead of those simpering ladies,' she continued in a floaty voice. 'I could never find the right female part.'

'Shakespeare didn't write any for crazy old ladies?' Stephen said under his breath.

'Why don't you weed the garden this morning, Stephen?' Granny Keane said in a sharper voice. 'It's getting so full of nettles I don't know what to do.'

That was the thing about Granny Keane. She might seem very dreamy, but she always got her way.

'Sure thing, Gran,' Stephen said, trying to hide the grumble in his voice.

'And you must help me sort through these books, Oisín. Grab a stack and come on up to the study as soon as you've had your breakfast. I've got so many on Pilates and Mediterranean ceramics and how to make the perfect origami garden and…'

Granny Keane was already off up the spiral staircase towards her study, where there were even more books and less space. Ordinarily, Oisín would have been happy to spend the morning helping her sort through which books she wanted to sell. Now, though, there was only one book that he wanted to look at and he didn't think he could do so while everybody else was around. Stephen was already eating the last of the cornflakes when Oisín got downstairs, leaving Oisín with Granny Keane's 'special' carrot and beetroot porridge. By the time he got to the study, his little sister, Sorcha, was already there. She had just turned seven and was more interested in practising ballet than in sorting through stacks of dog-eared paperbacks and faded cookbooks.

The morning passed slowly enough. Sorcha kicked up dust while she practised a pirouette. Out the window, Stephen was weeding in the garden, attacking nettles as if they were related to him. A stream of cars were headed into the Saturday shops in town. The tide was out and the rocks on the sand gulped up the sun while they could. In many ways, it was just like most weekends that Oisín spent at Granny Keane's.

Except for the little book in his hoodie. Oisín could sense it, even if he couldn't see it, and knew he had to examine it. Every time he tried to look at it, though, Granny Keane seemed to be behind him, even when he went down to the bedroom to fetch more books.

It was a couple of hours before he got his chance. Sorcha was getting more ambitious and knocked over several piles of books as she practised a leap.

'Oops!' she said as the books tumbled over like dominoes.

'Bit of fun for them,' Granny Keane said cheerily, stooping down to sort through the chaos.

'I'll get them,' Oisín said, crawling behind the large armchair in the corner to rescue some adventurous Charles Dickens paperbacks.

It was the perfect hiding place. Oisín pulled out the little book from his pocket and opened it carefully. He was reminded of his class visit to see the Book of Kells. Each page was filled with elaborate drawings and small handwriting in deep inks of different colours. Oisín pressed the book up to his nose, but he still couldn't read the writing. He shook it. Nothing happened. Maybe he'd imagined it. Maybe it had been the wind after all.

He was about to put the book back down when suddenly the pages flipped through to the very first page. It was blank except for a small picture of a creature Oisín didn't recognise, something with the head of a deer, bird feathers and a coiled-up tail like a snake. Oisín was trying to figure out what it was when it opened its mouth and out came its tongue, in ink as green as the creature itself. As the tongue slid across the page, it started to shift, changing into letters in front of Oisín's eyes until he was looking at a tiny inscription. He was surprised to see that it was in English and he could just make out the words. His heart gave a sudden loop. There, handwritten in dark green ink, were the ten *little words* that would change everything:

For Oisín Keane, the Keeper of the Book of Magic

What Oisín didn't see was the creature outside. A large raven was perched on the window ledge, as dark as shadows. It looked curiously in at the Book of Magic and the small boy holding it. With a glint of triumph in its glittering green eyes, it flapped its wings and began its long journey.

Chapter 2
Pearse Station

At first, Oisín didn't notice the ravens in Pearse Station. He was far too busy looking furtively at the Book of Magic. He turned it over and over in his hands like a pebble, waiting for it to do something. Maybe the Book would make him fly. Or turn Stephen into a rhinoceros. Or maybe it would just flip through its pages again. Instead, it remained perfectly still in his hands, as if it was the most ordinary thing in the world.

It wasn't, though. The Book was special and he was its Keeper. Oisín could feel its magic like a small pulse coming from its pages. He wasn't sure what being a keeper *meant*, but he liked the sound of it. It made him feel that it was OK to hold the Book, even when a small pang of guilt in his chest told him that he really should tell Granny Keane about it. She had said they could keep any book they wanted, so technically he wasn't stealing it.

Oisín had *meant* to tell her. But first Granny Keane had been very busy bundling her books together so she could sell them in town. Then they had been traipsing across Dublin looking for a second-hand bookshop that might want some of Granny Keane's unique selection. Even when they were having lunch in the Powerscourt Centre, it hadn't seemed like the right time. Now they were sitting on a bench in Pearse Station, waiting to take the DART home to Raheny. Oisín thought that he should say something. But something kept his mouth shut, some sense of a secret that was his alone.

Oisín was trying to decide what to do when he noticed a raven with green eyes. The Book of Magic shifted slightly, and something clicked in Oisín's brain: it wasn't the first raven he'd seen that day. There had been one staring in the window in Easons bookshop on O'Connell Street. He'd seen several ravens perched on Daniel O'Connell's statue across the road and even more sitting on the steps of the Ha'penny Bridge. He'd even seen one by the piano in the Powerscourt Centre, as if it had every right to be there amongst the pots of tea and lemon squares. Now that he thought about it, all of them had the same eyes, as green as grass, which he was sure ravens weren't supposed to have. A strange feeling came over him, as if somehow they knew about the Book.

'I think I might give my sandwich to the birdie,' said Sorcha. 'He looks hungry.'

Oisín turned to his sister. Sorcha was not a big fan of Granny Keane's banana curry and chickpea sandwiches.

'I don't know if he'll be able to eat that,' Oisín said quietly. 'Why don't you have a few more bites and then I'll finish it?'

It seemed like the sort of thing an older brother should say, even if the sandwiches weren't exactly his favourite kind either.

'No, the birdie looks hungry! Here you go, little birdie. Ow! He *pecked* me!'

Oisín sprang to his feet but the raven had already gone. Sorcha looked down at her ankle where the raven had pecked her. Her face faltered as if she couldn't decide whether or not to cry.

'Don't worry, Sorcha,' Oisín said, putting his hand on her shoulder. He hadn't read a book about comforting little sisters, but this was always what his mother did.

Sorcha's lip was still trembling, though, and Oisín knew he only had seconds.

'Here, why don't you sit down and I'll get you some Maltesers?'

Maltesers were Sorcha's favourite sweets, so she nodded her head and limped back to the bench. Oisín was sure his mother would have been fretting about tetanus shots if she'd been there, but Granny Keane didn't seem too bothered. She was staring into space, a box of books that nobody wanted to buy on the bench beside her. Stephen was playing a game on his mobile phone, hoping that none of his friends had seen him walking around town with his granny.

Oisín's hands shook as he put the coins into the vending machine. The next DART train was twenty minutes away, according to the electronic display. Oisín wished it was coming sooner. He was feeling strangely uneasy, as if somebody was watching him. Yet the train station was almost completely empty. There were a few workers, newspapers twitching in their hands. Spanish tourists leant against the wall and gazed up at the glass roof, hoping that the sun would reach them. Everybody looked quite normal.

It was the Book of Magic. That was why he was feeling so strange. He'd have to tell Granny Keane about it before they went home.

When he got back to the bench, Stephen and Sorcha were in the middle of an argument.

'Ravens don't have green eyes,' Stephen said, not looking up from his game.

'This one did,' Sorcha protested.

'It couldn't have.'

'It did.'

'What kind of bird did you say pecked you?' Granny Keane said, sitting forward suddenly on the bench, as if she was waking from a dream.

Usually Granny Keane's voice was quite light and airy, as if it belonged to somebody much younger than a lady in her eighties. People who saw her long wispy hair and bright turquoise beads sometimes thought she might be a little odd in the head and so she was always able to get a discount at the market or to convince the police that she could never have been speeding. Every now and then, though, her voice had a sudden sharpness, as if she was all too alert. This was the quality her voice had now.

'What kind of bird was it?' she repeated.

'A raven,' Oisín answered in a small voice.

'And what colour did you say its eyes were?'

'Green,' Oisín and Sorcha said at the same time.

Nobody could fail to notice the effect these words had on Granny Keane. A shadow flickered across her face, as if she was remembering some deep, forgotten sorrow. Her own big green eyes pulsed with a strange emotion, and Oisín thought he had never seen her look fiercer.

Are you OK, Gran?' he asked as she looked far into the distance.

It took a moment for Granny Keane's eyes to return from the place in the past where they had been. When they did, they focused on Oisín as if seeing him for the first time. She stared not at the packet of Maltesers in his right hand, but at the little book sticking out of his hoodie pocket.

Oisín pushed it out of view and sat down on the bench, handing Sorcha the Maltesers. Lots of feelings were tugging at his insides, but he couldn't give up the Book. Not yet.

When Granny Keane eventually spoke, it wasn't what Oisín expected to hear.

'Have any of you heard of the Morrígan?'

None of them had.

'Don't they teach you the old Celtic stories in school?'

'Some of them,' Oisín replied.

'Just the boring ones,' Stephen added. 'They're all about silly swans turning into children or old guys falling off horses. I don't know why we bother with them. Dad says that Irish will be obsolete in a few years – that means extinct.'

'Thanks, Dictionary-dot-com,' Oisín said under his breath.

'Remind me to thump you later,' Stephen growled.

Granny Keane ignored the pair of them.

'They never teach you anything useful at school,' she fussed, sounding a lot more like a regular granny than usual. 'Of course you haven't heard of the Morrígan.'

'What is this Morrígan thing?' Sorcha asked.

'She is the Great Queen of Battle Madness,' Granny Keane said.

'Is she a giant?' Sorcha asked.

'It's not her size that you need to worry about,' Granny Keane said. 'Something as small as a pea can hold all the trouble in the world.' She looked back towards Oisín and he had a strange feeling that she was looking right at the Book of Magic.

'What is she like?' Sorcha asked, her small eyes huge.

'She's the Queen of Shadows,' Granny Keane said and, once again, something strange and sad seemed to shift across her face. 'She feeds off all the despair of the world: all the bad thoughts and broken promises, all the little lies and unkind truths that make our world go round. She skulks in the shadows of the world, and when somebody is feeling at their lowest, she creeps over and makes them feel worse.'

Oisín shivered, thinking of some of the times he had felt sad. The day when Stephen's friends shoved him into the hedge at the bus stop and everybody laughed hadn't been great. Or when his best friend Jack had moved to the country three years ago, that had been a hard one. Or the day when Jack came back to visit last year, and was full of stories of his new friends and seemed like the kind of person Oisín would never have been friends with anyway, that day had been even worse. Oisín pulled down the sleeves of his hoodie, starting to feel cold all over. He couldn't imagine the kind of creature that would want to make you feel worse on your lowest day.

'Where did she come from?' Sorcha asked, captivated.

Sorcha usually loved to suck all the chocolate off Maltesers before eating them, but she hadn't even opened the packet yet.

'Have you heard of the Tuatha Dé Danann?' Granny Keane asked.

Oisín answered when Sorcha shook her head: 'The fairy people. The first people in Ireland.'

'Yes,' said Granny Keane. 'The Morrígan was one of them. A beautiful young girl. But then something turned her heart hard and she moved to a far-off mountain. During the great wars of Ireland, she swooped around the battle field as a crow, with her two bitter sisters, Macha and Badb. The three of them perched on the shoulders of soldiers and gave them the courage to fight on. The Morrígan cheered on *both* sides. She didn't care who won. All she minded was getting enough skulls to decorate her room with.'

'So she's a bird?' Sorcha asked.

'It's just a silly story,' Stephen said quickly. He shot Granny Keane a sharp glance, but nothing could stop her once she had started.

'She *can* look like a bird sometimes. She's a shape-shifter. Sometimes she looks like a wrinkled old lady. Sometimes she looks like a little girl. Sometimes she looks like the most beautiful woman in Ireland. No matter what she changes to, you can always recognise her by three things: the ravens that follow her, a terrible chill in the air around her and those green eyes of hers that will drown you in sadness.'

Even Stephen shuddered slightly. Oisín couldn't blame him. The temperature seemed to drop several degrees, as if the weather had decided that fine summer days weren't to be wasted on such stories.

'Does that mean you're the Morrígan?' Sorcha said, gazing into Granny Keane's green eyes with fascination.

A smile returned to Granny Keane's face and she gave a little laugh. 'Oh, no, dear. If I had all the power of the Morrígan, I wouldn't be trying to sell my books around Dublin.'

'What about you? Why aren't your eyes blue like mine and Stephen's?' Sorcha said, swivelling around to Oisín and inspecting his eyes.

It was something that Oisín had wondered himself. He was small with freckles, green eyes and hair the colour of sand. Both Stephen and Sorcha had black hair, blue eyes and not a freckle between them.

'It's complicated genetics,' Stephen began, but before he could explain what he had learnt about Mendel for his Junior Cert, Granny Keane had interrupted him.

'Lots of people have green eyes, love. Your cat, Smoky, he has green eyes, hasn't he?'

Sorcha nodded slowly. It was hard to imagine Smoky getting enough energy to leave his basket, let alone plot an evil scheme.

Granny Keane patted Sorcha's hand. 'I don't think you need to worry about any of us.'

'Or worry at all,' Stephen said, standing. 'It's just a story. Where is the stupid DART? Dublin Area *Rapid* Transit? A slug would get home faster!'

'What time is it?' Granny Keane asked.

'Almost five,' Stephen answered grumpily. He'd never been more ready to get back to his friends and his own house.

'It's too early to be getting dark,' Granny Keane murmured. In the middle of June, the sun never set until after ten, and yet the station was gradually getting darker and darker.

'Probably climate change,' Stephen said. That was what their father said whenever the weather went weird.

'No, no, it's nothing,' Granny Keane said quickly, standing up as if she'd suddenly realised something. 'Come on, let's get you a seat near the front.'

They did usually walk along the platform because it was easier to get a seat at the front of the train, but Oisín didn't think they needed to worry about that today. The few people at the station were leaving, whispering about the terrible state of train delays, the awful cheat of a summer where it started to get dark at five o'clock and how it was all probably something to do with the euro.

'Gran, are you sure the train's coming?' Oisín said, looking up to check the clock.

The train was still twenty minutes away and the neon seconds were flickering along towards five o'clock. But as soon as Oisín looked up he saw at once what had bothered Granny Keane and what was causing the unnatural darkness. Hovering over the glass roof were several creatures, their black forms blocking all the sun from the platform. Not one, not tens, but hundreds and hundreds of ravens, all of them pecking their beaks against the glass and looking down with terrible green eyes.

Chapter 3
The Underwater Train

Oisín's head told him to run. The problem was his legs. His legs were rooted to the platform as if they had decided it was time he learnt what *scared stiff* really meant. Oisín looked at his feet so he wouldn't have to think about the ravens, but he could feel them looking down at him, could feel the hairs on his neck stand straight as soldiers. The Book of Magic could sense them too. It was squirming in his pocket as if it wanted to get out. Oisín wasn't sure if it wanted to get away from the ravens or to join them. Stephen and Sorcha hadn't noticed yet. Sorcha was happy with her Maltesers (she had reached the sucking-the-chocolate stage). Stephen was playing intently with his mobile phone. The air around them got colder and darker.

Just when Oisín's brain had almost convinced his legs that it was time to get moving, he felt Granny Keane's hand on his shoulder. Her face was smiling tightly but he could feel her hand shaking. He had to tell her.

'Gran –'

'It's the train!' Granny Keane said, without hearing him.

'There's no train,' Oisín said. 'The clock still says it's twenty minutes away.'

But when he looked at the platform, the train was right there, as if it, rather than they, had been waiting all this time. It looked like a normal DART train with the same green checked cushions and yellow stripe on the side. Something wasn't right, though. It was eerily empty and hadn't made a single sound as it reached the platform. Oisín was beginning to feel like he didn't have enough hairs on the back of his neck for all this strangeness.

Stephen didn't seem bothered. He hurried Sorcha into the carriage and waited impatiently for Oisín. Oisín's legs were still staying put. He couldn't leave Granny Keane alone on the platform, even though she was planning on taking the 130 bus back to her own house in Clontarf.

'Why don't you come with us?' he asked.

A flicker of longing flashed across Granny Keane's face.

'No, dear, I'm staying here,' she said, patting Oisín on the shoulder. 'But you must go. Just remember –'

'Come on!' Stephen said, yanking Oisín by the arm.

'Wait!' Oisín said.

'Don't worry about me,' Granny Keane said quickly, as if she knew what Oisín was thinking. 'I can look after myself. But you must get on the train.'

Oisín looked into her deep green eyes. He had a thousand questions for her and he suddenly wished he had asked her about the Book of Magic as soon as he'd found it. What was it doing in her study? How could a book move? What was a Keeper? And what did it all have to do with the Morrígan?

Oisín struggled to find words to ask at least one of the questions, but before he could, Stephen pulled him into the train.

'Come on, Slowslime,' he barked, pushing the door-close button impatiently.

'Just remember your name,' Granny Keane said as the doors shut. 'Remember your name.'

Before Oisín could ask what she meant, the train had started to pull off, and in a second Granny Keane was left behind.

Sun streamed into the carriage. Oisín had forgotten that it was daylight and was surprised to see Stephen's face illuminated. He was even more surprised to see how worried his brother looked. Stephen ran to the window and looked out. When he looked back in relief, Oisín realised that Stephen had seen the ravens on the roof all the time, but he hadn't wanted to alarm Sorcha. Or to believe it himself. Stephen liked things to be normal. Normal didn't include his loser little brother or a roof full of ravens. It certainly didn't include magic books.

'What is that thing?' Stephen said, looking suspiciously at Oisín's Book of Magic.

'Just a book,' Oisín said, his voice catching. He wished he hadn't pulled it out of his pocket.

'Look, it's another birdie,' Sorcha said, pressing her nose against the window.

Stephen swallowed hard. Flying alongside the window was a raven with green eyes. Except these ravens were like ants. Once one appeared, it wasn't long before there was a trail of them.

'They're flying us home,' Sorcha said excitedly, seeming to have forgotten about the raven that had pecked her.

'Stay away from the window,' Oisín and Stephen shouted together.

Already, more ravens were appearing, blocking out the view of both Bram Stoker's house and Fairview Park with their dark, shadowy wings. Oisín wished the DART would go a little faster but it seemed, if anything, to be slowing down.

'*Déan deifir,*' he whispered to the train.

It was what Granny Keane always grumbled when she wanted her bus to hurry up. The DART didn't seem to care, chugging along at its normal speed. But the Book of Magic did, shifting in Oisín's fingers as if shaking off a long sleep.

Stephen's eyes bulged.

'Give me that thing,' he said, moving towards Oisín.

Oisín stood on the tips of his toes, trying to face Stephen eye to eye, which was hard, as Stephen was a lot taller than him.

'Listen, Bookmaggot, I've got hurling practice tonight and I just want to get back home without any trouble,' Stephen said.

Oisín wished that the Book of Magic wasn't acting so strangely. It had started to flick through its pages, as if it was getting ready for something.

'Give that thing to me!' Stephen said, lunging for the Book.

'No!' Oisín said, ducking out of the way.

Stephen grabbed it out of his hands. Oisín caught his breath. In a moment, Stephen would see the inscription in the Book and then he'd never get it back.

'It's *mine,*' he shouted desperately.

He didn't know why he said it. It wasn't as if he thought that the Book could hear him. It wasn't as though he expected the

Book to do anything. But that's exactly what happened. It snapped its pages shut on Stephen's finger and leapt through the air into Oisín's hands.

Oisín could feel something changing in the air, the tiniest of shifts. From the look on Stephen's face, it seemed that he could sense it too. The DART slowed down to a standstill. The ravens crowded closer. There was a clicking sound, the small unlatching of a carriage. And then the train started to move very quickly.

'They've gone,' Sorcha said, as the train suddenly shot through the cloud of ravens.

Oisín turned around. He could see the swarm of ravens coming after them. What he couldn't see was the rest of the train. Their carriage was running away on its own.

'Goodbye, Killester!' Sorcha shouted out.

A world of trees, houses, washing lines and annoyed people waiting on Killester platform whizzed by.

'It must be an express train,' Stephen said to himself, still trying to cling to a shred of a normal explanation.

The Book of Magic fluttered in Oisín's hands.

'Bye, Raheny!' Sorcha shouted out as more disgruntled passengers were left on the platform at Raheny.

Stephen paced up and down the carriage. He realised with a jolt that they were the only people on it.

'Bye, Kilbarrack!' Sorcha chirped.

'We can get off at Howth Junction,' Stephen said, running his fingers through his hair. 'The train will have to stop there.'

All the trains stopped at Howth Junction, no matter where they were going.

'Bye, Howth Junction!' Sorcha called out.

Oisín gulped. Instead of following the regular tracks, the carriage had veered off on its own. Oisín ran to the front of the carriage and looked out the window. There were the same wooden slats disappearing underneath the train as it powered along, but they looked a lot older, as if they hadn't been used in a very long time. The carriage kept going, travelling so fast that they couldn't see the ravens behind them any more.

Stephen strode forward and tapped on the window to alert the driver. The driver's compartment was empty.

'We're going to the sea!' Sorcha cried excitedly.

'We're not!' Oisín and Stephen shouted at the same time.

Sometimes, though, seven-year-old sisters can see things more clearly than their older brothers.

'We are,' Sorcha said stubbornly. 'We're going up Howth Head.'

She was right. Somehow the carriage was cutting through fields, trees and roads, all the time getting higher and higher. Surprised cows raised their heads at the green blur that had shot by them, but it was gone before they could let out so much as a moo. In seconds, the carriage had cut a path through the bright pink rhododendrons of Deer Park and was rushing towards the summit of Howth Head. If the carriage didn't stop, they'd fly off the edge of the cliff, the sea hundreds of feet below them.

'Stop!' Oisín whispered. He wasn't sure whether he was talking to the Book of Magic or the train. Neither of them was listening.

The carriage zigzagged through the gorse fields and kept climbing up the hill, not showing any signs of stopping. Sorcha looked out the glass window with a very serious face. Stephen jabbed at his mobile phone furiously, but it didn't have any reception. The edge of the cliff loomed. Stephen dropped his phone and held Sorcha's hand. He looked back and offered his other hand to Oisín.

Just as Oisín was about to take it, the pages stopped flapping and the Book opened at its centre. Three small words shone out clearly on the page, coming from the mouth of a bright speckled fish. It took Oisín a second to decide. He wasn't sure that he trusted the Book. He wasn't sure that the strange words wouldn't turn them into tadpoles. He wasn't even sure if he could read the small spindly handwriting. What Oisín was sure of was that he didn't want to plummet off the edge of a cliff without doing anything.

'*Téigh faoin uisce*,' he read quickly.

It was as if the train knew what he was saying, like it was a horse waiting to be tapped on its flank. The train dipped sharply down on a ninety-degree angle, flinging the children against the glass. They were too amazed to scream. One after another, tracks appeared on the cliff-face, as if they were appearing just for them. The tracks continued into the Irish Sea, running along the sandy bottom until they disappeared from view. Oisín knew that the carriage was going to follow them and sure enough it did, plunging into the water and chugging along the seabed, as if this was a perfectly normal thing for a DART to do. It showed no signs of slowing down and the windows seemed happy to stay shut.

'What's that?' Stephen asked.

Straight ahead was the strangest looking seaweed forest Oisín had ever seen. It looked like it was made of mist, and towered towards the surface. The tracks continued through it and the DART brushed through easily. The train was through the misty seaweed in under a minute but something seemed to have changed in the air. Oisín had a strange feeling, like when he entered somebody else's home for the first time and he caught the particular smell of the house. It was as though he had opened a curtain and now here he was, in magic's house. The Book of Magic settled into his palm, calm again.

'Look at the fishies!' Sorcha said, running to the window.

She didn't seem too bothered about what had just happened. Stephen sat on the floor, in shock. Things were so not-normal he didn't know where to start. Oisín could understand why. It wasn't just that the DART was travelling underwater. It was that the fish that swirled around the carriage were some of the strangest he had ever seen. There were bright little minnows that flashed on and off like Christmas lights. There was a huge salmon with goat horns on its head and long yellow seahorses that stretched out their necks like trumpets. Oisín had wanted to be an oceanographer when he was eight and had read lots of books about the sea, but he had never seen any creatures like the ones in front of him now. A strange sort of thought crept up on him – that these were the kind of fish you could never find in the Irish Sea, maybe even the kind of fish you could never find in this world.

Stephen buried his head in his hands as the carriage made its way through a gigantic kelp forest. The seaweed was as high as Liberty Hall and just as strange as the fish: towering lavender and turquoise stalks that swayed with the current, prickly pink plants that recoiled as the train went past, bushy blobs of yellow seaweed that puffed in and out.

The DART pulled out of the seaweed forest and continued along the ocean bed, as if it knew exactly where it was going. After about ten minutes, it started to climb out of the water, pulling back into the air and stopping at a sandy beach. The doors opened slowly.

'We must be in Wales,' Stephen said, struggling to keep his voice from shaking.

Oisín looked out the window at the strange island they'd arrived at. He'd never been to Wales but he had a feeling that it didn't have *any* palm trees. He knew Wales had mountains, but the white one in the distance looked much too big to be in the United Kingdom. And he was very sure that there weren't any volcanoes in Great Britain.

Stephen punched his fist against the window. He clung on to the one normal thing left: this was all his brother's fault.

'You did this,' he growled, glaring at Oisín and at the Book in his hands. Oisín didn't bother answering. He hadn't meant to make the train go underwater. He hadn't meant for the ravens to see the Book. But he had a feeling that there was no turning back now.

He held the Book of Magic in his hands, and for the first time, he felt how heavy it was.

Chapter 4
Antimony

As soon as Oisín found the Book of Magic, Antimony started in her sleep. Something had shifted in her magical universe, some small ripple from another world, miles and miles away. Probably nothing, she told herself, snuggling back into her moss duvet. Something tugged at her brain, though, like a pea bothering a princess through millions and millions of mattresses: something important was about to happen.

Antimony tried to keep her eyes closed. It was hard to sleep properly when you slept in a tree, though. As soon as the June sun peeped through the leaves, a host of buzzing insects and twittering birds zoomed in. Antimony pulled her duvet over her head as a bird pecked at her toes. Yet again, she imagined she was back in her real home in Nigeria and not living in a tree house with the strangest family she had ever met.

Maybe the Houlihans' house couldn't quite be called a tree house. Ordinary tree houses didn't have seven floors, or bamboo slides, or have segments missing so parts of the trunk hung in mid air. Of course, the Houlihans' house wasn't ordinary at all – it was magic. Antimony couldn't help admiring the Earth Magic that kept parts of the trunk suspended in mid-air. One flat-topped segment of trunk made a great dinner table and it was useful to be able to pass the salt without reaching around a giant hunk of oak.

Each floor, including Antimony's bedroom near the top of the tree, had the same round table in its centre, with the trunk continuing as normal towards the roof. It wasn't really Antimony's room, though. If it had been Antimony's room the table would have had something good on it. A moss trampoline. Or a fireball set. Or she would have left it bare so she could stand on it and pretend she was holding up the tree with her hands. Instead, the table was covered with herbs, small jars of strangely coloured liquids and lots and lots of books.

'Can you stop reading? I'm trying to sleep,' Antimony grumbled, burying her head in her pillow.

She could almost have liked the Houlihans' house if she didn't have to share a room with Caoimhe.

'Sorry.' It was Tom, not Caoimhe. That was how it was with those two. Tom was so good-natured he would apologise even when he hadn't done anything wrong.

'If you'd let me brew you a potion I'm sure you could sleep fine,' Caoimhe said, loudly turning another of the bark pages from the enormous book she was reading.

'No, thanks. I don't want you to poison me,' Antimony mumbled into her pillow.

She felt a peck at her toes, but she didn't know it was a raven. Otherwise she would have got out of bed. Antimony could always jump straight out of bed when something was important.

'Keep still, Tom!' Caoimhe said as Tom tried to pat his dog, Giant.

'Sorry.'

Caoimhe was practising on Tom again. She wanted to be a druid-doctor and was always reading herbal books and mixing medicines. As most of the Tuatha Dé Danann on the island were very healthy, they didn't have much need for medicine, especially when it was brewed by a twelve-year-old girl. Only Tom was too nice to refuse, even though he was a year older than Caoimhe and was setting a bad precedent for older brothers, in Antimony's opinion.

Even Tom was looking a little uneasy about the jar that Caoimhe was holding out. It looked like a brew of nettles, twigs, dandelion petals and something bright purple. Tom's face turned a pale shade of green.

'Are you sure I need to take this? I only scratched my arm when I was climbing.'

'Drink it!' Caoimhe said in a bossy voice.

'You definitely read the recipe right? You remember the time you thought you were going to stop my nosebleed and you turned my nose into a strawberry?'

'Keep still!' Caoimhe said, twisting her special pen. A strand of grass curled out from the tip and tied around Tom's arm.

'Not that I minded having a strawberry nose,' Tom continued. 'My snots were really tasty.'

'You can't swallow if you're talking,' Caoimhe said.

'Sorry,' Tom said, taking a gulp from the jar.

His face opened and closed as if it couldn't believe what it had been forced to drink.

'Keep still!' Caoimhe said, knotting the grass tightly.

'Sorry,' Tom managed to say, but this 'sorry' seemed a little more annoyed than apologetic.

Antimony didn't blame Tom. If Caoimhe had been *her* sister (her real sister, that is), she didn't know what she would do.

'Is my arm supposed to be growing twigs?' Tom asked.

Antimony heard the pages flick rapidly.

'Oh!' Caoimhe said in a small voice. 'Two drops of ash-tree sap, not two teaspoons.'

Antimony couldn't help poking her head out. Tom's arm was changing in front of her eyes. Small little twigs were popping out of his skin, his fingers were getting longer and thinner and all his goose pimples had been covered over in bark. Caoimhe had turned Tom's arm into a branch.

'Well, you definitely fixed that scratch I had. You'd never know it was bruised.'

Tom gave a big smile to show that he thought that having a branch for an arm was rather cool. Giant shuffled over and sniffed Tom's arm suspiciously. He was used to seeing Tom in strange states but he'd never seen him turn into a tree before. Tom ran his twig-fingers through Giant's shaggy coat.

'Maybe I can be a pirate now,' he said happily. 'Do you think pirates can have wooden arms as well as wooden legs?'

'You definitely have a wooden brain,' Caoimhe said as she flicked through her book. 'It only happened because you moved.'

'Yeah, that's it,' Tom said with a gentle shake of his head. 'It has nothing to do with the potion you gave me, just me moving. Careful you don't blink, Antimony, or your face will turn into a tulip.'

Tom gave Antimony one of his smiles, the sort that included her if she wanted to be included. Antimony turned back into her covers. If she *had* to have a brother, Tom wouldn't be so bad, she supposed. He was good for climbing trees with, and didn't care at all about books.

Only if she had to have a brother, though. But they weren't really siblings. How could they be, when they didn't look at all alike? The only thing they had in common was their green eyes. Tom and Caoimhe had the same pale skin and bushy mop of chestnut brown hair, though Caoimhe usually turned her hair green with magic grass. Antimony's black hair was plaited into long dreadlocks and, like everybody else in her real family, her skin was black. Or as her father used to say, it was dark brown but people who couldn't see colours very well called it black.

Antimony snuggled under the covers. She didn't like thinking of her family but she couldn't get back to sleep either. Caoimhe kept flicking through her book of herbal remedies as she searched for a cure and there was still the strange pecking at Antimony's toes. Antimony supposed it was Giant. Back home in Nigeria, her parents would never have allowed so many annoying animals to live with them. Her mother could have mixed some fire dust to fix Tom's arm in seconds. Antimony closed her eyes and told her brain to stop remembering. Her brain wasn't very good at listening to her, though. Once it had started remembering her parents it couldn't stop.

'Ow! Get that stupid dog off me!' Antimony shouted as she felt another nip at her ankle.

'It's not Giant,' Tom said. 'It's a bird.'

'Maybe I can practise on him,' Caoimhe said excitedly. 'I need to learn how to fix broken wings.'

'Fly away, raven, fly away,' Tom called out.

Antimony bolted upright as soon as she heard what kind of bird was at her bed. The raven looked at her with his big green eyes and disappeared back into the forest. Antimony knew what she had to do.

'You've scared it away,' Caoimhe said, disappointed that she wouldn't have a bird to practise on.

'I guess you must have fixed his broken wing,' Tom said, rolling his eyes.

'It's just a stupid raven,' Caoimhe answered. 'It shouldn't be flying this far south anyway. It means trouble.'

'Not all ravens are evil,' Tom said, hugging Giant as if he couldn't imagine how any creature could be bad.

While they were arguing, Antimony had already pulled her arms through her favourite orange T-shirt and had slipped into her purple jeans.

'Where are you going?' Caoimhe said. 'You know we have to help Mum with the hay?'

'I know,' Antimony said, slinging her special pouch over her shoulder.

'Want to play fireball later?' Tom asked.

'Maybe. Are you sure you want to play with a wooden arm, though?' Antimony said, looking for a large leaf to ride down the slide on.

'Sure,' Tom said with a laugh. 'I'll be tree-riffic.'

Antimony jumped onto the slide before Tom saw her smile. The bamboo slide was another good piece of Earth Magic and in a couple of seconds Antimony was on the forest floor. She quickly ran into a cluster of trees. Some of the other children would be searching for magic chestnuts or playing mossball in the clearing. She'd been on the island for six months now, but people still whispered when she walked past. Not on the side trails, though. None of the squirrels or insects cared how famous her parents were. Instead, the oak, ash and holly trees stretched towards the sun and towered above as if they were gentle guardians, looking out only for her.

As she got deeper into the forest, there were fewer spots of sun and she thought she could hear the bears and snakes that Tom promised were there. Antimony spread her arms wide and took in a gulp of forest air. Nowhere else could make her feel so safe and excited at the same time.

It didn't take Antimony long to find the tall hazel tree where she had carved out her initials. She'd been meeting Cluaiscín there once a week, so she was used to the routine. She picked up a piece of bark large enough to stand on, placed it beside the trunk, and reached into her pouch, which had everything important she'd taken from her parents' laboratory. She found her special slingshot and placed a couple of twigs inside. As soon as they started to glow, she shot the twigs at the bark and watched it begin to fizz. Antimony jumped on top and waited. Seconds later, there was a huge crackle and the bark whooshed up into the air. Antimony leapt sideways and clung onto a branch as the bark whizzed into the clouds.

She could have climbed the tree, but travelling by fire was much cooler. And it reminded her of her parents, of the first time her father had taught her the trick.

Antimony swallowed a sigh. Remembering was hard. Sometimes it made you feel better, as if memories were a warm blanket you could snuggle into. And then sometimes the blanket itched, scratched at feelings you didn't want to think about. Sometimes the memories made you feel cold instead of warm.

Antimony told her brain to stop and turned to the raven. Most people had to transform before they could speak to birds, but Antimony's mother had taught her Raven when she was five.

'Cluaiscín. This better be important for you to have woken me up.'

Cluaiscín flapped his feathers and shuffled his feet, looking very much like he would roll his eyes if that was something ravens did.

'Nice to see you too, Miss Antimony,' he said, hopping up and down on the branch. 'Cluaiscín has had such a long, cold journey with such big news. It's nice to be welcomed home.'

'What news do you have?' Antimony asked sharply.

'Such a long, cold journey across the sea,' Cluaiscín said, hugging himself with his wings. He looked down from the treetop at the sea which stretched out for miles without land in sight.

'OK, fine, but this better be good,' Antimony said, closing her eyes and concentrating. Smoke came out of her nostrils in a moment, billowing over to Cluaiscín and warming him immediately.

'So what's the news?'

'Cluaiscín had *such* a long journey. Not a scrap to eat for miles.'

Antimony crinkled her nose in annoyance but fumbled with her bag to pull out some worms. She held one out as Cluaiscín opened his beak.

'First, tell me what this is about,' Antimony said.

'I've found the Book of Magic,' Cluaiscín said.

Antimony dropped the worm, which couldn't escape Cluaiscín's beak in time.

'You're sure?'

'Positive,' Cluaiscín said through a mouthful of worm.

'Where did you find it?'

'Dublin.'

'Which way is it?' Antimony asked, standing up. She'd never heard of Dublin, but she figured it couldn't be that hard to find once she set off in the right direction.

'You shouldn't go there,' Cluaiscín said. 'It's across the ocean. Where the Milesians are.'

'The people who banished the Tuatha Dé Danann from Ireland? That'll make it easy. None of them know a thing about magic.'

'I'm not so sure,' Cluaiscín said, thinking of the boy with the green eyes who had found the Book.

'Whatever they can do, they haven't met me,' Antimony said, standing as tall as she could and flicking her dreadlocks back impressively. 'Are you going to tell me how to get to this Dublin place?'

'You shouldn't go there.'

'Don't tell me what to do.'

'No. You shouldn't go there because the Book's already coming here.'

Antimony gripped onto the branch beside her for support. After all this time, the Book of Magic was coming to her.

'Who has it?'

'Some Milesian boy.'

'Then it will be easy to take it from him.'

'It's not that simple. He's the Keeper of the Book now. You can't just take it.'

Antimony gritted her teeth. For years she'd been searching for this book. She wished her parents had told her more about how it worked.

'There is one time when the Book can be transferred,' Cluaiscín said, sensing another worm.

'When?'

'The Lughnasa festival.'

'That's more than a month away. Are they going to stay that long on the island?'

Cluaiscín shrugged. It didn't look like Antimony would be giving him any more worms.

'Then I need a way to make them stay here until then,' Antimony said, rummaging in her pouch to pick out something from the very bottom.

Cluaiscín's green eyes bulged when he saw the small jar she pulled out.

'Miss Antimony, you can't!'

Antimony ignored him and opened the jar. She turned her nose away from the wisps of indigo smoke that swirled out of it.

'Miss Antimony, that's deep magic, dangerous magic. Are you sure your mother would want you to do this?'

Antimony paused. She wasn't at all sure what her mother would have wanted. She remembered the first time she'd shown her *béal tine* in her laboratory. Antimony could hear her voice as if she was on the branch beside her.

'*Béal* is the Irish for mouth,' she had started. 'And *tine*, as you know, means fire.'

'Why do I have to learn Irish?'

Antimony bit her lip as she remembered. She wished she hadn't complained to her parents so much.

'Because it's one of the magic languages and you have to,' her mother had said in the voice she used when Antimony was being impertinent. 'And because *béal tine* is one of the most valuable things we have here. It can only be brewed in small amounts, just once a year, on the feast of Bealtaine.'

Antimony's mother had gone on about how Bealtaine was different from *béal tine*, even though they sounded a bit the same. At ten years old, Antimony hadn't cared about words, though. Not when there were things to be blown up.

'What is it? Fire that talks?'

Her mother had used her serious voice when she responded.

'*Béal tine* speaks the future that you desire. It has the power to change the course of events.'

On the hazel branch, three years later, Antimony's skin still prickled when she remembered what her mother said next.

'It's very dangerous to use. *Béal tine* can make something happen. But it never happens in the way you think.'

Antimony looked at the jar of dark, swirling flames. Would her mother have wanted her to use it? Would she have even wanted her to take it from the laboratory after the fire?

Cluaiscín's voice snapped Antimony back to the present.

'Miss Antimony, Cluaiscín has seen bad things, many bad things, but *béal tine* is always –'

Cluascín stopped talking and jerked from shock. Antimony had yanked one of his beautiful black feathers off.

'No, Miss Antimony,' Cluascín flustered, but it was too late: she was already sticking the feather into her arm. A single drop of her blood fell cleanly into the jar. Antimony broke the feather carefully into small pieces and sprinkled it on top. Because Cluaiscín had seen the boy, the pieces of his feathers were all that was needed to make a connection to him, and for *béal tine* to work. That, a drop of her blood, and a sacrifice.

Cluaiscín froze, wondering if after everything he had done for her mother, Antimony would...

'Relax,' Antimony said, as if she could read his mind.

She'd already taken a worm from her pouch. It plopped into the jar, trying to climb up the glass, as if it could sense what was coming.

Looking at the poor creature, Antimony almost felt sorry for it. This was the deepest magic she had ever done. She felt her skin tingle, from both excitement and fear. The worm pushed its body upwards. Antimony didn't have time to be sorry. She mumbled the words she wanted to happen and backed away.

A single, dark-blue flame shot out of the jar, brilliantly hot. It burnt out in seconds, leaving nothing in the jar but a small pile of indigo ash.

Chapter 5
The Tuatha Dé Danann

Oisín had never landed on a magic beach before. He stood at the edge of the DART carriage, wondering whether or not the ground would try to eat him. Not so bothered, Sorcha brushed past him and leapt off the train.

'We're on holiday,' she shouted happily to the winds. Her ankle was still sore where the raven had pecked it, so she hopped on one foot across the sand.

'Come back!' Stephen and Oisín shouted in the same older-brother voice.

Stephen shook himself, as if trying to remove any similarity with his strange younger brother.

'Don't get any ideas, Bookbrain. We're going home in a minute.'

Stephen looked around the strange island. They were surrounded by sea and forest. The DART train sat peacefully on the sand, as if it had always meant to end up there. Home had never seemed further away.

Encouraged that Sorcha was still in one piece, Oisín put his foot onto the sand and took a step. The sand felt as soft and scrunchy as any other beach he'd been on. He had almost forgotten the chilling feeling the ravens had given him. The Book of Magic nuzzled happily in his hoodie pocket. Oisín felt a rush of excitement: all he could see ahead was adventure.

'Careful!'

Sorcha had fallen over before Stephen's voice reached her. Hopping was not her strong point at the best of times, and a time that included a giant dog running into her could not really be considered the best.

'What is that thing?' Stephen said, racing over to help Sorcha up.

'Don't mind Giant. He's just chasing the chestnuts.'

The children turned to see a friendly curly-headed boy running out from the forest. The dog freed himself from Sorcha and bounded over to the boy.

'Here you go, Giant,' the boy said, taking out a couple of chestnuts from his jeans and throwing them into the air. They smashed against each other and exploded into coloured fireworks on the sand. Giant jumped up to catch the sparks while the boy stood still, as if chestnuts always burst into multi-coloured sparks where he was from.

'Hi, I'm Tom,' he said then, giving a friendly wave.

'Is your hand a tree?' Sorcha asked.

Tom blushed as if he'd forgotten something.

'Oh, yeah! Not really, my sister was mixing a potion to heal a cut and then this happened. She'll be able to fix it though. I hope.'

Oisín was about to ask what kind of potion could turn an arm into a tree when Stephen bustled over. He seemed determined not to notice anything out of the ordinary.

'Have you got a phone I can use? Mine isn't working.'

'What's a phone?' Tom asked.

'Like this,' Stephen said, holding up his mobile.

'You're not from this island, are you?' Tom said slowly.

'No!' Stephen said, appalled that anybody could mistake him for a native of a place where boys sprouted branches for arms.

'You're Milesians, aren't you?' Tom said, delight creeping onto his face. 'Can I have a look? I've never seen Milesian magic.'

Tom picked up Stephen's phone as if it was a rare, precious object.

'What's a Milesian?' Stephen said briskly. 'And where are we?'

Oisín answered before Tom could. As soon as he said it, he knew he was right: 'The island of the Tuatha Dé Danann. The island of the fairy folk. Milesians are the people who drove the Tuatha dé Danann out of Ireland.'

'No hard feelings, though,' Tom said with a smile. 'I mean, it was probably so many great-great-great grandmothers ago that we can call it a truce.'

Tom held out his hand and Oisín shook it. It was rather odd, shaking a twig, but Tom didn't seem to mind. Stephen took a step back as Oisín introduced them all. Tom was too busy talking to notice any rudeness.

'I can't believe you made it over here! What kind of magic did you use? Must have been some Water Magic to get that train across. Did the dolphins help you?'

Oisín felt the Book of Magic flutter in his pocket and was just about to tell Tom about it when something stopped him. Somebody else was watching. A girl with long dreadlocks stood at the edge of the forest, holding a slingshot to her chest as if she was deciding whether or not to use it.

'Oh, that's Antimony, my sister,' Tom said, catching Oisín's gaze. 'Antimony, come over and say hi. Milesians have washed up on the beach! Can you believe it?'

It seemed that Antimony could believe it, as she walked over very calmly. She had put down her slingshot but there was something about her stare that was much more troubling.

'You don't look very like brother and sister,' Sorcha said before Oisín could kick her.

'Adopted sister,' Antimony added.

'Auntie Money is a funny name,' Sorcha said, still deciding whether she meant 'funny' in a good sense.

'It's a chemical element,' Antimony said proudly. 'My parents were alchemists. And I pronounce it Ant-IM-onee.'

Stephen had no interest in how to pronounce strange names, especially when they belonged to stranger people.

'Can you take us to an Internet café or something?' he cut in.

'Is that a kind of magic place?' Tom asked.

'There's no such thing as magic,' Stephen snapped. 'Our train just got – lost. And we need to get back to Dublin. Can you take us to your parents?'

He was using the slow speaking-to-foreign-people voice that their father used on holiday in France.

'Is he OK?' Tom said, turning to Oisín. 'Maybe too much water got in his head or something?'

Oisín had to bite back a laugh before Stephen hit him.

'Come on, we're going,' Stephen barked. 'If you want to play games and pretend that your sister mixes potions and that your parents are alchemists or whatever that's grand for you, but we've got to get back to Dublin before dark.'

Something Stephen had said upset Antimony, because she stepped in front of him before he could move.

'Don't insult my parents,' she said slowly.

'Get out of my way,' Stephen responded.

Oisín was about to warn Antimony that he didn't think that Stephen would have a problem pushing a girl when he realised Antimony could look after herself. She closed her eyes and pinched her nose slightly.

'Don't believe in magic?' she asked.

Sorcha screamed before Stephen did.

'Fire! Your runners are on fire!'

Stephen looked up in amazement. Smoke was billowing out of Antimony's nostrils and sparking at his runners. Stephen dived to the ground and tried to put out the fire in the sand. Tom bolted over, rubbing a large dock-leaf on Stephen's shoes and making sure to keep his branch-arm away from the tiny flames.

'Antimony, you shouldn't be doing magic like that,' he spluttered.

'It's only fake,' Antimony said, crossing her arms. 'Next time it'll be real.'

'Sorry,' Tom said to Stephen, as if it had been his fault.

'Get off!' Stephen said, standing up again and feeling rather foolish to find that the flames weren't actually dangerous.

He started to back away slowly, thinking it best to keep an eye on somebody who could blow fire out of their nose.

'You shouldn't walk backwards, it's really not very healthy.'

It was a green-haired girl, carrying a stack of books and a small jar of red liquid.

'My other sister, Caoimhe,' Tom said to Oisín, who probably would have guessed that the girl with leaves in her curly hair was related to Tom in some way. 'Caoimhe, this is –'

'I made this for you,' Caoimhe said, holding out the jar. She didn't seem at all perturbed to find three strangers on the beach.

'Are you sure this will work?' Tom said, eyeing the liquid warily.

'Drink it up! It will fix your arm.'

Caoimhe gave it a quick stir with her pen and handed it to Tom, who gulped it down quickly.

'Delicious,' Tom said, screwing up his face to suggest quite the opposite. 'You should market this, Caoimhe. It's almost as good as Dad's seaweed stew. Whoa!'

Oisín stared at Tom's arm. Even after everything that had happened to them since the morning, he was still amazed at seeing magic. And whatever Stephen might say, there was no other word for what was happening to Tom's arm. The bark crackled and cracked, dropping to the sand like bits of metal. Tom's finger-twigs started to twist and thicken, hairs sprung up on his arm and freckles popped back like magic buttons. In a few seconds, Tom was moving an arm that looked just like Oisín's.

'Can I have some? I'm thiiiiiiirstyyyyyy,' Sorcha asked.

'Maybe that's not such a great idea,' Oisín said quickly. Magic was exciting but it wasn't really something for younger sisters to meddle with.

Sorcha gave a sigh and flopped down on the ground beside Giant.

'Do you like chocolate?' Tom asked, crouching down to her.

Sorcha nodded solemnly.

'We can get you some back on the farm. Dad's been grow-ing chocolate bees. He'll be excited to see you all – we never get Milesians here – and maybe they'll even know if they can find one of those phoney things.'

Stephen rolled his eyes, but didn't bother to correct him. He hoped that Tom's and Antimony's parents were slightly more normal than their children.

Tom held down his hand and pulled Sorcha up. He turned back to his sister.

'Caoimhe, am I supposed to have six fingers?'

★★★

Stephen's hopes that the Houlihans would approach 'normal' were disappointed. Sometimes their father said people were 'eccentric' if they were so different from him that they got on his nerves. Their neighbours who grew their own vegetables instead of buying them at Supervalu were eccentric. Mr Jones, who could sometimes be seen talking to his Great Dane, was a little eccentric. Granny Keane was definitely eccentric. When Oisín met the Houlihans, he wondered if they were so eccentric that his father might have to think up a new word.

For a start, when Tom's mother held out her hand to introduce herself, she insisted they call her Cathleen instead of Mrs Houlihan, laughing and saying that it made her sound old. Neither of Tom's parents seemed very old to Oisín. Cathleen wore large wellies, jeans and a loose checked shirt. Bits of wool and bark poked out of her long red hair. Jimmy Houlihan was the spit of his son, with the same easy smile, but with rings in his nose and ears. Both Jimmy and Cathleen carried on about their kitchen as if it was perfectly normal to have three children drop in off an underwater DART, and the only problem was whether or not there was enough dinner to go round.

'You're in luck: fresh seaweed stew with lemongrass cabbage today,' Jimmy Houlihan said as he stirred a vat of bubbling green soup and prodded some yellow cabbage.

'Dad likes to experiment with food,' Tom whispered. 'Sometimes it tastes really good.' Which made Oisín wonder if today was one of those times.

Cathleen dipped her finger in the pot of soup and tasted.

'Interesting,' she said, and Jimmy tickled her affectionately before giving her a kiss, which Oisín had never seen his parents do and wasn't in any hurry to see either.

Cathleen picked a piece of wool from her hair and used it to attach a bundle of cutlery to a small-wheeled contraption, which looked a bit like a miniature unicycle.

'Mum likes to invent things,' Tom explained as the wheel used the cutlery like skis to propel it towards the table and then deposited a knife and fork at intervals. Oisín thought it might have been easier to set the table by hand, but he didn't say anything. Stephen was less concerned with being polite.

'Can you invent something to get us home?' he asked Cathleen.

It was clear the Houlihans' tree house made him uncomfortable. It was hard to pretend he was sitting down to a regular dinner when the table was a suspended slice of tree trunk. It was even harder to pretend that things were normal when Cathleen's inventions bustled about in every corner. A cluster of staplers snapped at insects like a Venus-fly trap by the window, tubes turned rainwater into washing-up liquid and what looked like mechanical frogs croaked in the corner.

'They're supposed to be clocks,' Tom whispered to Oisín in a tone that suggested that Cathleen's inventions had the same success rate as Jimmy's cooking.

Cathleen pulled a hair from her soup and considered Stephen's request to make something to take them home.

'There is my hot-air bicycle,' she said, chewing on her hair as she thought.

'Mum, that thing couldn't make it to the top of our tree,' Caoimhe said.

'That was a prototype,' Cathleen answered briskly. 'Or I had that idea for the water-skis made out of ironing boards. You just have to bewitch the iron and then you can charge them and –'

'Sink to the bottom of the ocean,' Caoimhe said, raising her eyebrows.

'Maybe you should spend more time researching how to fix your brother's hand,' Cathleen said in a thin voice. Tom had five fingers now, but no thumb.

'Don't worry about it all,' Jimmy said. 'Madame Q is coming over. If anybody'll know how to get you back to Dublin, she will.'

'Why is she coming?' Antimony said quickly.

Oisín had almost forgotten about Antimony. She'd sat there silently for the whole meal, tracing swirls in her soup rather than eating it. She hadn't forgotten about him, though, and continued to look at him carefully.

'Because I asked her over,' Jimmy said in a firm voice.

Oisín could feel the unease around the table.

'Dad, she's mad creepy,' Tom said between slurps of seaweed.

'She's the smartest druid on the island,' Jimmy answered calmly.

Tom's face suggested that she could still be the creepiest. Antimony looked uneasy, as if she wanted to leave the table.

'Does she have to come over?' Tom continued. '*Eachtra* launches tomorrow. We'll be seeing plenty of her then. And she'll be saying we should have been practising magic all year.'

Caoimhe saw the look of confusion on Oisín's face.

'*Eachtra* is a magical ship. Its name means adventure –'

'And every summer it goes on a different adventure,' Tom interrupted her. 'The druids on board take on kids to help run the ship.'

'*If* you pass the test,' Caoimhe added. 'It's hard work but it's the best chance to practise the different kinds of magic.'

'Or have some fun,' Tom said. 'If you're on *Eachtra* you get to meet the magic horses and go to the coolest parts of the island. You know, last summer one of the kids rode on the Great Elk in the Enchanted Forest!'

'I heard two druids were eaten by dragons,' Antimony added in awe, as if being eaten by a dragon was the highest honour a druid could hope for.

Caoimhe raised her eyebrows.

'Of course this will be the first year for all of us, so none of us really knows what it's like. And it'll only be if we make the cut: it's very competitive. Though *some* of us *have* been practising all year.'

Oisín thought about helping to steer a magic ship and fighting dragons. It sounded a lot more exciting than a summer sorting Granny Keane's books. When he broke out of his daydream, Tom was complaining about Madame Q again.

'I don't like the way she looks at you. Like she can see right through you. I swear she's got eyes on the back of her head.'

'Thomas Houlihan, I assure you that my eyes are firmly on the front of my head. You, however, might wish to invest in an extra pair: it might help you avoid offence.'

Everybody turned around to see an imperious older lady standing behind them. From the way Tom gulped and slowly turned green, Oisín knew that this must be the famous Madame Q. She was at least as old as Granny Keane, but much taller and thinner, with her silver hair towering towards the ceiling in a tight beehive hairstyle. She wore a long indigo cloak, the colour of the night sky, with silver stitching so fine that it almost looked invisible. Oisín wondered if he should stand up when she entered the room.

He wasn't the only one. Jimmy Houlihan bent his knees uncertainly, stooped somewhere between sitting and standing.

'Thank you for coming, Madame Q,' he said reverentially.

Madame Q batted him down with an impatient flap of her hand. 'It's always a pleasure to visit your ... house.' Madame Q looked uncertainly around the Houlihans' tree, as if she were unsure whether or not it could really be called a house. 'Especially when you have such distinguished guests.'

Her eyes turned to Oisín. He saw at once why Tom found them creepy. Her irises were the same shade as the stitching on her robes: gleaming silver that pulsed with each flicker of the light.

'You must be the Milesian,' she said, looking at Oisín as if Stephen and Sorcha weren't there.

Oisín nodded uncertainly. He had the same uncomfortable feeling that Tom had mentioned, as if Madame Q was looking right through him.

'Please, Madame, we were hoping that you could help us get home,' Stephen said, standing.

'All in good time,' Madame Q said briskly. 'But first I have to talk to your brother.'

She made another hand motion, as if swatting a fly, and Stephen found himself back on his stool, his cheeks burning. Oisín looked at Madame Q uncertainly.

'So you're the Keeper of the Book of Magic,' she said finally.

Her nose crinkled slightly, as if she might have expected somebody better.

'I guess so,' Oisín mumbled.

'Very well. Do you think I could see the Book?'

Oisín could see Tom and his parents share a glance, and he wished that he had told them about the Book. He reached into his hoodie pocket to pull out the Book of Magic. Everybody leant forward eagerly. Oisín paused.

'Well?' Madame Q said with an impatient twinkle.

'I can't,' Oisín said, feeling his stomach lurch horribly.

He reached into his pocket again to make sure. His hands grasped at the folds of his hoodie: the Book of Magic was definitely gone.

Chapter 6
The Great Queen

Oisín's heart thumped against his chest. Even though he'd only found the Book a few hours ago, he felt its absence keenly, as if he was missing a limb.

'It's gone,' he said, struggling to keep his voice level. 'The Book of Magic is gone.'

'It can't be,' Madame Q said sharply. 'I can feel its energy. It's in this room.'

Oisín stood up and looked around wildly. How could the Book be in the room? He hadn't told any of the Houlihans about it. He caught Antimony's eye.

'She has it,' Antimony said slowly.

Oisín turned around. It wasn't Madame Q that Antimony was looking at, though.

'Sorcha?' he said.

Sorcha had her hands behind her back and a guilty expression on her small face.

'Sorcha, did you take the Book of Magic?' Oisín asked.

Red rose to her cheeks. Oisín felt his own cheeks burn in anger and had to stop himself from jumping over the table and grabbing it.

'It's not a toy, Sorcha.'

'I know that!' Sorcha's face was even redder. 'But it's not fair that you get to have it. I want to do magic too.'

'It's mine!' Oisín cried.

It was the second time Oisín had said those words about the Book of Magic, and again the force in his tone surprised him. The Book of Magic jumped out of Sorcha's hands and skidded across the table. Oisín snatched it quickly, feeling a rush of happiness as he held the little book again. Sorcha looked miserable.

'Do you want a chocolate bee-sting?' Tom asked.

Jimmy was breeding magic bees that produced edible stings the way that hens laid eggs. Tom eased the sting from a large

41

bee and collected cubes of different flavours from a jar beside it, as if it was a kebab stick.

'Dark chocolate, honey and horseradish,' Tom said, bringing it over to Sorcha.

'I don't want any!' Sorcha shouted, pushing his arm away roughly.

'Sorcha!' Stephen said in a voice that their mother might have used.

Sorcha ignored him and scratched her ankle instead. The raven's bite had spread and a thin circle of black radiated out like a cobweb.

'Is your ankle OK?' Caoimhe asked, suddenly interested. 'I could mix up a remedy. Dock-leaves are good for bites and I have a few drops of lavender oil.'

'I want to go home!' Sorcha screamed.

Madame Q clapped her hands with an air of impatience. 'Why don't you go outside and play, child?'

'Come on, I'll show you the jelly trees,' Tom said.

'And you can be my apprentice druid-doctor,' Caoimhe said, bundling up her books. 'I need some help squeezing out the lemon jelly.'

Sorcha didn't seem thrilled about this, but went anyway, dragging each foot slowly to show how unfair the world was. Stephen stood up, unsure whether or not to go.

'She's not usually like that,' he said to Madame Q. 'She's just rattled because of everything that's happened. We need to get her home.'

He said the last word slowly, picturing the solid bricks of their Raheny home and the firm ground of Dublin, and wondering if the word itself was enough to charm them back. Madame Q ignored him and turned to Oisín.

'Now we can begin,' she said, flexing her fingertips.

Oisín put the Book of Magic on the table, feeling a small tingle as he pulled his hand away.

'What is that thing?' Stephen asked as Madame Q picked up the Book.

'One of the most extraordinary and dangerous books in our world,' she said, caressing the Book's leather spine as if it were an old friend.

Madame Q held the Book very respectfully and opened it slowly. For a second, Oisín was sure her eyes changed colour, flashing to a bright green. But when she returned her gaze, her eyes were as silver as ever.

'It's the real thing,' she said finally.

Oisín couldn't quite read her expression. She was definitely impressed by the Book, but there was something else there – fear or excitement, he wasn't sure which.

'So what is this Book of Magic? Can it get them home or not?' Cathleen Houlihan said irritably. She didn't seem to have much time for books in general.

'Of course it can,' Madame Q said.

'I'm its Keeper,' Oisín said. 'Does that mean I can control it?'

'If it wants you to.' Madame Q gave a strange smile, pleased by her answer.

'Is that thing good or evil?' Stephen asked.

Madame Q looked at him as if he were a particularly unimaginative student. 'That isn't the question at all! The Book of Magic is powerful, that's what matters. It's like magic itself. It isn't good or evil – it's both.'

'Where did it come from?' Oisín asked.

A small snort flared from Madame Q's nostrils as if she wasn't used to storytelling and found all these questions rather tiresome.

'You've heard of the Dagda?' she began.

'He's like the god of the Tuatha Dé Danann, right?' Oisín said, scratching at the back of his brain for what he could remember.

Madame Q gave another snort.

'Thinks he's a god!' she said. 'More like a large, fat old man with too much time on his hands.' Jimmy Houlihan looked a little shocked, so Madame Q moved quickly on. 'A long time ago, the Dagda made a huge cauldron in which he placed the great gifts of Ireland. The Stone of the High King. The Harp of the Four Seasons. An Freagarach, the sword that can never be beaten.' Madame Q reeled through these amazing items as if they were of little importance to her. 'There were also six books in the cauldron, governing the five different kinds of magic of the Tuatha Dé Danann.'

'What are the five kinds of magic?' Oisín asked.

Madame Q looked as if her patience for storytelling was stretching.

Jimmy Houlihan answered for her. 'Earth, air, fire, water and Quintessence,' he began. Seeing Oisín's blank expression, he started to sing in a lilting voice:

The first child is born of air
Of atoms and inventions, of clouds and consequences.
The next child comes of water
From music and memory, drops and prophecies.
A third child twists from earth
All soil and toil, all feeling and healing.
Another is forged of fire
Made of spark and swift, of force and fury.
The last child tilts from the worlds' edge
A Quint quite unlike the others
Of moons and mysteries, of blanks and histories.

'What a delightful performance,' Madame Q said with some asperity. 'I haven't heard the Song of Magic since my youth.'

Oisín was torn between imagining a young Madame Q and trying to decipher the strange song when Cathleen interrupted.

'It doesn't have to be too cryptic,' she said brusquely, picking up her invention that was turning rainwater into washing-up liquid. 'Air Magic is about the mind, for example. It governs magical mathematics and shape-shifting. Earth Magic is what looks after this house. And our farm. And Caoimhe's healing. It's all about the body.'

'Water Magic draws on the seas,' Jimmy said. 'It's about using your emotions and reading the future and –'

'Fire Magic is the best,' Antimony said suddenly. 'It's using your spirit to be a warrior and avenge your enemies.'

Oisín had forgotten that she was still sitting there. She was no longer staring at him, but looking at Madame Q with a strange expression. If Madame Q minded, she didn't show it, taking over the story in her own grand fashion.

'And Quintessence is the most important kind,' she said, pronouncing the strange word slowly, as if it held mysteries too delicate for any tongue to fully unravel.

'Er, what is *Quintessence*?' Oisín asked.

'The fifth element,' Madame Q said with an elegant smile. 'The study of everything and nothing, of the swirl of the stars across our sky, of the design at work in the smallest snowflake. Only the most advanced druids study it.'

Oisín didn't really understand what she was saying but found himself captivated nonetheless. He had a sudden, ridiculous vision of becoming a druid, learning all about Quintessence, using the Book of Magic to uncover the mysteries of the universe.

'And what does this Book of Magic do then?' Stephen said, bringing them all back to earth. From the irritated look on her face, it didn't seem that Madame Q thought Stephen was of the right calibre to practise *Quintessence*.

'The Book of Magic was the sixth book in the Dagda's cauldron,' Madame Q said briskly. 'It has sections on each of the five types of magic.'

Madame Q flicked through the Book slowly and Oisín started to understand. There was a section full of pale blue fish and tear stains which Madame Q announced was the Water Magic section. The pages with dirt and green writing had to be Earth Magic, and the section with gleaming orange words and tiny dragons was Fire Magic. The pages towards the back, which Oisín assumed had been empty, turned out to have very fine silver writing: Quintessence.

'So if the Book of Magic can do everything, why would you need the other books?' Oisín asked.

'Because they are full of deep magic that this book only scratches,' Madame Q said. 'On its own, the Book of Magic can do some strong magic, very powerful magic. But its real purpose is to unlock the other books. None of them can work without the Book of Magic as well.'

'They're all lost, though, aren't they?' Antimony said, suddenly quite interested.

'Everything from the Dagda's cauldron has been lost,' Madame Q said. 'The Dagda was in a relationship.' Madame Q said the word 'relationship' as if it were a head-cold – she clearly didn't approve. 'He was in one with a grasping woman who wanted the contents for herself. They fought and the Dagda mustered a great wind, scattering the contents across Ireland. Over the years, some of the items have cropped up. Every warrior in Ireland claimed to have An Freagarach at some stage. There have been rumours about the books, but none has been found. Until now.'

Oisín felt the air in the room getting heavier, the way it did when it was about to rain. How could the strange little book he had found in Granny Keane's study be so important?

'Why am I its Keeper?' he asked, feeling responsibility creep over him like clothes he wasn't sure he could fit into.

'The Dagda was the original Keeper of the Books,' Madame Q said. 'The Keeper of a magical book is the one responsible for it. Unless dark dealings are involved, the Keeper is the only one who can use it to its full capacity. The Keeper also has the power to sign the book over to another owner. Whoever had this book last signed it over to you.'

'But why him? What does he know?'

Oisín glared at Stephen, but the question was one he wanted answered himself.

'That I don't know,' Madame Q said, continuing to fix her silvery eyes on Oisín. 'But I'm sure we'll find out. It's not everybody who has a book for their *croíacht*.'

Oisín had to ask. 'What's a cray-och-thingy?'

'Cree-ocht,' Jimmy said gently when Madame Q ignored the question. 'It's related to *croí*, the Irish word for heart. Which is sort of what it is: your magical heart.'

Jimmy pulled out a small wooden spoon from his apron.

'Every druid has one special item that helps them do magic,' he continued. 'Once you've found your *croíacht*, it starts to become part of you. It means you can do all sorts of different magic.'

Jimmy stirred the spoon in his soup. Slowly, the yellow liquid started to change, growing roots and stretching upwards. Jimmy continued to stir until a small tree popped out of the bowl, sporting bright yellow cabbage flowers. Jimmy picked one off and bit into it happily. Oisín thought about the feeling he'd had when he had picked up the Book of Magic, as if his body was suddenly whole.

'So anything can be a *croíacht*?' he asked.

'Pretty much,' Jimmy said. 'Usually it's an ordinary object that's been waiting for the right owner. Sometimes it takes a while for a druid to find the right fit. Tom hasn't found his yet, but he will soon enough.'

A look passed between Cathleen and Jimmy, as if this was something they worried about.

'Usually your *croíacht* relates to the kind of magic you want to do,' Jimmy continued. 'So Caoimhe has a pen that she uses to heal. Cathleen has a wrench for her inventions. Antimony has a slingshot. And … er … Madame Q has –'

'Had quite enough of this chatter,' Madame Q said quickly.

'Can't we just use this thing to get back home?' Stephen said, impatient with all the talk.

'Yes, that is possible,' Madame Q said after a pause. 'Though I'm not sure it wants to go back yet.'

'Well, he can just sign it over to you and we'll head back to Dublin and leave you to it,' Stephen said, standing up as if he'd solved the problem.

Oisín glared at him again and wished he'd got the DART on his own. He couldn't part with the Book yet. Thankfully, Madame Q didn't want him to either.

'That wouldn't quite work,' she said, pushing the Book back towards Oisín. 'The Book must stay with its Keeper for the moment. It can only be transferred on a day of special magic, during one of our festivals. We've just celebrated Bealtaine in May so the next will be Lughnasa.'

'Is that in August?' Oisín asked, remembering a Celtic calendar from school.

'We're not waiting over a month!' Stephen said when Cathleen nodded. 'You'll have to find another way to get us back.'

'Getting you back is easy,' Madame Q said, waving her hand through the air. 'Protecting the Book is another matter. The Morrígan will already be looking for it.'

'The Morrígan wants the Book?' Oisín asked, remembering the chilling story Granny Keane had told about the Great Queen of Shadows.

'Of course,' Madame Q said. 'She was the one who tried to steal it in the first place. All those years ago, when she was in a relationship with the Dagda.'

Oisín wondered if Madame Q had been alive then, but remembered that it wasn't polite to ask how old a lady was. Granny Keane always laughed when he did, saying she was old enough that she didn't want to remember.

'But why would the Morrígan want the Book?' Oisín asked. 'I thought she could already do whatever magic she wanted.'

'The Book is the key to unlocking all the others,' Madame Q said. 'If the Morrígan managed to get hold of it, she could find the other lost books. If she could become Keeper of all six books, she'd be able to control all the magic in the world.'

Oisín felt the air in the room grow cooler as they all imagined that kind of power and what would happen if it fell into the wrong hands. Madame Q looked at him with a shrewd expression.

'What do you know of the Morrígan?'

'Nothing,' Stephen answered quickly, but Oisín ignored him. He had the uncomfortable feeling that Madame Q could find out what happened anyway, so he told her about the green-eyed ravens.

Madame Q stood very still, considering her thoughts as if they were a fine wine to be savoured. 'So one of the ravens pecked at your sister. That could be useful. Perhaps we could talk to her.'

Stephen was about to protest when Tom and Caoimhe came rushing in. Words barrelled out of them.

'It happened so fast. I thought it would be funny to surprise Caoimhe –'

'You were going to squeeze lemon jelly all over me.'

'Because you kept going on about it, as if you're an expert –'

'I *am* an expert! And you were –'

'What happened?' Cathleen's voice cut in.

Tom looked as if he wanted the ground to swallow him whole.

'It's your sister,' he said turning to Stephen and Oisín. 'She's disappeared.'

★★★

Sorcha was feeling very grumpy. Oisín had a magic book and she'd been fed cabbage soup instead of Maltesers. Her ankle was still itchy and her mother wasn't anywhere to be seen.

She slumped down beside a tree. She could hear them all calling for her, but she wasn't going to come out yet. They'd have to be really nice to her and not send her off like a stupid baby. She'd teach them a lesson.

'Are you a princess?'

Sorcha looked up in surprise to find a beautiful young lady in front of her. The most beautiful lady she'd ever seen.

'I'm Sorcha,' she said slowly.

'What a beautiful name that is. You must be a ballerina, look at those long legs you have. You'd like to be a ballerina princess, wouldn't you?'

Sorcha nodded her head. She thought she'd never seen such beautiful sleek black hair and hoped hers might be as long as the lady's one day.

'You know, Sorcha, I've been waiting to meet a little girl just like you so I can find my next princess.'

The lady's voice was soft like melted chocolate. She was much better than Cathleen Houlihan with her messy hair and man's shirt.

'I've been waiting to meet a princess because I have a very special gift for you.'

'Is it Maltesers?'

'It's much better than that.'

'Can I see?'

'I keep it in my kingdom. Do you want to come and get it?'

'Is it far?'

'Oh, no,' the lady said, smiling. 'All you have to do is climb onto my back and we'll be there in seconds.'

Sorcha could hear Oisín calling for her in the distance. She'd teach him to keep the Book all for himself.

'You don't want to stay the night in a smelly tree, do you? Not when I have a nice big bed that can be all yours. And a very special gift that's all for Sorcha. One that you won't have to share with anybody else.'

Sorcha hesitated. She really wasn't supposed to go off with strangers. But then again, they probably weren't supposed to go on underwater trains either, and wasn't this nice lady much less strange than people who lived in a tree and ate lemon cabbage?

Sorcha heard Stephen calling her name. Probably trying to steal my present, she thought, scratching her ankle and holding her hand out to the beautiful lady.

'Are you a real queen?' Sorcha asked as she climbed up onto the lady's back.

The lady gave a little smile as she flashed her emerald eyes and the ground swirled below.

'Of course I am, my dear. I'm the Great Queen.'

Chapter 7
The Plan

Oisín thought he was going to be sick.

'Drink some tea,' Caoimhe said, placing another mug of hot nettle tea on the table. There didn't seem to be any herbal remedy for an evil witch kidnapping your sister, so Caoimhe kept on making tea. It was what her parents always did in a crisis. Several mugs of tea sat in front of them on the table, cold and strangely sad.

Oisín pushed the latest mug away from him and went over to the sink for what felt like the hundredth time. Instead of two taps, several thin pipes hovered over the sink, reminding Oisín of a church organ. Each pipe dropped a different liquid into a jar below. Caoimhe explained that druids communicated by Water Magic, so each pipe transported messages. The one that dribbled drops of rain told the weather. Another, dropping chunks of ice, told news from Caoimhe's friend in New Zealand. A bright orange stream filled one jar with a recipe for orange juice curry from Jimmy's mother. There was only one jar that Oisín was looking at, though: one filled with thick black liquid. Oisín tapped his finger against the jar. A sickly sharp woman's voice came out.

'Bring me the Book of Magic by Lughnasa, or never see your sister again.'

'We know what it says,' Stephen snapped.

Stephen continued to pace around the kitchen. The adults had all gone upstairs, but no matter how hard he twisted his neck, Stephen couldn't hear what they were saying.

Oisín was still staring at the thick black liquid. Every now and then it shifted shape so that it showed the face of a beautiful woman, who was smiling in triumph. Beside her, a small girl was sleeping.

'At least she's safe,' Caoimhe said.

Stephen glared at her. 'Why don't you swap with her then?'

Caoimhe turned pink and went over to make another cup of tea. Oisín hoped she was right, that at least Sorcha was safe. Madame Q had explained that Sorcha was in an enchanted sleep, deep in Cnoc na gCnámh, the Hill of Bones far to the north of the island, where the Morrígan lived. Nothing bad would happen to her. As long as they gave over the Book.

'Why didn't she just take the Book?' Oisín said. 'Or just take me?'

'That's not how she works,' Tom said grimly. 'She wants to cause the most pain possible.'

Oisín could tell that both Tom and Caoimhe felt horribly guilty. They all did. Even Antimony looked uncomfortable, though it could hardly have been her fault at all. He turned away from the sink and looked down at his little book with a mixture of dread and disgust. He hated the Book for causing all this trouble. He'd give it over to the Morrígan in a second if it saved Sorcha. Yet it wasn't the Book's fault, was it? And if he gave up the Book, what would the Morrígan do with it? And what would he do without it?

'Give me that thing, Dirtface.'

'It's not yours,' Oisín said, standing up to Stephen.

'I'm taking it up north. Hand it over!'

Stephen lunged for the Book but Oisín had been ducking from him long enough to know how he worked and dived under the table. Stephen jumped on top of him, trying to wrestle the Book out of his hand. Oisín heard a mug smash, saw nettle tea pool across the floor. And then Stephen screamed.

Oisín pulled himself up and saw Caoimhe quickly dipping her pen in the nettle tea and shooting a stream towards Stephen's jeans. They had been on fire. For a second, Oisín had a terrible feeling that the Book of Magic had caused it. Then he saw Antimony's slingshot.

'I told you it would be real next time. Leave the Book alone.'

'Stay still,' Caoimhe said, before Stephen could respond.

A small pair of scissors had emerged from the tip of her pen and she was cutting the frayed bottom of his jeans so that they were even. Oisín hadn't noticed how unusual her pen was until now. It was made of thick bark, with circles inside like the rings of a tree trunk. Each circle had a different kind of material, which Caoimhe could shoot out and retract with a swish of her hand. One moment she was dabbing Stephen's ankle with dock-leaf, the next, grass had emerged from the tip and she was dusting ash from his runners. He didn't seem to be hurt, which Oisín had to be thankful for. Whatever he felt about Stephen, with Sorcha missing, he needed all the siblings he could get.

Stephen was still staring at Antimony, who kept her slingshot in the air. Before either of them could do anything, the adults clambered down the ladder. Jimmy Houlihan swept his eyes over the spilled tea and charred table leg but decided not to say anything. He placed his hand on Oisín's shoulder, the way people did at funerals. Oisín sat down, feeling even sicker than before.

'Chin up, boy, chin up. Help is at hand!'

Oisín looked up at the stout elderly lady who had come in behind Jimmy and Cathleen.

'Mrs Fitzfeather,' said the woman, bustling over and shaking Oisín's hand vigorously. 'Captain of *Eachtra*. We'll sort it all out for you.'

Mrs Fitzfeather was short, with an eyepatch, lots of bright shawls around her and a variety of facial hair that matched her white curls. Madame Q stood beside her with a grimace, which made Oisín suspect that she was too delicate for Mrs Fitzfeather's booming voice.

'Keep up the courage, boy!' Mrs Fitzfeather shouted, pumping Oisín's hand as though this might make him feel better.

'Perhaps we can get to the plan, Mrs Fitzfeather?' Madame Q said in a crisp tone.

'Of course, of course,' Mrs Fitzfeather said, pulling her shawls around her and moving her hand away from Oisín's. It paused in mid-air, hovering slightly above the table.

'This is the Book, is it?' she asked.

'Yes.' Oisín nodded.

'Such a troubling thing,' she said, her fingers drifting towards the Book's cover. 'So powerful and so dreadful.'

Her stubby fingers rested inches from the cover and Oisín had to restrain himself from pulling it away.

'Mrs Fitzfeather?'

Madame Q's voice broke Mrs Fitzfeather's concentration. She jerked her hand away from the Book.

'Yes, yes, looks like the real thing,' she said finally. 'That does make things more difficult. I wonder if we shouldn't destroy it.'

'We can't destroy it,' Madame Q said quickly. 'At least not until Lughnasa.' She turned to Oisín with a curious expression. 'Then you could transfer it to somebody more suitable.' She weighed each word slowly, as if imagining herself as Keeper of the Book of Magic.

'You know that's not what we agreed,' Mrs Fitzfeather snapped. 'Transferring the Book is not part of the plan.'

'What is this plan? What are you going to do to save my sister?' Stephen asked, pounding his fist down on the counter in frustration.

'Don't worry, boy,' Mrs Fitzfeather said gruffly. 'We have it under control. As some of you know, *Eachtra* travels north every year. While we don't normally like to travel so close to the Morrígan's territory, we could do it this year.'

'What?' Oisín asked. 'Are we going with you on *Eachtra*?'

'Not a bit of it, boy, that's far too dangerous!' Mrs Fitzfeather said, laughing at the idea of such an enterprise 'You're both Milesians, you'd be sizzled in a volcano or strangled by an octopus in no time.'

'But won't the Morrígan want to see me?' Oisín asked. 'I'm the only one who can give away the Book.'

'He has a point,' Madame Q started.

'We agreed on this!' Mrs Fitzfeather said in a sharp tone, which suggested that they hadn't agreed about much at all. Her one green eye flashed with fury. She turned back to Oisín and attempted another smile. 'Far too dangerous for you to face the Morrígan, boy. But *Eachtra* has a shipshape crew. Our Keeper of Books will guard it in our library.'

'What about Sorcha?' Stephen almost shouted.

'Do sit down, young man,' Madame Q said. 'The finest druids in the world travel aboard *Eachtra*. I can assure you that we are more than a match for the Morrígan. We'll find a way to release your sister without giving up the Book.'

Or a way to just keep the Book, Oisín thought. When it came to it, he knew that Madame Q wouldn't give up the most powerful book in the world for a seven-year-old girl. Frustration boiled up through his body.

'And what are we supposed to do? Just wait here?'

The last hour of waiting had been agonising. He didn't think he could face a whole summer watching tea grow cold while Sorcha was trapped in the Morrígan's chamber.

'That's exactly it, boy. You will just wait here.' Mrs Fitzfeather said, as if Oisín had solved a particularly difficult sum. 'We'll have to convince your parents that you're all away at the Gaeltacht, but a little magic dust on the envelope should persuade them that this is perfectly normal. And the Houlihans have agreed to look after you, just don't be clogging up their kitchen.'

'It's the best option,' Jimmy said, avoiding Cathleen's gaze.

'I don't need to be babysat,' Stephen said. 'Just show me which direction the Morrígan's mountain is in, and I'll be off.'

'Technically, Cnoc na gCnámh is a hill, not a mountain,' Madame Q said, supremely unconcerned with Stephen's frustration. 'Although, certainly, it is as impressive as any mountain and often referred to as such.'

'I don't care if it's a hill, a mountain or a mongoose,' Stephen shouted, his clenched knuckles turning white. 'Just show me which direction it's in. I don't need any book: I'll kill her with my bare hands.'

'You'll have to stay put,' Madame Q said firmly. 'There's no way you can make it up north by Lughnasa on your own.'

'If it's that far, how can Sorcha already be asleep up there? I knew you were lying to us!'

'I did no such thing,' Madame Q said icily. She clapped her hands together and produced a cloud of silvery smoke. A map of the island appeared instantly.

'We are here,' Madame Q said, gesturing to the bottom of the map. 'Cnoc na gCnámh, the Morrígan's Hill of Bones, is up here.' Madame Q stretched her arm to the tip of the map, where a large mound of bone loomed. 'Cnoc na gCnámh is protected by the Morrígan's dark magic – only she can whisk there in seconds. Unless you are a far superior druid to myself, which I somehow doubt, it will take you weeks to travel that far north.'

Madame Q's finger traced the path from the Houlihans' beach up to the north of the island. 'Then there are the obstacles that *Eachtra* faces. There's Sliabh na Gaoithe, the Mountain of Wind; Linn an Bhróin, the Pool of Sadness; the Forest of Shadows; and, of course, the fire-fields in the north.'

Oisín looked at the silvery map with awe. Madame Q's fingers moved slowly over huge mountains, across deep rivers, through dark forests and finally across a series of flames to the bare mound of bone where the Morrígan lived. He couldn't believe Sorcha was so far away. Madame Q clapped her hands and the map dissolved.

'We'll come on your boat, then,' Stephen said.

'*Eachtra* is a magical vessel, not a *boat*!' Mrs Fitzfeather said with a touch of wounded pride. 'We don't have room for any Mileseans who can't do magic. You'll be much safer here. Think of it as a summer holiday.'

Stephen clenched his fists, as if he was considering whether it was ever appropriate to fight with elderly ladies. He seemed to decide against this course, storming out of the room and into the forest instead.

'It's understandable,' Cathleen said. 'He just wants to do something.'

'We agreed, it's safest for them to stay here,' Jimmy said in a calm voice.

'Sometimes you can't afford to be safe,' Cathleen said, looking out into the forest.

Jimmy placed his hand on her shoulder but Cathleen shrugged it off.

'Ah, leave me, Jimmy. I know what the plan is.'

She shot a dark glance at Madame Q and Mrs Fitzfeather and stalked off into the forest. Jimmy's shoulders dropped, as if he'd been punched.

It was already causing divisions, Oisín thought. He'd only had it for a day and already everybody was fighting over the Book of Magic. Could it be that great if it caused so much trouble?

'Best get this thing aboard *Eachtra*,' Mrs Fitzfeather said, standing by the edge of the table.

'Maybe I should look after it,' Madame Q said, stepping forward.

For a second, Oisín saw the desire in both their eyes, the strange hold the Book of Magic had over people. Mrs Fitzfeather caught his gaze and started as if she had been surprised by a mouse. She pulled her hand back from the Book.

'Maybe neither of us should take it,' she said. 'It isn't something that a powerful druid should get too close to.'

'I can mind it for the moment,' Antimony said, a little too quickly.

'That won't be necessary,' Madame Q said. 'Jimmy, you will look after it. It should have no effect on a druid of your level. You can bring it when you drop off your children tomorrow.'

'Sure,' Jimmy said, too distracted to be offended that Madame Q didn't think him a good enough druid to be tempted by the Book.

He winced apologetically at Oisín as he picked up the little book and put it in his pocket. His green eyes flashed for a second, but he seemed mostly immune from the Book's power.

Oisín gripped the table. He felt a tug at the Book being taken from him, but he didn't have enough energy to resist. How did he think he could ever be its Keeper or have a *croíacht*? He didn't know anything at all about magic and now his little sister was in trouble because he couldn't just leave the Book on the floor. It was all his fault.

'I'm going to bed,' he said.

'Don't worry, boy, we'll get your sister back,' Mrs Fitzfeather said, slapping his back as he walked towards the ladder.

He turned back to find Madame Q looking at him. It didn't matter if she could see through him, it was pretty clear what he was feeling at the moment. He dragged his feet up the ladder, taking the kind of slow steps that Sorcha took when she didn't want to go to bed. Oisín felt a terrible pang at the thought of her, miles and miles away in a cold cave.

On an ordinary night, Oisín would have been blown away by Tom's room where Jimmy had made him a moss bed. At the very top of the tree, it was full of Cathleen's inventions and the wonderful smell of outside. Oisín couldn't muster up any excitement, though, even when the leaves moved from side to side like windscreen wipers to keep out the rain. He dug his head into the pillow and wished he could get to sleep.

'Oisín!'

Oisín turned to see Tom and Caoimhe crouched beside him.

'I don't want any tea.'

'We've got a plan.'

Oisín leant back on the pillow and looked at Tom.

'What kind of plan?'

'We feel really bad about letting your sister run away like that,' Tom said, looking at the floor.

'It's not your fault,' Oisín said quickly. 'What's the plan?'

Tom and Caoimhe looked at each other. They both seemed a little unsure how to broach the subject.

'It's not that we don't trust Madame Q,' Caoimhe started.

Tom coughed a little, to show that he didn't entirely agree.

'But …'

'We just don't think we should leave the adults with that book.'

'But what can I do? I can't go aboard *Eachtra*.'

'Maybe you can,' Caoimhe said, sharing a glance with her brother.

After they had told him their plan, Oisín found it even harder to get to sleep. He listened to the rain pattering against the leaves, wondering if he was about to do something very stupid.

Chapter 8:
Sliabh na Gaoithe

'Nothing can possibly go wrong,' Tom said, giving Oisín a quick thumbs-up before throwing a blanket over him.

Oisín lay down in the boot of the Houlihans' van and groaned. 'Nothing can possibly go wrong' was exactly the kind of thing that you weren't supposed to say before you went through with a plan. Especially a plan that involved lying to every adult Oisín had met on the island.

'Where's Oisín?' Cathleen Houlihan asked from the front. 'Doesn't he want to say goodbye?'

'We said goodbye upstairs,' Caoimhe said sweetly.

It was agreed that she was better at lying than Tom, who, Oisín was sure, was blushing at that moment.

'Bye, Stephen!' Caoimhe called out.

Oisín felt a twinge of guilt. They hadn't told Stephen about the plan. He'd be standing in the tree-house, getting smaller and smaller as the van bumped its way down the Houlihans' road.

Oisín tried not to think of the names Stephen would invent for him when he found out that he'd been abandoned. This was easy enough, as it took most of Oisín's energy not to get sick. The vehicle that he was hiding in wasn't really a van, but a contraption that Cathleen had made out of twigs and branches. Gramophones and old hoover pipes collected sunlight on the roof and Cathleen used her wrench *croíacht* to steer. Even the wheels were mostly wooden, which made for a very bumpy ride. From the sharp twists and turns, it seemed like they were climbing up a mountain road, and Oisín thought it better not to know how close to death he was each time Cathleen swerved around a corner at the last minute.

At least he had the Book of Magic. The twinge of guilt expanded to fill his stomach as he held the Book. It had been Caoimhe's idea to give her father a few drops of forget-me-not potion. Oisín had been worried that Jimmy's head would turn midnight blue or he'd never forget anything, which had sounded more likely, given the name of the flower. However, it had worked ('Of course it did,' Caoimhe had snapped) and Jimmy Houlihan was now sitting in the front seat happily, without any idea that he was supposed to deliver the Book of Magic to Mrs Fitzfeather.

'It's just a precaution,' Caoimhe had said. 'Once you get to the top of Sliabh na Gaoithe, they'll have to take you on board. But if you have the Book, maybe that means you can keep it. And it will help you if you have any problems.'

Oisín didn't want to think about what the problems might be. Caoimhe and Tom had both been very hazy about what Sliabh na Gaoithe actually was.

'It just means the Mountain of Wind,' Tom had said, shrugging his shoulders as if this was no big deal.

'Remember, I'm going to make a ladder out of ivy,' Caoimhe had reminded him. 'All you have to do is climb up.'

Right, Oisín thought to himself. All he had to do was climb an ivy ladder up a mountain of wind, making sure that nobody tried to take the Book of Magic. Or saw him. No problem.

Oisín's head was so full of things he was trying not to think about that the three hour ride flew by. Before he knew it, the van veered around another tight corner and came to a stop.

'Here we are,' Cathleen announced.

Oisín swallowed a gulp. They'd made it to the mountain already.

'Tom! Watch it!'

That was Tom spilling his blackcurrant juice all over Caoimhe's bag. Oisín's cue to get out of the boot.

'Stop making such a fuss, Caoimhe,' Cathleen said brusquely.

Oisín only had a few seconds. He lifted up the blanket, gently pushed up the lid of the boot and jumped to the ground.

Snow crunched beneath his feet. Oisín ran towards a large rock, hoping everybody was too distracted by Tom and Caoimhe's argument to notice. When he peeped from behind the boulder, he saw Jimmy Houlihan smiling absently as he walked round the car.

'Guess I left the boot open,' he said, scratching his head and closing the boot. Caoimhe must have given him quite a lot of forget-me-not potion.

Oisín tried to ignore his stomach, which was squirming guiltily now. He felt the Book of Magic nestle into his hands and wondered yet again at the things it made people do. He pushed the thought away and looked over at Sliabh na Gaoithe.

Any excitement Oisín might have had about magic was quickly fading. He thought of Sorcha and stopped himself from running back to the van. It wasn't just that Sliabh na Gaoithe rose towards the clouds until he couldn't see the top. It wasn't just the enchanted winds, which whipped ferociously around the mountain while the air a few feet away was perfectly calm. It was the group of about thirty children standing at the bottom, shuffling their feet in the snow and waiting. Oisín had been getting on alright with Tom and Caoimhe but he'd never been one to make lots of friends. Something about the group of chattering children made Oisín feel just as nervous as the mountain of wind in front of him did.

Oisín watched as Tom, Caoimhe and Antimony joined the group. Tom had told him that *Eachtra* accepted children over twelve from all of the magic islands around the coast of Ireland. There was a red-haired girl who sounded like she was from one of the western islands. A chubby boy with expensive-looking runners had a Northern Irish accent. Another boy who was kicking a football sounded like he lived closer to Dublin. Oisín had never heard of any magic islands, so he was amazed to see so many children his own age who had grown up in such a different world.

He was even more surprised to see how many children had come from magic communities in other countries. The red-haired girl made everybody say where they were from and Oisín could barely keep up with the different destinations that children had travelled from. There was an American boy, playing a flute. A small Japanese girl was blowing on her hands to keep them warm. A pair of Guatemalan twins shared squares of magic hot chocolate. An Australian boy popped one into his mouth, looking like he wished he'd worn something more than Bermuda shorts and a T-shirt. They had all been practising for ages to join *Eachtra*. Did Oisín really think he could just climb up a ladder?

He tried to listen to the snatches of conversation to distract himself.

'Canada?' the red-haired girl said to another girl, not sounding very impressed. 'I didn't know there were druids in Canada! Of course, not everybody gets accepted as part of *Eachtra*'s crew. Although, if you can't use Air Magic to climb this thing, you might as well go home anyway! I'm just waiting until Madame Q picks her new Quints …'

'Me too,' the chubby Northern boy announced. 'All the McIntosh clan have been Quints. I'll be the thirteenth Conor McIntosh to travel aboard *Eachtra*.'

'Oh, you're a McIntosh, *congratulations*,' the red-haired girl said with a hard laugh. Two curly-haired girls giggled behind her as if she'd said something very funny.

'I'm Medb Gaultney,' she said, playing with a curved gold necklace around her neck. 'From the Gaultney goldsmiths. And yes, this is a real torc.'

Oisín was starting to feel cold inside. It wasn't just the snow: he didn't know anything about magic or Quints or where anybody came from. At least Medb couldn't see him to quiz him. Antimony wasn't so lucky.

'No need to ask where you're from,' Medb said. 'I heard the Ogonis' daughter was on the island.'

'What's it to you?' Antimony snapped.

'I heard standards were slipping. But I didn't think *Eachtra* would ever let traitors' children aboard.'

Antimony looked like she was about to set something on fire, but at that moment a pair of huge white wings swooped down from the mountain. Oisín gazed at the giant swan: it was six feet tall with wings the size of front doors. And it was talking.

'I'm Angus Óg,' the swan said in a grand voice. 'I'll be piloting *Eachtra* through the magic mountains. As you know, only the bravest and brightest of children will be selected to join the crew. Your first task stands before you. You may use any means at your disposal to ascend Sliabh na Gaoithe. Those who do not make it will not board *Eachtra*. You have two hours. Begin.'

Without so much as a 'Good luck,' Angus Óg was gone, flapping his huge wings and disappearing into the clouds. Oisín noticed quite a few nervous gulps in the crowd and saw that, unlike Tom and Caoimhe, not everybody had realised how difficult the first task was going to be. One girl was walking further and further away from the mountain, searching to see if her parents had left yet. Others were getting started. Antimony had already put some fire-sticks in her slingshot. Tom was making strange animal sounds. Conor McIntosh was whispering to his runners, which were starting to grow wings. Medb picked off a ruby from her necklace. It looked like one boy was trying to scale the mountain with his bare hands, though Oisín could hardly see with the wind whirling around.

Oisín tried not to think about all the incredible magic and turned towards Caoimhe. The grass from her pen had made a tent to keep off the winds and she was crouched on the ground, tickling a small patch of ivy with her pen. It curled lazily into a crevice, as if it wanted another few minutes in bed. Caoimhe persisted and, bit by bit, the ivy stretched into a ladder. It wasn't the most stable of structures with which to scale a giant mountain beset by ferocious winds, but it was something. Oisín promised himself that he wouldn't look down.

'Watch out!'

Oisín and Caoimhe dived out of the way as soon as they heard Antimony's cry. There was an enormous crash as a huge chunk of the mountain fell to the ground and flattened Caoimhe's tent, smashing into several pieces of snow and ice as it landed and leaving jagged rocks scattered along the base of the mountain.

'What do you think you're doing?' Antimony shouted. 'You're not supposed to use dynamite magic. You could have killed us all.'

Medb stroked her necklace. Oisín had a feeling that each jewel was very dangerous.

'Any means at your disposal,' Medb said in a sweet voice. 'Besides, I thought your family was the expert on murder.'

Before Antimony could do anything, Medb was already performing some sort of Air Magic on one of the chunks that had fallen, whispering to it until it rose off the ground like a kind of icy magic carpet. She hopped on and smiled, not at all bothered about the wreckage she had left below.

'Oisín!'

Oisín turned to where Caoimhe's voice came from and realised with a sickening jolt what had happened. They had jumped in different directions and now there were several giant boulders between him and Caoimhe – and her ladder. Caoimhe could still climb up to the top of the mountaiian, but there was no way Oisín could reach her ladder. Caoimhe looked at him desperately over the rubble, flicking through one of her herbal books as if it might provide some solace.

'The problem is that nothing grows here,' she said in a tight voice. 'I can't change the direction of this ladder and I've left most of my herbs at home. Tom's already turned into a mountain goat, so he can't help either.'

Oisín had no idea how he could climb Sliabh na Gaoithe. He didn't have a board to surf up the mountain like the Australian boy. Nor was he able to charm a flock of seagulls to carry him like the American boy. He certainly couldn't turn into a crane and fly like the Japanese girl.

'You'll have to use the Book,' Caoimhe said.

'But I don't know how!'

'Of course you do – you're its Keeper.'

Caoimhe looked at her ladder, which was stretching up into the air, clearly torn. She wanted to help Oisín. But she'd been waiting to board *Eachtra* for as long as she could remember. Now that she'd got her first potion right (even if it was a mild poison on her father) she couldn't turn back, could she?

'Go on,' Oisín said, sensing her struggle. 'I'll use the Book. I'll be grand.'

Caoimhe gave a relieved smile.

'I'll see you at the top.'

The winds almost stole her words and in a few seconds, she'd disappeared up the ladder. Oisín looked up at the mountain hopelessly. Everybody else was using their *croíacht*s. Conor McIntosh's runners had sprouted wings and were fluttering tentatively. One of the giggling curly-headed girls had pulled out knitting needles and was knitting a magic rope. The Guatemalan boy was quickly sketching an escalator with his magic brush *croíacht*. Even the boy who was climbing the mountain with his bare hands was getting closer to the top.

Oisín thought about jumping on the escalator, but the boy was rubbing it out as he went up. Oisín picked up the Book of Magic and shook it. Nothing happened. He could feel Sorcha and *Eachtra* slip further and further away from him. He moved closer to the mountain. The wind knocked him over in seconds, whipping mercilessly through him, as if it was playing a triumphant song with his teeth as its instrument.

It was easy for the wind, Oisín thought bitterly, all it had to do was blow.

And then, as he sat there in the terrible wind, something clicked in his head. It was like the moment when they'd started algebra in fifth class. At first, the blackboard had been a swirl of letters and symbols and Oisín couldn't understand at all what the alphabet had to do with sums. Then one day, he saw beyond the chalky letters and understood the meaning. He felt as if he was stretching, reaching for something on a shelf several feet above. And when he grasped the shelf, when it all made sense, it was like he had learnt a different language.

That was sort of how he felt now, sitting in the wind at the bottom of Sliabh na Gaoithe. Before this, he had just done what the Book of Magic had wanted. Suddenly, he had his own idea of how magic worked – it was a shelf almost within reach. He flicked quickly to the Air Magic section.

'Wind, wind, wind,' he whispered to the Book. If it was easy for the wind, why not *become* it?

Nothing happened. Oisín wasn't concerned. He *knew* he was right, even if he couldn't say why. He just wasn't speaking the right words. Or the right language. Most of the other words in the Book had been in Irish. But what was the Irish for wind? Oisín wished he'd spent less time looking out at the clouds in Irish class. *Scamall*, that was the word for cloud, but that wasn't any use. *Spéir. Bogha báistí. An ghrian ag taitneamh.* Lots of weather words spun through Oisín's head but not the one he needed. How was he supposed to climb *Sliabh na Gaoithe* if he couldn't think of the word for …

Sliabh na Gaoithe! Of course!

'*Gaoth*!' Oisín shouted.

He repeated the word to the Book, sure he was onto something. The Book shifted slightly, the tiniest of movements. Oisín whispered the word again, concentrating as hard as he could. Just when he was about to give up, the pages started to move, flapping in time with an invisible wind of their own. When they stopped, Oisín saw a picture of a tiny cloud blowing five words across the page. He peered at the page to read them: *Rith ar nós na gaoithe.*

Oisín searched his brain. *Rith* was the Irish for run, that was easy. *Nós* was harder. He remembered Granny Keane saying something about *sean nós* music, and he knew that meant 'old style' music. Run in the style of the wind?

'Run like the wind!' Oisín shouted, and seconds later that was what he was doing, legging it around the mountain as fast as he could manage. He ignored the wind whooshing at his face, concentrating instead on the words, *rith ar nós na gaoithe*, calling them again and again.

Oisín wasn't exactly sure how or when it happened. One moment he was running, the wind whacking him in his face, the Book of Magic fluttering in his hands. And then the next, he couldn't quite feel the ground underneath his feet or the weight of his hands. He'd had dreams before where he'd been running and jumping and then suddenly he was flying and this was a little like that, except much, much better. He couldn't feel his legs or hands because he didn't have any: he'd turned into the wind.

Oisín gasped (or he felt like he did, since he wasn't sure if he still had a mouth to gasp from) as he looked down and saw the road Cathleen's van had swerved along far below. He was about halfway up the mountain face, but he was being pulled further and further from it by the gusts of wind. Oisín twisted whatever particles he was made up of now and found a current that was going in the right direction. *Up*, he thought, and tried to turn his wind-self up towards the clouds. It was harder than he might have thought, but he managed it and then he was zipping along with the wind, travelling faster and faster, up and up and up.

It was the most wonderful feeling he had ever had. Snow-covered fields and icy rivers were far, far below and he was high above the ground in the open air. He was the air, at once himself and part of everything around him. He did a little loop-the-loop through the wind currents with joy, suddenly feeling very free. Oisín might have continued flying and flying if he hadn't seen the top of Sliabh na Gaoithe coming into view. Making his way into a downward current, he focused on reaching the mountain top where he could see Angus Óg and a number of figures. Down, down, he thought to himself and then he was doing it, dipping like a plane approaching a runway. The ground gulped up to meet him, closer and closer and then it was right in front of him and –

'You might need to work on your landing,' a crisp English voice said.

Oisín had bowled into a tall blond boy. He was about fifteen and impeccably dressed.

'Sorry,' Oisín said, glad to see that he still had his voice, and the rest of his body for that matter. The Book of Magic was still in his hands, the words already invisible as if nothing had happened.

The boy stood up, dusting snow off his blazer and casting an appraising glance at Oisín.

'Wind Magic is very advanced. How did you manage it, Pipsqueak?'

'It's Oisín.'

'Right. But what's your secret?'

The boy's blue eyes landed on the Book of Magic. He checked himself and held out his hand.

'I'm Lysander Quicksilver,' he said in a confident voice. 'One of Madame Q's Quints.'

Lysander shook Oisín's hand very formally, as if he were fifty rather than fifteen, but his eyes remained fixed on the Book.

'Lysander? Are you keeping time or not?'

It was Angus Óg, flapping over towards them. Lysander rolled his eyes.

'Of course I am,' he said, pulling out a sleek silver pocket watch from his blazer. Lysander's clear voice rang across the mountain.

'All right, everybody, ten seconds before this party is closed to all losers.'

Oisín looked around the mountain. Most of the other children had made it to the top. Caoimhe gave him a smile. Tom beamed at him with curled horns still on his head. Antimony looked at him in surprise. Medb Gaultney gave him a curious look, as if she hadn't quite decided where he slotted into her life.

'Nine, eight, seven.'

Oisín scanned the crowd. He couldn't see any sign of Mrs Fitzfeather. She'd have to let him stay once the deadline had passed.

'Six.'

The two curly-headed girls heaved themselves up their woollen rope in a fit of giggles. Angus Óg flapped his feathers irritably.

'Five, four, three, two ...'

'One.'

Lysander turned to see which voice had stolen his line.

'He made it!' the boy with the magic football cried in admiration as everybody turned around to see the last child who had made it up the mountain. It was the boy who had climbed up with his bare hands, which were now chafed and cut with the cold. He didn't seem to want to relish his moment, hiding his face in his hood.

'This doesn't count,' Lysander said, irritated. 'You have to climb Sliabh na Gaoithe by magic.'

'No,' Angus Óg said with a slow shake of his head. ' "Use any means at your disposal." That is the phrase. It's never been interpreted in this way. But that is the phrase. You've made it just in time.'

The boy nodded, as if that had never been in doubt.

'Well, this is a day of firsts!' Angus Óg continued. 'One boy turns into wind, another climbs the mountain without magic! Well, whatever your methods, you have passed the test. What is your name?'

The boy sat down on the snow and answered in a defiant voice that was very familiar to Oisín.

'Stephen Keane.'

Chapter 9
Snakes in the Snow

Oisín felt as if he was back at school. Stephen was surrounded by a group of admiring children, dying to hear about his bare-handed climb up the mountain. Oisín was sitting with the Book of Magic, almost as invisible as when he'd turned into the wind. The only people who weren't listening to Stephen's story were Lysander Quicksilver and his friends – and Antimony, who continued to watch Oisín carefully.

'But how did you get to the mountain?' Caoimhe asked.

'Your mum gave me that air bicycle of hers,' Stephen said.

It looked as if he was tiring of his fame. Every time he spoke, Nuala and Noreen, the two curly-headed girls, repeated what he had said as a question.

'You got here on an air bicycle?' they gushed excitedly. They seemed incapable of speech that didn't end in fits of giggles.

'I knew Mum was up to something,' Tom said. 'Probably why she didn't notice our plan: she was too busy thinking about helping you. But why didn't you just ride that thing up to the top of the mountain?'

'It's not the most stable device,' Stephen said, in a tone that suggested his feelings about magic hadn't changed all that much.

'You know, nobody's ever climbed Sliabh na Gaoithe without magic before,' the boy with the magic football said in a tone that suggested he had a new hero.

'Well, I wouldn't recommend it,' Stephen said, rubbing snow into the many cuts on his hands.

'You wouldn't recommend it?' Nuala and Noreen chorused.

'No,' Stephen said, walking away to get some fresh snow and a little bit of quiet. For a second, Oisín thought Stephen was coming over to talk to him. Maybe now that Oisín had climbed Sliabh na Gaoithe, Stephen would have some respect for his brother. Instead, Stephen glared as he walked past. Oisín braced himself and approached Stephen, hoping the right words would come.

'What's up, Windboy?' Stephen said, not looking up from his cuts. 'Did you have fun with your little book?'

'I just want to help Sorcha,' Oisín said carefully.

'Yeah, well, I hope she's having as much fun as you are,' Stephen said, dusting snow off his jeans. He walked away, looking like he wished Oisín was as easy to shake off.

Oisín swallowed and imagined the kind of patterns a snowball would make on the back of Stephen's head.

Tom came over, his goat horns still on his head.

'He'll get over it,' he said hopefully.

'Being an idiot is not something you get over.'

'At least the plan worked. You're part of *Eachtra*'s crew now, whatever Fitzfeather says.'

'Yeah,' Oisín said, feeling strangely empty.

He didn't want to disappoint Tom, so he asked about Lysander and his cluster of friends to distract himself.

It was clear they were some sort of group. All four boys were dressed identically in pale blue shirts, dark grey trousers and indigo blazers, which were stitched with the same almost-invisible threads as Madame Q's dress. They were also all standing in the same way, with their hands in their pockets, their noses in the air and their striped ties loosened just enough to show that they were far too cool to be bothered with young kids. There was only one girl and she looked like a female version of Lysander: tall, with sleek blonde hair, a pale blue blouse, a grey pleated skirt and a stylish silver scarf that flapped around in the wind.

'Who are they?' Oisín asked.

'Quints,' Tom said, spitting out the word as if it was dangerous. 'They're Madame Q's special crew. Usually some of the older teenagers help out the younger ones. Just our luck to get stuck with Quints.'

'That red-haired girl said she wanted to be a Quint,' Oisín remembered.

'She's just the type,' Tom scoffed. 'Quints usually come from the richest families and my Granda always said that the Gaultneys have more gold than good in them. She'll have to wait a while though: Madame Q only ever has five Quints at a time and most keep coming back until they're eighteen.'

'Do you know these ones?' Oisín asked.

'Sort of,' Tom said. 'Sometimes they stay with Madame Q on our island during the year. Those two are the Washington twins: Ben and Brad. Their family owns most of the magic islands off America's east coast.'

The two American teenagers certainly looked like they were from a very rich family. Ben had a silver calculator with tiny diamonds for buttons and Brad had a variety of gleaming gadgets. Oisín had the impression that he was trying to show them off: one moment he was rocking back and forth on a silver skateboard, the next he was playing with his special sunglasses, which had a comb as part of their frame.

It seemed that the other Quints weren't that impressed with Brad's toys. A tall Quint snatched the silver baseball that Brad had started to toss up and down.

'Leave my *croíacht* alone!' Brad shouted, but the boy had already rolled it across the snow. Brad skateboarded after it, looking like he was used to this treatment from the other Quints.

'That's Raqib Paro,' Tom said, as the tall boy hi-fived Lysander. 'His family have an adventuring air-balloon in the Himalayas, but they wanted him to come here. They're some sort of chemists. And then there are the Quicksilvers.'

Tom pointed at Lysander and the girl who had to be his sister.

'Their family has a second castle on this island. They're worse than Caoimhe: think they know everything and don't mind telling you.'

'How come there are so many magical siblings here?'

'There's *supposed* to be a special bond between siblings,' Tom said, as if his sister were proof that this couldn't be true. 'Magic is stronger when they're together.'

Oisín was thinking that Stephen would be another exception to that rule when he realised that the Quicksilvers were coming towards them.

'All right, Pipsqueaks,' Lysander said in his superior tone, 'you are fortunate enough to be in our group.' He took in Tom's horns and smiled. 'Perhaps the pack animal can lead the way.'

'You'll have to forgive my younger brother,' the blond-haired girl said swiftly. 'He hasn't quite perfected the Quicksilver charm.'

She turned to Oisín and flashed him a dazzling smile.

'I'm Cassandra Quicksilver. It's a pleasure to have you in my group.'

Oisín shook her hand. She had the same piercingly blue eyes as her brother, the same flecks of silver glittering in them like snow in the sun. There was something else, a sort of cold in her handshake, that made Oisín shiver for a second. Cassandra pulled away and turned to Stephen, who was also in their group.

'Here, this will help your hand,' she said, wrapping her scarf around his scars like a bandage.

Stephen grunted a sort of thanks, Cassandra's smile seeming to override any objections he had to using magic.

'Are you supposed to be in charge?' Antimony said, folding her arms and tapping her foot. 'Or should I just lead the way?'

'Your mother was Ngozi Ogoni, wasn't she?' Lysander said, looking at Antimony like she was a juicy fish he'd just caught.

'So what?'

'She was one of the finest druids of this century. You're lucky.'

'Yeah.' Antimony didn't seem to know what to do with a compliment and flicked her dreadlocks so they covered her face. 'Can we leave before my feet break off?'

The walk to *Eachtra* was slow going. There were several snowy mountains to cross and the afternoon sun made everybody tired. Oisín began to miss the Houlihans' bumpy van and wondered why the younger children weren't allowed to use magic to get to *Eachtra*.

'It's part of the tradition,' Cassandra Quicksilver said briskly, melting snow into drinking water with her *croíacht*, a tiny silver telescope. 'Being part of *Eachtra* is as much about hard work as adventure.'

Medb Gaultney didn't agree.

'My father will be appalled when I tell him we had to walk to *Eachtra*. He was going to send me to one of those summer camps on the American islands, but we thought Madame Q would be horrified to lose me. He'll definitely be having a word with her.'

The good thing about Sliabh na Gaoithe was that the wind drowned out most of what people said, so Oisín was able to ignore Medb's complaints. He was glad of the walk to distract him. Tom didn't like the Quints, the Quints didn't like the Houlihans, everybody knew who Antimony's parents were but Oisín had no idea what had happened to them. It was all too bewildering to think about. At his school, Oisín didn't have any friends any more, which made things easier. He'd just sit with a book and read during lunch and he wouldn't have to worry about who was fighting with whom. Now he had been plunged into another world without really understanding the rules. Even the thought of starting secondary school in September seemed less daunting. Perhaps because there was less chance of getting killed at St Paul's, no matter how hard Stephen tried.

Oisín looked up at the sky and ignored the chatter. It was perfectly clear, not a cloud or a raven in sight. Yet Oisín couldn't shake the uncomfortable feeling that somebody was watching him. He tried to observe the rest of their small group, wondering if any of them had designs on the Book. Everybody was pretty busy keeping one foot following another.

Eventually Cassandra Quicksilver ran to the edge of a snowy cliff and clapped her hands in delight. Oisín looked at the vessel in the valley below.

'That's *Eachtra*?'

'No, Pipsqueak, it's the Taj Mahal,' Lysander said.

Oisín had never been to the Taj Mahal, but he had a feeling it would look less strange than *Eachtra*. *Eachtra* was shaped like a ship, with masts made out of telegraph poles and bright sails that looked like they were stitched together from lots of different bedsheets. But it also looked like *Eachtra* was built to move on land when it needed to: huge bicycle wheels came out of portholes on the hull and a dozen brightly coloured horses stood on the ground, as if it was no problem at all for them to pull a giant ship. The horses looked like they came from a merry-go-round and Oisín had a hunch there was something magic about them.

'Mum says a lot of leftover things from the Milesian world end up here,' Tom said, grinning at the sight of *Eachtra*. 'I guess they use them all somehow.'

There were certainly a lot of ordinary objects in unusual places: umbrellas were twirling as fans, enchanted toothbrushes cleaned the multi-coloured windows and frying pans scooped snow off the deck. Oisín was positive that one of the socks making up the ladders down the side was the Spiderman sock he had lost in the wash years ago.

'We're nearly there,' Oisín whispered to the Book of Magic, which was flapping its pages excitedly as if it could feel the pull of the magic.

'All right, calm down,' Oisín whispered, feeling odd talking to a book as if it were a pet.

It didn't seem to have any effect. The Book of Magic continued to writhe in his hoodie pocket. Oisín had a familiar feeling that something strange was about to happen. He looked down at *Eachtra* but everything seemed peaceful: the horses were chewing clover and there wasn't a bird in the sky. And then it happened.

'The ground is moving!'

Oisín looked down, expecting Medb Gaultney to be exaggerating. Instead, he saw that the snow was shifting under his feet. Flakes of snow started to clump together like grains of sand, twisting this way and that into thin, narrow ridges.

'Snow-snakes!' Tom shouted, stepping back.

'Away from the edge!' Cassandra screamed, pulling Oisín and Medb backwards.

'Give me my scarf!' she shouted at Stephen.

Oisín wasn't sure why Cassandra Quicksilver was worried about her appearance when the snow was shifting under their feet. He felt a shape slither under his foot and backed away. The Book of Magic flapped uncontrollably.

'We have to run,' Medb Gaultney said, shaking as several shapes darted past her underneath the snow.

'Stay still,' Lysander shouted, but Medb had already started to move. The snow-snakes were not happy to be disturbed. One emerged from the ground and reared up, ten feet tall and terrifying, with ice blue eyes and a darting icicle of a tongue pointed right at Medb Gaultney.

SNAP!

A thin silver rope whooshed through the air and sliced into the snow-snake. The snake dissolved instantly, crumpling to the ground in a shower of powder.

Oisín looked over to see Cassandra whipping her scarf through the air like a weapon.

'Stay still,' she shouted, smashing another snow-snake with her scarf. Another flash of navy and silver filled the air. Lysander had turned his tie into a rope and lassoed a snow-snake as it coiled up behind Caoimhe.

'Got one!' Stephen shouted, diving to the ground and thumping a snake with his fist. It hissed at him, squirming madly and thrashing its tail through the air.

'Idiot,' Lysander shouted. 'You'll only make them angry. Don't move!'

It was hard not to move when the ground was wriggling below you, though. Soon it seemed as if there were hundreds of snow-snakes swarming towards them. Everybody fought to keep them off. Lysander and Cassandra swirled silver ropes, Antimony shot fiery snowballs from her slingshot and Stephen rolled across the ground like a commando, intent on punching every snake he could. Even Nuala was knitting a rope to attack them with.

Oisín was determined to be helpful. He pulled the Book of Magic out of his pocket. The pages flapped backwards and forwards uselessly. Oisín searched his brain, but he couldn't think of anything he could do. He could turn into wind again and escape, but that wouldn't help the others and he wasn't sure if he'd be able to run. He could try, he supposed.

The only problem was that he couldn't move his leg.

Oisín looked down and saw his fears confirmed: a thin snow-snake was winding its way around his leg. He tried to wrench it free, but the snow-snake was locked firm. While he was trying to free his right leg, another snow-snake had latched onto his left one.

Oisín gasped as he was tugged down to the ground. He felt his arms being pulled to the side, as two more icy snakes wreathed around them. The Book of Magic dropped to the ground. Oisín willed it to open, but it sat there quite happily, as if it didn't mind at all if its Keeper was eaten by snow-snakes. It wouldn't take them long. Oisín was already sinking into the snow. He tried to call for help but a small snow-snake had slithered across his mouth, binding it shut. He shook his limbs desperately, but that only seemed to make the situation worse, helping the snakes as they dragged him under. Soon only his head was above ground, the Book of Magic resting serenely on the snow, as if it was happy to mark his grave. Oisín looked around but everybody else was busy fighting the other snow-snakes. He was all alone.

The snow-snakes tugged hard. Oisín had one last glimpse of bright blue sky before his head was pulled under the snow. It was a horrible feeling. Cold snow shot up his nose and into his ears. He tried to struggle but kept on being pulled further and further into a world of white, until he wasn't even sure which way was up any more.

Liathróidí tine.

The muffled words seemed to come from very far away. The fire was very real, though. Oisín gasped as searing balls of fire scorched into the snow. The snow-snakes scattered in seconds. Oisín felt a hand yank him onto the surface and saw the last person he had expected to save him standing over him: Antimony, her slingshot in her hand and a scowl on her face.

'Where's the Book?' she said quickly.

'Here,' Oisín said, pulling it up from the snow.

It had stopped moving. The snow had too. It lay perfectly still, like a child in a deep sleep. Oisín stared at it, wondering why the ground had attacked them. Was it all because of his Book? Why hadn't the Book helped him when he had needed it?

'Let's go, Pipsqueak,' Lysander said, fixing his tie. 'Perhaps you can all work on not dying before you set foot on *Eachtra*. I have a bet on how many of you will get eaten by the Enormous Octopus and I'd hate to spoil my odds.'

Nobody said anything for the rest of the journey down the mountain. Everybody seemed to feel shaken until they reached *Eachtra*. It was hard to feel anything other than wonder the first time you arrived at *Eachtra*, even if you'd just been attacked by snow-snakes. Oisín couldn't decide where to look first. There were the crimson and gold horses that pulled *Eachtra* and looked like they belonged in a fairground. There were the strange portholes made up of scraps of coloured glass and plastic. The rooms inside looked even more interesting: Oisín glimpsed a room full of pipes which looked like the mail room. Another room seemed to be the kitchen and had several druids stirring mistletoe berries into large cauldrons. One porthole was filled up with a giant eye, belonging to a creature that Oisín suspected he didn't want to meet.

'Come along now, we're already late,' Cassandra said, pulling Tom away from the horses and ferrying the rest of them up the sock ladders. Oisín had to climb several rungs at a time to keep up with the Quicksilvers and was out of breath by the time they reached *Eachtra*'s deck. They had climbed up by the stern, where a twisting silver tower curled elegantly towards the sky. Lysander slipped inside it and Oisín spotted him talking to Madame Q.

Up at the front of the ship, Mrs Fitzfeather and Angus Óg were addressing the other groups. A large wooden statue of a bird was at the prow of the ship, looking out towards adventure. Oisín noticed tiny statues of birds beside it, stretching around *Eachtra*'s rim, like gargoyles in a Cathedral.

'So, again, congratulations,' Mrs. Fitzfeather said. 'It takes a lot of courage to climb Sliabh na Gaoithe. You'll be needing much more over the next few weeks, though. We have a serious quest on our hands this year. You're not children any more: for the next four weeks, you're Wrens.'

'What's a Wren?' Oisín whispered to Tom.

'It's just what they call the young druids on *Eachtra*,' Tom said.

'So it's like being a cub or a scout or something?'

'Er, maybe,' Tom shrugged, confused. He was distracted by what was happening in front of them. Angus Óg had made a complicated hand motion and some of the tiny statues of birds came to life, fluttering from *Eachtra*'s side and flying over to the children. Each statue had an old shoelace attached to it, so it could loop around the children's necks like a pendant.

'Nice,' a girl named Graciella Gambaro said as a tiny wren announced her name and fastened around her neck.

The wrens flew over to each of the children, chirping their names ceremonially. Oisín worried that he might not have a wren: he wasn't supposed to be on board *Eachtra*, after all. Would it mean he couldn't stay?

'Any chance we could get a cooler bird?' asked Dimitri Moran, the boy with the magic football. 'Maybe a hawk or something?'

'Wrens are the coolest,' Orion Jones, an American boy with a flute *croíacht* said. 'They've got one of the sweetest songs in the sky.'

'They're a bit small, though,' Dimitri's friend Pádraig said.

'While other birds might be more powerful, wrens are the official king of the birds,' Angus Óg said, ruffling his swan feathers with some irritation.

'You should never underestimate small things,' Mrs Fitzfeather said. 'Many a time, wrens have come to *Eachtra*'s aid. And besides, it's part of the tradition here.'

Mrs Fitzfeather said 'tradition' as if it was a word not to be argued with. Not everybody was convinced.

'Do I have to wear this ugly thing? I don't think it matches my torc,' Medb Gaultney complained.

Mrs Fitzfeather's face turned red. She bustled over towards Medb, pulling her shawls around her. Then she caught sight of the two people behind Medb and her face somehow turned even redder.

'Never in my life! What a business: Milesians sneaking up the mountain like stowaways! Jimmy Houlihan sent me a message and I can't believe the cheek of the lot of you! You'll have to go back!'

'I'm not going back until I find my sister,' Oisín said, hoping his voice sounded more confident than he felt.

'I am the Captain of *Eachtra* and I say who comes aboard.'

'Actually, you don't,' Madame Q said coolly, emerging from the silver tower behind them. 'The Captain serves *Eachtra*. And *Eachtra* is bound by the *geasa*, the old customs of the Tuatha Dé Danann, to never refuse a child that has made it up Sliabh na Gaoithe in the given time.'

'Yes, but in this case −'

'There are limits to power, even ours. We can no more break the geasa than split the sky.'

Madame Q turned to Oisín with the sliver of a smile.

'So it seems that I was right after all. We cannot have the Book without the boy.'

Oisín felt a different kind of cold rush over him, one unrelated to the snow wedged between his socks.

Mrs Fitzfeather looked as if she wanted to protest. Just then, two wooden wrens flew over to Oisín and Stephen and announced the two newest members of *Eachtra*'s crew. Warmth rushed over Oisín as the pendant settled against his chest.

'I don't want to be a wren-boy,' Stephen said, attempting to wriggle away from his wren.

'Being a Wren is nothing to do with that Milesian nonsense,' Mrs. Fitzfeather said grumpily. 'On *Eachtra* we don't hunt birds, we look after them.'

She rearranged her shawls and glared at Madame Q.

'Well, I suppose there's nothing I can do. You'll both have to pull your weight, though. A bunch of the horses need delousing, as it happens.'

'No,' Madame Q said. 'There's something else we must do first.'

She turned to face her Quints.

'Lysander, you know what to do.'

Chapter 10
The Keeper of Books

'We're going to a library?' Oisín asked as he read the sign on the tiny oak door in front of him.

'What did you think I was going to do, Pip? Sacrifice you?' Lysander said.

Lysander had escorted Oisín through *Eachtra*'s winding corridors at a pace that suggested he had far better things to do with his time. He opened the door and half-crawled through.

Even Oisín had to stoop a little to enter, so he was surprised to find himself standing in the largest room he had seen on board *Eachtra*. He was reminded of the trip his class had made to the Long Room in Trinity College, though this library was even bigger than that, with large stained-glass windows and books stretching up for what seemed like miles.

It was the most incredible room that Oisín had ever seen. Pools held waterproof Water Magic books, which older Wrens pored over with sticks, as if they were stirring soup. The Fire section had books that belched fire and turned into ash. Earth Magic books were housed in a lovely grassy mound in the west corner, where Wrens lay on leaf hammocks and thumbed through the leafy books. The Air Magic books floated near the ceiling and Oisín could just make out Wrens lying on clouds as they read about the secrets of magical flight and inventions. He looked at the rows and rows of beautiful books and thought that he could stay there for ever and be happy.

'Come on, Alice, we'll never make it through Wonderland at this rate.'

'Is this magical mathematics?' Oisín asked, trying to understand how the giant room fitted behind the little door.

'Suppose so,' Lysander said with a bored shrug, as if magical mathematics was far too basic to be of interest to Lysander Quicksilver.

'Hurry up, Pip, we've got to get that book of yours taken care of.'

'It's Oisín.'

'Whatever.'

Lysander removed a silver key from his blazer and waited as a glass lift descended slowly from the ceiling. Before the lift arrived, a boy came skateboarding down one of the banisters along the stairs and nearly knocked them both over.

'Sorry, dudes,' he said, picking up his skateboard. 'Hey, I'm Brad,' he said, starting a complicated handshake that Oisín failed to follow.

He was another Quint, one of the rich American twins that Tom had pointed out. Oisín suspected that Brad's position as a Quint might have been due more to his parents' money than his magical abilities.

'Awesome work changing into the wind,' Brad said, flashing a smile at a couple of older female Wrens as they walked past. 'I can show you round *Eachtra* if you want. The library's the most boring part. There are some wicked rooms near the bottom.'

'We're on a mission,' Lysander said drily.

'Need a hand?' Brad said as the lift arrived.

'I think we'll survive without your expertise,' Lysander said, stepping inside.

'Later, little bro,' Brad said, leaning in to give Oisín a complicated hand salute goodbye. He whispered something else as he did so, in a voice that sounded serious.

'Be careful.'

Oisín wasn't sure if he'd imagined it. Brad waved goofily as the lift took off, adjusting his balance on his skateboard. For a second, Oisín thought he saw a dark expression pass across his face, but again he couldn't be sure.

Lysander dug into his trouser pockets and took out a pale silver apple.

'Hungry, Pip?'

Oisín shook his head. A strange silence settled around them. Oisín thought of the way his mother would chat about the weather to strangers in the lift in Dunnes or, with a pang, how Sorcha always liked to count the seconds it took. This lift was very slow. Oisín was sure that Sorcha would have reached double digits.

'Have you always been able to turn your tie into a weapon?' he asked finally.

'It's elementary magic,' Lysander said.

He looked through the glass at the other floors below and Oisín felt like a small kid that Lysander had the misfortune of babysitting.

'Did you really turn into the wind to get up the mountain?' Lysander said after a moment and, though his voice stayed casual, Oisín could feel something beneath it.

'Yeah, kind of,' Oisín said. 'It was –'

'The Book of Magic?' Lysander said quickly, and this time his voice wasn't at all casual.

'Yeah.'

'It must be pretty amazing,' Lysander said, looking over at the spot where the Book was in Oisín's hoodie.

'I guess so,' Oisín said, wrapping his hoodie around him. It was getting colder as the lift climbed higher.

'Do you think I could have a look?'

Oisín tried to focus on the books floating by the window or the book about dragons that fizzed and sparked as a girl looked at it.

'I'm not sure,' he said, feeling the Book twist in his pocket, as if it might actually want to be held by somebody else.

'Just a little peek,' Lysander said very softly.

Oisín turned to look at him and saw that he had his most persuasive smile on.

'Come on, Pip, what are friends for?' he said, holding out his hand confidently.

Oisín wasn't sure they were friends at all. Still, it couldn't hurt to let him have a look.

Lysander reached over and gently took the Book from Oisín's hand. Oisín felt a sharp pain, as if he had just got an electric shock. Lysander's blue eyes turned silver. The whole elevator seemed to twist upside down as if gravity was taking a couple of seconds off.

As quickly as it happened, things returned to normal: Lysander was looking at the Book and the lift was slowly ascending. Lysander was so absorbed in the Book that he didn't seem to notice anything else. He didn't seem to be finding what he expected either, though, and his pale forehead crinkled into a frown as he turned the pages. Oisín had a sudden urge to grab the Book back.

Luckily, the lift stopped at that moment. Lysander looked up as if from a daze and handed the Book to Oisín, as if he wasn't sure what it was any more.

'The Keeper of Books should be on this floor,' he said vaguely.

'Aren't you coming with me?' Oisín asked, stepping out of the lift.

'No, I'm very busy,' Lysander said, seeming a little confused and suddenly eager to get away from the Book. 'I've got to go to the Quintessence section.'

Oisín followed his gaze upwards, but there didn't seem to be any more floors, only a thick layer of clouds.

'Maybe you'll be able to go up there some day,' Lysander said with a twinkle, his confidence returning.

The lift disappeared into the clouds and Oisín was left on the almost empty floor. Towers of very old books were stacked all around the walls and several centuries of dust hung in the air. Oisín started to walk down a corridor of tall bookshelves, unsure what to do. He could feel the magic in the air, like a thick layer of summer heat.

'Now, you must be Oisín Keane.'

Oisín turned around to find a very old lady pottering through the bookshelves. She hadn't bothered to turn to address him.

'Er, yes,' Oisín answered, craning his neck to get a better view of her. She was very small, with thick glasses and a frayed woollen cardigan wrapped around her.

'Are you the Keeper of Books?'

'Of course,' she said, her eyes focused on the shelves. 'My *History of Magic Rebellions* keeps on running away, but I suppose it is true to form.' She laughed and waddled towards Oisín.

'Would you like a cup of nettle tea? You look like you could use some warmth. I keep telling Mrs Fitzfeather that we need some more heating up here, but of course it would interfere with the books. They need to be kept at the right temperature, you know.'

She stroked her books as she said this, as if she were tending a flock of sheep. Oisín was surprised to see that some of their spines rippled as she did this.

She poured Oisín a steaming mug of nettle tea. Oisín took a sip and hoped that the lady was better at looking after books than she was at making tea.

'Now, you must be looking for a home for the Book of Magic,' the Keeper said, peering at Oisín uncertainly through her giant glasses.

'I guess so,' Oisín said, holding the Book in his pocket and not at all sure that he wanted to leave it behind.

'*Muise*, I was wondering when you'd get here,' she said.

Of all the old ladies he had met, the Keeper of Books seemed the most similar to Granny Keane. She even said the same country word, *muise*, that Granny Keane sometimes said to herself and which meant nothing, as far as Oisín could tell.

'That book needs to have its magical protection,' the Keeper continued. 'Who knows where it's been all these years and not even at the right temperature?' The Keeper of Books wrung her hands at the horrors that might face books, before turning to Oisín sharply. 'Where is old Fitzfeather, anyway? Is she still avoiding me because she hasn't returned the copy of *Magic with Mead*? If she thinks she can get away with not paying library fines because she's the Captain, she has another think coming.'

The Keeper of Books crinkled her nose to show that, for her, overdue library books were as severe a crime as you could find.

'She said she'd rather stay outside in the air,' Oisín answered, and went on to explain how he had found her.

'Really?' the Keeper said, opening her eyes wide when she heard that Lysander had escorted him. 'Well, well, that is interesting,' she murmured to herself and started to fuss at the shelves.

'So the Book of Magic has a shelf here?' Oisín asked, wondering if the bursting shelves could fit even something as small as the Book of Magic. As if on cue, a book dived off the shelves and fell to the floor a few rows back.

'*The Kamikaze Guide to Magic*,' the Keeper of Books said with an affectionate sigh. She poured herself a cup of tea and tried to focus on Oisín. 'I can't believe Mrs Fitzfeather didn't tell you this! Or Madame Q. Every great book has a shelf here or, in this case, a drawer. The six from the Dadga's cauldron have been long lost, but their drawers remain. The books can leave, but they need to come back, otherwise their magic won't work properly. Outside influences could get hold of them.'

The Keeper of Books pursed her lips and Oisín wondered what or whom she meant by outside influences.

'So it's like having a mobile phone plugged into a charger?' Oisín asked, trying to figure it out before he realised that the Keeper of Books probably didn't even know what a phone was, let alone a charger.

'Oh, yes, *Modern Wonders of the Milesian World* does mention that device,' the Keeper said as she scanned her brain for what the book said. '*Muise*, we must get your book to its home.' She stood up very quickly and started to follow a thread of her cardigan through the winding corridors.

Oisín struggled to keep up. For an old lady, she was quite fast.

'Do you always stay up on this floor?' he asked.

'I try to avoid downstairs,' the Keeper replied with a shudder, as if downstairs was a dangerous foreign country. 'Now, where are we? Yes, the Book of Magic is in the exclusive section of course, next to all the most dangerous books, including *The Book of Love*. What I wouldn't have given to have my own copy of that when I met Lir Mac Fois!'

The Keeper gave a deep sigh. Oisín had seen Granny Keane give similar sighs, and hoped that it wouldn't take all day for the Keeper to come back to earth. Thankfully, it seemed that books were a lot more important to the Keeper now than whoever Lir Mac Fois was and she recovered herself until she had reached a special section full of miniature books in drawers. She pulled out a dark chestnut drawer which was labelled 'The Book of Magic'.

Oisín felt the Book tremble in his hoodie, as if it didn't want to be imprisoned in a drawer. Oisín thought he understood what it meant: he was its Keeper, not this old lady, so shouldn't he keep it?

'You don't want to give it up,' the Keeper of Books said with a knowing smile. 'Yes, that's often the way with other Keepers. But the Book needs a library to work properly. It's the only way you'll be able to find your sister.'

Oisín held out the Book with a pang of guilt. How could he think of keeping the Book when he had Sorcha to save?

'Do you want to put it in?' he asked, holding the Book out to the Keeper.

For a second, a shadow passed across the Keeper's face and her green eyes bulged through her glasses at the sight of the Book of Magic so close. It was an expression that Oisín had seen on many people the first time they had laid eyes on the Book: Stephen, Sorcha, Madame Q, Lysander.

'No, no. You put it in,' the Keeper said quickly, her face flushing slightly. 'Some books are too dangerous for me to handle. *Fitzwater's Fireworks* was a disaster – that was when I was still a junior librarian here and I thought they'd *fire* me after all the damage.' She gave a little laugh at her joke and seemed to return to her normal self.

Oisín couldn't help noticing that she caught her breath when he placed the Book of Magic in the drawer and closed it. He felt his stomach tighten as the drawer closed.

'Will I still be able to use it?' he asked. He felt a bit silly asking if it would still be his *croíacht*, but he'd need all the help he could get if he was going to face the Morrígan.

'Of course,' the Keeper said. 'In fact, you must come and visit. It's very important that you keep your connection with the Book.'

She gave a glance around the shelves to see if anyone else was there and moved closer to Oisín.

'And I must tell you, it's very important that you don't let anybody else visit the Book either. You are the Book's individual Keeper. Nobody else can open that drawer, not even me.'

She took another look over her shoulder and Oisín felt a chill at her next words.

'The Book of Magic is one of the most powerful books of the Tuatha Dé Danann. There are quite a few people here who might want to use it, even those who seem close to you, but you mustn't let them.'

'If the Book is so powerful, why am I its Keeper?'

The Keeper of Books looked at him for a moment and smiled.

'There's only one name on the Book of Magic. And it isn't your brother and it isn't a Quint or even the Captain of *Eachtra*.'

Oisín gave a little smile back, but he wasn't sure that he felt all that much better. He felt strange without the Book, like walking to school without a bag on your shoulders. He had been used to carrying a weight and now it was gone. The strangest thing was that Oisín missed the weight.

'You'll come back,' the Keeper said, as if reading his mind. 'Now, you'll have to take the stairs back down. Do you want to take some thread to remember the way?'

'I think I'll be OK,' Oisín said, worried about what would happen to the Keeper's cardigan if she unravelled it further. 'Won't you be here, though?'

'Sometimes, of course,' the Keeper said. 'But you must come even if I'm not. Just make yourself at home. I have lots of nettle tea.'

Oisín thanked her and walked down the many stairs to the bottom of the library. The ground floor was a bit of a shock, like stepping on to a busy city street after being down a side alley. He squinted at the light streaming in and bumped into an older Wren carrying a stack of books. The books dropped to the ground and one immediately started to hiss.

Oisín stooped to help pick up the dark books and started when he saw who they belonged to.

'Typical,' Stephen muttered under his breath, making sure not to look at his brother.

'What are you doing?' Oisín asked, surveying the stack of dark books.

Stephen pulled them to his chest defensively.

'None of your business, Dirtface.'

Oisín spoke before his brother had a chance to turn. 'It's not my fault that you're jealous.'

'Jealous!' Stephen scoffed. 'Look, Birdbrain, let me get this clear: I don't want to play with your little book or be part of your stupid magic club.' He pulled at the wren pendant around him, though it was bound with a magic he couldn't shake. 'I'm here because my little sister is missing. Because *someone* couldn't keep his hands off a stupid book.'

Oisín could feel a gap widening between him and Stephen, a chasm that he wasn't sure they could ever bridge.

'You wish it was me that was taken instead of Sorcha. You wish the Morrígan took me instead.'

Stephen met his gaze, but he didn't say anything, just stalked back off into the bookshelves. Oisín thought it was just as well he didn't have the Book of Magic with him, because he could easily have turned Stephen into a toad there and then without a single regret.

Chapter 11
The Raven's Secret

Antimony curled into her hammock and wished that it was already midnight. When she looked at her watch, though, it was paying attention to the clockwork of the universe rather than her desires. 10.55 p.m.

Somehow time had a way of slowing down just when it should be getting faster. Antimony didn't know if she could wait another hour. Cluaiscín had been clear though. He could only meet her after midnight.

Antimony held her mug of firecocoa and let it warm her. It was the good kind, where small chillies danced around the warm chocolate liquid and exploded like fireworks when you had a sip. Graciela Gambaro, who was in the hammock below Antimony, had brought some with her from Guatemala. Antimony could tell she wanted to be friends, but Antimony had put her off. Before the fire, Antimony had had no problem making friends. Before the fire, a lot of things had been different. Antimony rested her mug against her lip and breathed in the warmth. Graciela was playing with Medb Gaultney, bewitching their ponytails so that they could talk. Antimony turned over and faced the wall. They'd been on board *Eachtra* for a week now and she still didn't feel settled. She told herself that she didn't need friends. Especially when all they did was play with ponytails and worry about spots.

'Are they supposed to be blue?' Nuala Nugent asked. Caoimhe was healing her acne.

'They're like beauty spots now,' Caoimhe said in a tone Antimony had heard many times before. Nuala's friend Noreen Moriarty giggled.

'But why are they getting bigger?'

Antimony heard Caoimhe flick through her book and mutter a guilty-sounding 'Oops.'

After hearing Nuala complain about her skin for an eternity (or four minutes according to her watch) Antimony jumped out of her hammock and went for a walk. Maybe she'd work on her Air Magic. *Eachtra* couldn't make it through the snowy mountain range without a lot of Air Magic. Mrs Fitzfeather had showed them which Magical Inventions helped defrost the windows and keep the horses warm. Another druid had helped them to calculate the magical mathematics necessary to enable *Eachtra* to fold in and out like an accordion so it could fit through the narrow gaps between mountains. Angus Óg was teaching them how to transform into birds so that they could fly ahead and scout. So far Antimony hadn't managed to plot the shape of a magical cupboard or sprout a single feather. If she wasn't careful, she'd have to make her own way to Cnoc na gCnámh.

Antimony looked out a porthole at the dark clouds. Maybe it didn't matter. Soon they'd be at the lake and using their Water Magic. That was one of the best things about voyaging on *Eachtra*, her father had said, exploring the different types of magic in the right environment. Antimony could remember how excited she had been to hear about his time as a Wren. He had made her promise that she'd work hard at all the different types of magic, even though they both knew she'd be waiting for the final week when she could show off her Fire Magic. That promise had been before the fire, though. Everything was different now. Now all that mattered was getting hold of the Book of Magic.

Antimony reached the supply room. It was just a dusty old room full of crates and sacks of food, but it was where the younger Wrens liked to hang out. Dimitri Moran and Pádraig Price had made a table out of stacked crates and several Wrens were playing ping-potato across it. Antimony found a crate in the corner. It was pretty noisy so nobody paid much attention to her. Orion Jones gave her a small smile as he played his flute. He was trying to be friendly, maybe because he was the only other new Wren who was black, but Antimony just picked up her book. Orion turned back to Billy Lewis, the Australian boy who was trying to invent a guitar that flew into your hands.

Antimony flicked through her copy of *No Fuss over Feathers: Bird Flight in Thirteen Steps*. Maybe if she could turn into a raven that would be handy. Then she might not need Cluaiscín to do all her spying. Not that she could really get rid of him. He'd always worked for her mother. It was nice to have something to connect her to her past life, however small.

Every day that *Eachtra* moved north, Antimony felt herself pulled further and further from her past. That morning, she couldn't remember whether the curtains in her old room had been red or orange. She wasn't sure if her father used to have two or three sugar cubes in his firecocoa. Soon her parents' faces would be like clouds, shifting in and out of focus, hard to pin down exactly.

'Careful!' she shouted as a magic football rocketed above her head.

'Sorry,' Dimitri Moran said, heading the ball back to his group of friends. Before the fire, Antimony might have joined in. Now, though...

'Watch out, would you?'

This time it was Stephen, shouting at Rachel Humphreys because she'd sent a potato in his direction. He flung it back (he was a much better throw than any of them) and returned to his stack of dark books. Antimony caught his eye from the other side of the room. She looked away quickly, picking up her book as if bird-transformation was suddenly fascinating. Her insides squirmed, the way they always did when she thought of Sorcha. She hadn't known what would happen when she burnt the *béal tine*. It was what her parents would have done. Except maybe it wasn't, a small voice in her head said. Maybe getting the Book of Magic wasn't what her parents would want her to do at all.

Stephen was still looking at her. He was suspicious. His little brother had no idea what was going on but Stephen always saw her in the library, as they both watched Oisín visiting the Book of Magic.

Antimony felt safer with the Book locked up in the library, biding its time until Lughnasa. She didn't want Oisín to bond too much with it. He was in the other corner now, *helping* Tom befriend the magic mice that lived in the supply room.

Antimony could tell he missed the Book, though, could see that he was calculating the hours until he could go back to the library. She'd be *helping* him by taking it. She wouldn't think of Sorcha or Stephen then.

'Twelve o'clock. The time is twelve o'clock.'

Antimony looked down, surprised to see the little green dragon on her watch puffing out twelve circles of smoke. Midnight had crept up on her as soon as she'd stopped waiting for it. She bolted up and headed for the door, knocking over Billy Lewis's air-guitar, which seemed much happier to be on the ground anyway.

Antimony hurried up the sock-ladder to the deserted deck where Cluaiscín was waiting for her, fluttering his feathers nervously.

'Well,' Antimony said, slipping into Raven. Her mother had always told her not to apologise to ravens.

'Not well, Miss Antimony, Cluaiscín is not well at all! *Eachtra* is no space for ravens, not nice for ravens at all! Poor Cluaiscín working so hard and not a bit of food.'

Antimony rolled her eyes. He was so predictable sometimes. She fished in her pouch and pulled out a jar of iridescent beetles that Gabriela's twin brother Gael had traded her.

'Look what I got for you,' she said in what she hoped was a kind voice. 'Bright beetles all the way from Guatemala.'

'I hope they're not poisonous.'

'I had to swap two fire stones to get these!'

Cluaiscín seemed to decide not to protest further and gulped down a couple of beetles. He shook out his beak, feeling fuller if nothing else.

'Well,' Antimony said, impatient to get started. 'What have you found out?'

'Sssssh, Miss Antimony, not so loud!'

Cluaiscín looked over his shoulder skittishly as if he expected somebody to emerge from the shadows.

Antimony had never seen him look so nervous.

'Bad times, Miss Antimony, bad times. Miss Antimony should never have burned the *béal tine*.'

'Don't tell me what to do,' Antimony snapped, hoping she sounded like her mother.

'Bad deep magic. No good will come of it.'

'It's too late to change it now. Did you just come here to tell me off or do you actually have some news?'

Cluaiscín checked over his shoulder yet again before he spoke. When he did, his voice was as small as it could be.

'She's here.'

'There's nobody here.'

'No. *She's* here. On *Eachtra.*'

'Who?'

Cluaiscín gave a nervous flutter of his wings, shifting his feet uncomfortably.

'The Morrígan.'

Antimony felt a nip in the air, was suddenly aware of every sound as the ship moved through the mountains.

'There's no way the Morrígan could be here,' Antimony said, thinking of all the druids present.

'She is. In disguise.'

Antimony felt another shiver, as if just talking about the Morrígan made the air grow cooler.

'She wants the Book?' Antimony asked.

Cluaiscín nodded.

'There's something else, isn't there?'

Cluaiscín shifted his weight on his feet, torn between fear and loyalty.

'Somebody here is helping her?' Antimony guessed.

Cluaiscín nodded.

'A druid? A Wren? A Quint?'

Cluaiscín looked behind him again.

'Cluascín, there's nobody there. You've got to tell me. Who's helping the Morrígan? Who's she disguised as? Cluaiscín?'

'Very bad times, Miss Antimony, very bad times.'

'Cluaiscín, tell me what you know!'

Cluaiscín looked like he was about to say something when they heard footsteps. Cluaiscín disappeared into the air in seconds. Antimony turned around sharply, searching in her pouch for her slingshot.

'Caoimhe!' she said as the figure walked into the moonlight. 'What are you doing here?'

'I could ask you the same question,' Caoimhe said calmly. 'Rachel said you ran out in a rush. I thought I'd make sure you were OK.'

'You don't need to spy on me.'

'Who were you talking to?'

'None of your business.'

Antimony glared at her supposed sister, at that moment hating her as much as she ever had hated anybody. She was about to storm off when another figure appeared: Cassandra Quicksilver, her pale face rather flushed.

'Girls, what are you doing out so late?' she said, looking over her shoulder.

Antimony was about to ask her the same question when Caoimhe stepped on her toe.

'We're just stargazing,' Caoimhe said quickly.

'Oh, me too,' Cassandra said, although she had to reach in her bag to pull out her telescope *croíacht*. 'It is a beautiful night for it,' she continued, strolling over to the railing and turning her telescope up to the stars. 'I just wish they weren't so sad.'

'You can read the stars?' Caoimhe asked.

'It isn't exact, of course. But I can get a reading.'

'And something's strange tonight?' Antimony asked.

Cassandra turned to face Antimony. In the moonlight, her pale skin was very striking.

'Of course, it could be nothing,' Cassandra said, pulling her scarf around her and looking back at the stars. 'Come on, let's get back inside before Mrs Fitzfeather catches you and something truly tragic happens.'

She attempted a little laugh but there was no hiding it. Cassandra Quicksilver was definitely worried about something. Or, Antimony thought with a shudder as they walked back, she wanted them to think she was worried.

***

Later that night, Cluaiscín still couldn't get to sleep. He'd fly far off in the morning, he told himself. Staying loyal to Antimony's mother was one thing, but the girl was pushing it. To think what he'd almost told her! He'd be off in the morning, somewhere nice and hot. Preferably where he could get more of those nice bright beetles.

'Cluaiscín.'

Cluaiscín froze as he heard somebody creeping into his hiding place at the back of *Eachtra*. It was a voice he couldn't forget, one like a knife wrapped in velvet.

'I hope you're not trying to hide from me?'

'Of course not,' Cluaiscín said, starting to feel very nervous.

'I don't like my little birdies to fly too far away.'

Her green eyes were the only thing that Cluaiscín could see in the dark. He'd never got used to how cold they were, as if just looking into them could banish all happiness.

'Of course not, O Great One,' he flustered.

He felt a sharp fingernail tap at his side, inches from his heart.

'You haven't been telling secrets, have you?'

'No, no, no!' Cluaiscín said, keenly aware of the sharp nail pressed at his side. 'The Great Queen knows that all ravens serve only her, serve always her!'

'But sometimes they get hungry, don't they?'

Her voice was soft but Cluaiscín could hear the steel behind it.

'Cluaiscín said nothing, Cluaiscín knows nothing!'

'The Ogoni girl, she wants the Book, doesn't she?'

Cluascín felt the nail digging harder into his side. He gasped for breath.

'Come on, Cluaiscín, you don't want to keep any secrets from me. She's planning to take the Book, isn't she?'

Cluaiscín gave the smallest of nods. He tried not to think of Antimony's mother, of the promise he'd made.

'Please, O Great One,' he said as he felt the nail pressing into his feathers. 'Cluaiscín will go away!'

The Morrígan gave a little laugh, somehow light and terribly heavy at the same time.

'That's exactly what you're going to do.'

Cluaiscín gasped as the sharp fingernail stabbed expertly into his side. The last thing he saw before he crumpled to the ground was a pair of green eyes, glittering terribly in triumph.

Chapter 12
Shadows in the Water

After a week of travelling through the mountains, *Eachtra* reached a series of lakes and its wheels morphed into rudders. In the mountains, *Eachtra*'s umbrella-fans had used the winds to keep it moving when the horses got tired. Now that *Eachtra* was acting more like a real ship, the Wrens needed to practise Water Magic to help it run. While Air Magic involved learning a lot of equations and memorising the right words to say, Water Magic relied more on their eyes.

'Your gaze is very important,' Cliodhna, a druid with eyes like whirlpools, told them in a dusty room at the bottom of *Eachtra*.

She concentrated very hard on the jars of water in front of her and swished her hands around quickly. One by one, the jars started to hum a haunting melody. It wasn't just beautiful. The sound-waves set a series of cogs in motion, propelling *Eachtra* through the lake. Unfortunately, Oisín wasn't very good at magical music (he'd already smashed several jars by looking at them too hard) so he allowed his mind to wander as Cliodhna showed them the magical scale.

One morning, Oisín had decided that magic was just like electricity. He remembered one time when he flicked a light switch in his bedroom back in Dublin. It was just like the other umpteen times when he had done this everyday action, but for some reason it made him wonder how electricity worked. He had understood the basic idea, but he hadn't been sure what all the wires in his house did or how a pale white bulb suddenly burst full of colour when one switch moved. He was pretty certain that he wouldn't have been able to make a new internet system or even an electric kettle if people suddenly forgot how those things worked. And then it had hit him, most of the things he did every day – getting in a car, watching television, Googling something – were mysteries. It was as if the rug underneath his life had slipped and all the furniture was slowly rearranging itself.

'That's just how it works.'

That was what Oisín's mother had said when he had pestered her about electricity. It was exactly the same phrase that Tom used whenever Oisín asked about magic.

'That's just how it works.'

Tom shrugged when Oisín asked how lights popped on magically when they walked into cabins. Magic was just like electricity for the Tuatha Dé Danann. It was all around them, but they never really thought about it unless they had to.

'You have to concentrate! If your gaze is strong enough, you can use a wave to push you all the way to the other side of the world. But if you keep looking out the porthole, for example, none of us will ever leave this lake.'

Tom gave Oisín a sharp nudge. He'd hadn't been paying any attention to whatever Cliodhna was saying about magical scales and Cliodhna's intense eyes were currently focused on him.

Oisín tried to look equally focused and Cliodhna returned her attention to the jars of water humming in perfect pitch. Oisín managed to smash another couple of jars before the morning was through, making him especially glad when they broke for lunch.

As usual, Oisín went to the library to visit the Book of Magic after he'd wolfed down some surprisingly tasty algae curry. He wasn't surprised to see Stephen on the ground floor. Despite his suspicions about magic, Stephen worked hard every day, turning red as he attempted to transform into a puffer fish, nearly drowning as he wrestled an octopus. He spent all his free time in the library, looking through stacks of dark books. Currently, one of the books had turned into a mosquito and was doing its best to torment Stephen.

Lysander Quicksilver walked by with the Washington twins and laughed. 'Not a magical bone in his body.'

Oisín was glad Stephen couldn't hear Lysander (Stephen definitely had punching bones in his body) but he couldn't help agreeing with the statement. The truth was that Stephen didn't seem to be very good at magic.

And Oisín was. Not at everything – his head still hurt when he tried to master magical equations and he wasn't much better than Stephen at wrestling an octopus – but every now and then something clicked. A feather sprouted out of his fingers when he concentrated very hard on transforming. A drop of water froze when he looked at it correctly. More and more, magic began to feel like electricity, like something that was part of his world.

'Of course you can do magic,' the Keeper of Books said to him when he reached her floor. 'You'd hardly be a Keeper if you couldn't!'

'I suppose,' Oisín said, taking a polite sip of her twigleaf tea and gazing out the small window as *Eachtra* sailed through a long ribbon-lake.

'And you have green eyes,' the Keeper said, as if that clinched it.

'You don't have to have green eyes to do magic,' Oisín said, thinking of the Quints.

'Ah, but the best druids all have emerald eyes!' the Keeper said, patting her white hair. Her own green eyes looked enormous in her giant glasses.

'Don't tell Madame Q that.'

'I won't get a chance,' the Keeper said in a rather icy tone. 'She wouldn't be bothered coming to check in on boring old books.' The Keeper shuddered, the way she always did when she imagined people treating books poorly. 'Though I suppose at least that keeps her away from your book.'

Oisín wasn't so sure. Every now and then, he thought he saw a flash of silver in the bookshelves. Yet whenever he checked, the corridors of books were as long and empty as ever.

'You should get going,' the Keeper said, looking at him indulgently, understanding how hard it was to part from a book. 'Unless you want some more tea?'

'No,' Oisín spluttered, putting down his mug of steaming, undrinkable liquid. 'Thanks. We've got to get through the Underwater Caves today.'

'Ohhhh,' the Keeper said, as if remembering something. 'I have a book on underwater algae somewhere, but I can't remember if it's shelved under D for "Don't eat" or Z for "Zoospores and their homes".'

With that, she was off into the stacks again, and Oisín had a rare moment of peace with the Book of Magic, the delicious feeling when the door closes and an empty house is all yours. Oisín told himself he'd just stay a minute, but as he looked at the Book of Magic, he couldn't help staying longer. The more he understood magic, the more pages of the Book made sense. He now knew that several of the diagrams were plots for magical rooms and that some of the faint blue notes were special song-spells. The Book seemed to sense that he understood it better, and snuggled into his hands affectionately.

After what seemed like far too little time, Oisín put it back in its drawer and raced through *Eachtra*'s corridors towards its southern exit. He jumped out and found Tom waiting at the archway to the underwater caves.

'That book,' Tom said, shaking his head.

Tom was perhaps the only person on *Eachtra* who didn't understand the appeal of the Book of Magic.

'Where is everybody else?' Oisín asked.

'They've all gone in,' Tom said.

Oisín must have been in the library longer than he thought. The Book of Magic had a way of swallowing time, so a whole afternoon could vanish just looking at it.

'Not to worry, at least we don't have to listen to Medb Gaultney talking about how her dad would never allow Wrens into filthy caves,' Tom said as he clambered into the archway, his usual smile returning.

Oisín followed, and they sloshed their way through the winding Underwater Caves, which were lit by patches of phosphorescent moss. *Eachtra* would sail across to the other side of the caves, so the Wrens had to find their own way through. The water was only up to their ankles in most of the narrow caves, but some chambers were deeper. A giant wave rushed down one of the corridors and Oisín remembered the hand motions to change the path of water just in time. Another chamber had a huge organ made out of shell pipes and a door which would only open when you hummed the right scale. Thankfully, Tom had been paying more attention to Cliodhna than Oisín.

They could have got through the caves faster if Tom, who missed Giant terribly, didn't stop whenever they passed any magical animal. Tom already spent his mornings looking after the merry-go-round horses (who didn't like it when *Eachtra* behaved like a real ship and seaweed got in their manes). Now he insisted on befriending every scuttling creature they met, several of whom left 'affectionate' bite marks on his arm.

Tom had turned towards a snapping turtle when Antimony strode over to them, dripping water and irritation in equal measure.

'I need to talk to you,' she said to Oisín.

'OK.'

'Privately.'

Tom smiled good-naturedly. 'You guys go on. I'll stay and help this fellow.'

Antimony pulled Oisín into a side corridor before he could protest. 'The Morrígan is after the Book of Magic,' she said as soon as she was sure they were alone.

'Um, I already know that.'

'No. Here. The Morrígan is in disguise on board *Eachtra*.'

'She can't be.'

'She is. And somebody else is helping her, one of the other Wrens, I think.'

Oisín had a terrible feeling that maybe Antimony could be right. He shivered, feeling something brush against his feet. When he looked down, though, nothing was there except water flowing along innocently.

'Why are you telling me this? Is this about that bird?'

Antimony had been looking for a raven for the past few days, muttering darkly that something must have happened to him.

'The Book of Magic needs to be protected,' Antimony said, as if she wasn't sure she could trust Oisín to do that. 'We need to find out who's working with her. I bet it's one of the Quints –'

'Oooh, sorry. Having a special moment, are we?'

It was Medb Gaultney, followed by Nuala and Noreen.

'Get lost,' Antimony said.

'Careful not to get too wet – you might spoil your lovely hair,' Medb said, her green eyes fixing on Antimony's dreadlocks with malice.

'We're going this way,' Oisín said, grabbing Antimony's arm and pushing past Medb and her friends, who departed in a chorus of giggles.

'Just because I don't want to swim,' Antimony said. 'Anybody can swim. Just wait until we get to the firefields, I'll scorch that smile off her –'

'Stop! Can you feel the water moving?'

Oisín stood still, trying to figure out what was happening. They had walked into another side corridor, where the water seemed to be flowing a lot faster. Oisín definitely felt something brushing against his feet this time. He looked down and squinted at the water in the dim mosslight.

'Shadow-fish,' Antimony said after a moment.

Oisín looked closer and saw with horror that it wasn't the water that was moving fast, but a series of tiny fish, as dark as shadows.

'We need to turn back,' Antimony said.

'I can't turn around! They're moving too fast.'

Antimony couldn't either. It seemed like there was an endless stream of shadow-fish brushing against their ankles and pulling them along with the current.

Antimony tried to send some smoke from her nostrils but she couldn't.

'I can't do Fire Magic here,' she said in a panic. 'The Water Magic is too strong.'

'Just walk slowly. We can get out.'

But even though her brain told her that she should walk very slowly, Antimony's body had other ideas. Her legs felt the slithery shadows slipping past them and they tried to shake them off. Her arms felt as if the shadows were all around, and waved about frantically. After a moment, her hands thought it would be a good idea to cling to the slippery sides of the cave for support.

'Antimony!'

It was too late. Antimony toppled over with a crash and was carried down with the shadow-fish current in seconds. Oisín hesitated. More and more shadow-fish were streaming past him, whooshing in the direction that Antimony had gone in. He couldn't leave her alone.

Surrendering to the flow, Oisín dived into the water and let the current of shadow-fish pull him along. The passage got narrower and narrower, until Oisín felt as if he was in a water slide at a funfair. Except this slide was more terrifying than fun. Oisín felt the strange shadow-fish slip around his arms and had the horrible feeling they wanted him to drown. After a couple more twists and turns, the passage turned into a proper chute and plummeted towards an opening. Oisín closed his eyes and braced himself.

For a moment, he was thrown into the air, his limbs flapping about like crazy. Then, just as suddenly, he landed in a dark pool with a hard splash. His head bobbed under water and he saw hundreds of tiny shadows, glinting at him with small green eyes. He pushed his head back to the surface and spluttered. They had been expelled into a huge cavern. It was almost completely dark, except for a strange orange glow that came from the wall. Magic was in this place like a current, deeper than any Oisín had ever felt. He called out Antimony's name but only heard his echo in return.

Then he heard a thrashing sound, the noise of somebody slapping shadows. Oisín swam over quickly.

'Hold on to me,' he said.

'There's no way out,' Antimony gasped, gripping Oisín's hoodie.

'Breathe, breathe!' Oisín said, feeling himself being pulled under by the shadow-fish. 'You can do this,' he spluttered, feeling his head bob into the dark water. More and more shadow-fish were streaming into the cavern and the water was getting deeper and deeper. 'Just kick your legs and move your arms like you're making a big circle. Don't worry about your dreadlocks! Breathe with me!'

The shadow-fish made it much harder to stay afloat than usual. Every time one of his legs slowed down, Oisín could feel the shadow-fish latch on and try to drag them under. After a couple of very long minutes, during which Oisín was sure they would both drown, Antimony was able to tread water on her own.

'OK,' Oisín said, feeling his legs tire as he pushed against the shadow-fish. 'Now we have to get out of here.'

The already cold water had just dropped several degrees and he was worried that the flapping wings he had heard above belonged to ravens.

'Is that an opening?' Antimony said, peering towards the other end of the cavern. 'Yes, look, there's a ledge and an archway and –'

Oisín understood why Antimony had stopped. Far away, at the other end of the cavern, Oisín could just make out a creature unlike any he'd ever seen. It was sort of like a stingray, with a flat black body like a long slippery rug. Several long tentacles emerged from its sides like snakes. What worried Oisín, though, were the green eyes on its head, which gleamed like glittering emeralds and seemed to be looking right at him.

Oisín felt the shadow-fish pulse with energy as the creature slithered into the water. Soon all Oisín could see were its two green eyes, gleaming terribly in the darkness. They floated on top of the water, moving closer and closer. Oisín felt the water rise around him. He could hear Antimony panicking, forgetting again how to tread water. Oisín barely noticed. He was hypnotised by those eyes, remembering Granny Keane's words: *She's a shape-shifter. No matter what she changes to, you can always recognise her by three things: the ravens that follow her, a terrible chill in the air around her and those green eyes of hers that will drown you in sadness.*

Oisín swallowed a gulp of cold water as the shadow-fish gripped his legs. He knew before Antimony whispered in his ear: he was looking into the eyes of the Morrígan.

Chapter 13
An Freagarach

Oisín wished he had the Book of Magic with him. Without it, he felt useless. The Morrígan's green eyes were getting closer and closer. The shadow-fish wound around his legs, trapping him in the water. Oisín couldn't think of a single thing to do. Magic felt a lot less like electricity and more like a puzzle that he could never hope to solve.

The Morrígan's eyes pierced into him and Oisín felt her stripping away his foolish hopes until all that was left was a terrible cold despair. He craned back his head, staring at the cavern's ceiling. He'd look at anything to avoid the Morrígan's gaze.

There was a layer of stalactites on the ceiling, or was it stalagmites? Oisín had never paid attention in geography class and now he was going to die without knowing the difference, which seemed a strange thing to worry about.

A thought flashed in Oisín's brain. He looked up at the stalactite ('c for ceiling', that was it!) and remembered what Cliodhna had told them about freezing. If he concentrated really hard...

Concentrating was very difficult when hundreds of fish were trying to drown you. Oisín kicked them away and tried to ignore the sound of the Morrígan's tentacles lapping through the water, getting closer and closer. He focused on the stalactite, picturing the ice in the freezer at home. The tip of the stalactite gleamed white and started to crackle. It was working. Oisín kept his gaze firm but focused. Water Magic was all about the gaze. If he could just concentrate...The stalactite plunged from the ceiling, stabbing into the water as an icicle. It hung suspended on top of the water, and a circle of ice spread slowly around it.

'Antimony, freeze the ceiling,' Oisín spluttered. 'We have to get out of this water.'

He focused on another stalactite. It created another circle of ice as it landed. Oisín kicked the shadow-fish from him and clambered up on to the ice. The shadow-fish squirmed below, pushing their dark shapes against the underside of the fragile ice. Oisín pulled Antimony up.

'She's getting mad,' Antimony said, staring at the Morrígan's green eyes, still coming towards them and flashing with irritation.

'Don't look at her.'

Antimony picked up one of the fallen, icy stalactites and put it in her slingshot. She aimed it at a pile of loose stones. They turned white and plunged towards the ground, spreading another layer of ice across the water. Oisín felt a surge of hope. Soon the whole ceiling was snowing and ice sealed off the passage they had come in through, stopping the flow of shadow-fish and trapping the green-eyed creature under ice. For a second, Oisín felt safe.

Then he heard a tremendous crackle. Oisín and Antimony watched in horror as a tentacle shot through and the Morrígan pulled herself on to the ice. She transformed in front of their eyes, contracting her tentacles until they were part of a long black cloak, worn by the most beautiful woman Oisín had ever seen.

'Nice try,' the Morrígan said with a light, fluttery laugh that sent shivers into the air. 'But you can't ever hope to beat me. Not without your little book.'

'You'll never win,' Oisín spat out.

'Let's see what your sister thinks about that. She's very fond of me, you know.'

'Leave Sorcha alone.'

Antimony pulled Oisín's shoulder back before he could move forward. The Morrígan gave another little laugh and tossed back her black hair, which curled down her head like tentacles.

'So brave, so young. I admire that. But no need for bravery just yet. It's actually your friend I want to talk to.'

The Morrígan fixed her terrible eyes on Antimony. Antimony felt the fire return to her veins.

'You want me, come and get me,' she said, stepping forward.

The Morrígan smiled and flicked her hair. In a second, one of her curls had actually turned into a tentacle and it whipped through the air, heading for Antimony.

'No!'

A body leapt from the side of the cavern, launching onto the Morrígan just in time and pushing her to the ground.

'Stephen?' Oisín gasped, staring at the figure tackling the Morrígan.

The Morrígan transformed back into her terrible stingray form, sending her long tentacles crashing across the ice. One smashed down inches from Stephen's head.

'It's me she wants,' Antimony shouted, shooting smoke out of her nostrils.

The Morrígan didn't seem to care at that moment, and was intent on dealing with the irksome creature confronting her. She backed Stephen into a corner by the wall and raised one of her tentacles. This time she wasn't going to miss.

It happened before Oisín had time to do anything. Stephen gripped the rock for support, the tentacle drove through the air, it landed with a sickening smack and there was a flash of light and a terrible scream.

Stephen stood up, a long stone gleaming in his hand. The Morrígan's tentacle lay slumped on the ice where Stephen had cut it off. Stephen held up the granite stone he had pulled from the cave. It was shaped like a sword. Oisín realised it was the source of the orange glow he'd seen earlier.

The Morrígan looked at it with furious eyes. Oisín was sure she was going to raise another tentacle to attack, but she seemed to decide otherwise, and slunk off into the shadows.

Stephen stood staring at the stone in his hand in confusion.

'Get her,' Antimony said, looking at the shadows into which the Morrígan had disappeared.

Stephen shook himself and ran towards the archway. Before he could get through, he crashed into somebody coming out.

'Cassandra!' he said, steadying her.

Cassandra Quicksilver looked very dazed and her beautiful face was more worried than ever.

'What happened?'

'Later,' Stephen said, heading for the archway again.

This time he ran into Mrs Fitzfeather, who looked almost as worried as Cassandra.

'What's all this business, boy?'

'It was the Morrígan,' Antimony said, looking over at the spot on the ice where the tentacle had already dissolved into black dust.

Mrs Fitzfeather pulled her shawls around herself as if she was the one who needed protection.

'No! That can't be possible! The Morrígan couldn't have been here.'

'I'm afraid she could. You know the kind of deep magic these caves hold.'

It was Madame Q, emerging suddenly out of the shadows. Oisín wondered how long she had been standing there. She stared at him with her strange silver eyes.

'You made a snowstorm in this cavern?'

Oisín nodded.

'Without the Book of Magic?'

Oisín could see her searching the magical air for the Book's presence. He nodded.

'That's very advanced magic,' Madame Q said carefully, unsure if this was a good thing. Her eyes swivelled over to Stephen.

'Where did you get that?' she said, looking at his stone sword.

'It just came out of the wall when –'

Stephen stopped, hearing footsteps behind them. Instinctively, he stretched out his arm, holding out the sword and its surprisingly sharp point.

'New toy? I'd have thought you might be too old for that kind of thing.'

'Lysander, stop!'

Lysander turned around and saw his sister beside him. He smiled.

'Nobody told me we were having a party. Bit chilly, though. Perhaps I should magic up a fire?'

'That won't be necessary,' Madame Q said curtly.

Oisín wondered how they had all happened to be so close to the cavern and yet none of them had come while the Morrígan was attacking him and Antimony.

'What is that?' Cassandra said, walking over to look at Stephen's sword. She caught her breath. 'No, it can't be.'

'It is,' Madame Q said with a grim smile. 'An Freagarach. '

Oisín saw the confusion on Stephen's face. 'It's the lost sword from the Dagda's cauldron,' he said slowly.

'The sword that can cut through any enemy,' Antimony said in awe.

Lysander's eyes flared with envy. 'An Freagarach is one of the most magical items that exists. That lunk couldn't have just *found* it.'

'Don't call me that.' Stephen's voice was level, but An Freagarach was stretched out, its tip resting against Lysander's chest.

'Try it,' Lysander said with a twinkle in his eyes.

'Stop it!' Madame Q said irritably, parting the two of them with a quick flick of her wrist. 'That sword is not to be trifled with. It could change everything.'

'It could kill the Morrígan,' Stephen said in a strange voice, looking down at his new sword.

'It could kill everybody,' Mrs Fitzfeather said in a worried tone. 'I'm not sure it's a good … *Cassandra!*'

Everybody turned to where Cassandra had fallen on the floor. For a terrible second, Oisín thought she had brushed against An Freagarach.

'She's having a prophecy!' Mrs Fitzfeather said. She looked around the cavern as if seeing it for the first time. 'We're in the Pool of Prophecy. That's why the magic is so strong. We can't let her get to the water, you know the charge it has.'

Madame Q seemed to have the opposite opinion.

'Lysander, help her,' she said quickly, cutting a small circle in the ice with a flick of her fingers. The shadow-fish had all disappeared and the clear water gleamed. Lysander eased his sister in, supporting her arms on the ice. Cassandra closed her eyes as the water wrapped around her body.

'Get her out of there,' Mrs Fitzfeather barked.

'No, we have to hear the prophecy,' Madame Q said firmly. 'Lysander, hold her.'

Lysander gripped onto his sister as she started to shake. Oisín wondered if Mrs Fitzfeather wasn't right. Whatever was happening to Cassandra didn't seem very pleasant. After a moment she stopped shaking. Her face was completely blank and her eyes had turned silver. The words came out in a low, flat tone:

Calamity creaks towards us
A shadow passes across the land
Woe will circle woe before the crash of corn
Brother will fight brother, siblings sunder
The children of the golden hair will split
The dearest of the deer will be lost
War rears its head
Good and evil fade, strong fights stronger
The six that will not be found shake free
What would be kept must be given away
The Queen of Shadows –
'That's enough!'

Mrs Fitzfeather pushed Lysander out of the way and gripped Cassandra. She was surprisingly strong and had Cassandra out of the water in seconds. Cassandra coughed, her face returning to normal.

'You should never interrupt a prophecy!' Madame Q said in a terse voice.

'Teenagers shouldn't be giving prophecies,' Mrs Fitzfeather flared.

'She's my Quint!'

'And she's *my* responsibility!'

For perhaps the first time, Oisín could see why Mrs Fitzfeather was the Captain of *Eachtra*.

'Or perhaps you're afraid what the prophecy will reveal.' Madame Q said, looking at Mrs Fitzfeather curiously.

'I don't have to listen to prophecies to know how to lead my life,' Mrs Fitzfeather responded.

A series of glances passed between the two old women and Oisín was sure a lot was being communicated. It was Lysander who broke the silence.

'Maybe next time you can try something cheerier, sis? Perhaps something about kittens?'

Nobody laughed. Oisín looked at Stephen swirling An Freagarach through the air, as if it were an extension of his arm. He felt a chill pass through him. Oisín hadn't understood most of Cassandra's prophecy, but a couple of words rattled in his head. *Brother will fight brother. Siblings sunder. Before the crash of corn.* The Lughnasa Festival was approaching with its harvest.

Oisín gulped. Whatever trouble the prophecy told of, it was coming soon.

Chapter 14
Deirdre of the Sorrows

If there was any benefit to being attacked by the Morrígan and her legion of shadow-fish, it was that Oisín gained another friend. Not that being Antimony's friend was exactly easy. Antimony spent half the day scowling at the other Wrens (all of whom she was certain were helping the Morrígan) and the rest of the day grumbling about how boring Water Magic was. As Antimony had previously spent her days silently following Oisín, this was an improvement. Especially now that staring at Oisín was everybody else's favourite hobby.

Although Mrs Fitzfeather had sworn everybody to secrecy, by the next day the whole of *Eachtra* had heard about the prophecy. Oisín and Stephen got even more attention, especially as Stephen had started carrying An Freagarach in a scabbard over his jeans.

Antimony was an expert in avoiding unwanted gazes and showed Oisín the small cabins and corridors where you could rely on quiet on *Eachtra*. Unlike Tom and Caoimhe, she also understood how important the Book of Magic was. Caoimhe was too busy practising medicine on lake slugs (who could move pretty fast when they saw her approaching) and Tom still didn't trust the Book. Antimony did, though, and helped Oisín to race through his morning tasks so he could spend more time in the library.

In the quiet corridors of the twelfth floor, Oisín didn't have to worry about the other Wrens or prophecies. A small part of Oisín almost resented *Eachtra*'s steady movement towards Cnoc na gCnámh because each day they got closer, the moment when he would have to part with his magic Book also came nearer.

That changed when they reached Linn an Bhróin. It was their last afternoon before they entered the Enchanted Forest. Linn an Bhróin was a semi-circular pool on the edge of the forest, surrounded by slender trees and a large waterfall.

'Real weeping willows,' Tom said in awe as they sat on the edge of the pool and waited for a druid to appear.

It took Oisín a second to see what he meant. Instead of leaves, the trees around Linn an Bhróin grew small tears, which dangled off their branches like jewels. Every now and then, one dropped gently into the water and another appeared on the branch. Something stirred in Oisín as he put his toes into the cool water. He remembered Sorcha all alone with the Morrígan. Suddenly, he felt terrible for reading the Book of Magic all day and wishing that *Eachtra* would travel slower.

Antimony did not seem quite so affected by the pool.

'The Pool of Sadness,' she said with a snort. 'What kind of a stupid name is that? You know, in Nigeria, most druids don't even *use* Water Magic.'

'You might have mentioned it,' Caoimhe said.

As usual, Antimony ignored her.

'Or anything except Fire and Air. I mean, I don't see the point of it. Why would you –'

'Use that anger, my child, use it!'

Everybody turned to see where the voice had come from. The water started to ripple strangely. Slowly, it pooled together until the outline of a body emerged: a very large woman with big cheeks and long hair, made entirely out of water.

'I am Deirdre of the Sorrows,' she said in a commanding voice. When nobody did anything she added, 'The *very famous* Deirdre of the Sorrows.'

Some people gave little gasps of awe, which seemed to be what Deirdre of the Sorrows wanted, but Oisín could hear a few 'Who's across the bench. Antimony's was the loudest.

'My dear,' Deirdre of the Sorrows said, wading over towards Antimony with an expression on her face that was at once tragic and greedy. 'You must have so many sorrows. Think of it, the child of the infamous Ogonis! What you must have inside you!'

'I don't have anything inside me. I didn't have breakfast this morning.'

There was some laughter, which Deirdre of the Sorrows pretended not to hear.

'Oh, but you must be full of pain!' she said, swooping a hand back dramatically. 'Let me see, dear.' Deirdre of the Sorrows turned her watery eyes on Antimony, as if she were a doctor examining a patient. 'Ah, yes,' she said. 'So much anger and betrayal! My dear, you must quench this fire with the water of sorrow.'

'Why do we have to come here?' Antimony complained. '*Eachtra* doesn't even travel through this pool.'

'My dear, travelling through the past is the ultimate adventure,' Deirdre of the Sorrows exclaimed. 'Wrens always visit Linn an Bhróin. It's a special treat!'

Oisín didn't think it was much of a treat but it seemed that some of the other Wrens disagreed.

'Look at that!'

Everybody followed Medb Gaultney's pointing finger. The running waterfall had turned into a sort of television screen. Oisín saw a couple of adults who looked very like Antimony, mixing magical potions in a laboratory. The picture changed and a child was at their feet, spitting out her first sip of fire-cocoa. The man laughed, a big, booming laugh. Another picture. The woman was standing talking to a raven, her hands on her hips, very much in control. Oisín looked over at Antimony who seemed hypnotised by Deirdre of the Sorrows' gaze. Oisín realised what was happening: Deirdre of the Sorrows could project Antimony's memories onto the waterfall just by looking at her.

'Dig deeper, dear,' Deirdre of the Sorrows said in a soft voice.

A new picture came up, quite different from the others. A figure was running away, a cloak catching in the breeze. The two parents were looking out a window, fear on their faces, fire lapping at the bottom of their house. They were helping their child out, magicking her to the ground. The child looked up, crying. The adults were still at the window, fire creeping closer. The child started to scream.

Oisín dived into the water before he could think about it. He could see Antimony shaking, could hear Medb whispering to her friends. He had to stop it.

'Oh, my dear, how clumsy!' Deirdre of the Sorrows said, almost toppling over in the water. She looked rather irritated until she stood up and saw Oisín in front of her.

'Oh, my poor child!' she said. 'The brother of the missing girl! Too overcome with grief to be able to stand up straight!'

Oisín blushed and wished he was able to move away from Deirdre of the Sorrows as easily as he had stepped over towards her. There was something about her gaze, which seemed so sympathetic and kind. Oisín had a hunch that all his feelings were being shown on the running sheet of water.

'None of the rest of you can know how this boy feels,' Deirdre of the Sorrows announced. 'Imagine the sorrow of having your sister murdered by the Morrígan!'

'She hasn't been murdered,' Oisín blurted out.

'Or she might have been eaten or tortured or be cold or crying or – oh, the woes that are probably happening!' Deirdre of the Sorrows said, stretching a watery hand out to Oisín.

Oisín tried not to think about Sorcha, but as soon as Deirdre of the Sorrows mentioned it, he pictured her, way up north, asleep with only the Morrígan for company. She'd be cold and thirsty and having bad dreams and –

'Let it out, child, don't keep it in,' Deirdre of the Sorrows said as visions of Sorcha came up on the waterfall. Oisín could hear everybody whispering.

'Oh, the things that are buried here,' Deirdre of the Sorrows continued, seemingly intent on making Oisín as miserable as possible. 'Oh, what sorrows you have seen!'

Oisín squirmed and felt sadder and sadder. He thought of things apart from Sorcha – sitting in the yard on his own at break time because nobody would talk to him, the day that Stephen had stuffed him into a rubbish bin 'as a joke'. He could feel his cheeks burning. He knew everybody was watching him on the waterfall.

'Yes, nobody here could match these sorrows!' Deirdre of the Sorrows said, seeming to get happier the more misfortune she encountered.

'Surely *you* could.'

It was Antimony, looking at Deirdre of the Sorrows with a defiant gaze. Her hunch paid off. At the mention of her own troubles, Deirdre of the Sorrows immediately broke away from Oisín and wobbled over to a more central spot.

'Of course, my dear. Nobody can match the pain of Deirdre of the Sorrows!' she said, tossing her hair back dramatically.

A shell full of chocolate truffles rose up from the water and Deirdre of the Sorrows popped one into her mouth, as if chocolate were the only way to cope with being so sad.

'Oh, how lucky you plain girls are never to know how hard it is to be the most beautiful woman in Ireland!'

The waterfall screen changed to show a very pretty young girl – Deirdre, before she had eaten quite so much chocolate. Once Deirdre of the Sorrows had started talking about her own sorrows, there was no stopping her. After a long history of how hard it was to grow up as the most beautiful girl in Ireland, whom everybody wanted to marry, she moved on to the moment she had met Naoise.

'The most handsome warrior in the country,' she said as the image of a young man came up on the waterfall. 'I knew as soon as I saw a raven drinking blood in the snow that that was what I wanted: a man with skin as fair as snow, with hair as black as a raven and with cheeks as red as blood. Oh, the pain of loving the most beautiful man in the world!'

'Is this important to know for Water Magic?' Conor McIntosh asked.

'The only important thing is to learn not to interrupt a beautiful story,' Deirdre of the Sorrows said, sounding not quite as sorrowful as usual. 'Of course, if you want to really make it in Water Magic, you'll have to be able to make good tears. Air Magic is all about the brain and Earth Magic is about your body and Fire Magic is about your spirit but Water Magic is about your … heart!'

Deirdre of the Sorrows pointed dramatically at her heart and started to sob.

'Many enchantments require magical tears. Luckily you all have me to produce so many of them.'

Tears started to stream down Deirdre of the Sorrows' watery face, so that it looked like she might dissolve back into the pool.

'My Naoise was the most handsome warrior in the country and then he was murdered by the High King of Ireland because he fell in love with these beautiful eyelashes!'

Oisín thought that whatever happened to Naoise sounded quite sad, but it was hard to be too sympathetic when Deirdre of the Sorrows was blubbering like a baby.

'Oh, and his lovely legs were broken,' she wailed as the water started to rise with her tears. 'And then those beautiful bones were trampled on by boars and crumpled into the ground until they were mushed up. His lovely legs, no more!'

Dimitri and Pádraig stopped playing football at the thought of somebody's bones being mushed up. The weeping willows drooped, adding to the tears.

'And his pale skin, no more! And his beautiful black hair, no more! And his lovely red cheeks, no more!'

'And our poor ears, no more,' Tom said.

Oisín tried not to laugh, which was getting easier as all the tears were sending water up to his mouth.

'And his lovely smile, oh, his lovely smile, twisted off his face!' Deirdre of the Sorrows sobbed. Her tears built into a crescendo, until her whole body was a running stream of tears and eventually she dissolved into the water. She waited a moment for dramatic effect before suddenly reappearing, fatter with tears than ever.

'Thank you, thank you,' she beamed at her audience as if they were clapping wildly instead of looking confused. 'I do think that was one of my best performances.'

'That cute warrior guy looks like Stephen,' Medb Gaultney said, tossing back her ponytail and smiling at Stephen.

Stephen looked at his sword as if it might be able to transport him somewhere else.

'No, his name was Naoise. Such a beautiful name! And so doomed!'

Before Deirdre of the Sorrows could start to cry again, however, she caught sight of who it was that Medb and her friends were giggling at and opened her watery eyes wide. 'Oh, but, my child, the resemblance is something!' she said in a fluttery voice and quickly glided across the water towards Stephen. 'My, what lovely black hair you have! But my Naoise would never have spiked his hair like that.'

Ignoring the giggles from the rest of the Wrens, Deirdre of the Sorrows continued to gaze admiringly at Stephen.

'Such lovely black hair and such pale white skin and such bright red cheeks!'

The last part was definitely true. Oisín had never seen Stephen blush so much.

'Oh, if you could have seen me all those years ago,' Deirdre of the Sorrows said, twirling her long hair in the water and attempting a giggle. She nearly toppled over, and held onto Stephen's sword to steady herself.

'What is *that*?' she gasped. 'An Freagarach!' she whispered before he had a chance to answer, clutching onto the sword.

Stephen leant back, half afraid she was going to hug him, but instead she just touched the blade of the sword very gently, as if feeling for something.

'This sword can only be used by the greatest warrior in Ireland, which used to be my Naoise,' she said in a shaky voice. 'And here is the mark he made on it all those years ago.'

Something was etched in tiny writing inside a small heart on the sword.

'"Naoise and Deirdre for ever." And now he's dead!'

Oisín was waiting for Deirdre of the Sorrows to start listing all of Naoise's body parts that had been stamped to nothing again, but instead she clasped her hands to her mouth and backed away from Stephen as if something much worse had happened.

'Oh, my child! You have An Freagarach! Nobody has ever had that sword and lived a long life!'

A ripple of interest passed across the pool, but Stephen wasn't concerned.

'I'm just holding it for the moment,' he said coolly. 'Once I get my sister, I'll be gone.'

'Oh, no. The sword holds you. You can't be rid of it. And your sister will –'

Deirdre of the Sorrows returned her hands to her mouth and she turned around to Oisín.

'The calamities! The two brothers have arrived!'

Oisín didn't know what she was talking about, but at that moment his image had just appeared alongside Stephen's on the screen. A large whirlpool formed in the centre of the room and Deirdre of the Sorrows crouched on the edge and stirred it, peering in as if she was checking on soup.

'The Well of Woes has always told of two brothers,' Deirdre of the Sorrows said in a sad voice.

Oisín remembered Cassandra's prophecy with a lurch.

'It doesn't even look like a well,' Antimony said loudly.

'Too worried about your parents to see clearly!' Deirdre of the Sorrows cried out. 'Oh, my children, the Well has always said that two brothers will come, one with a sword, the other with a book. Our land will be saved, but they will destroy the ones they love.'

With those words, the two brothers on the waterfall screen started to fight. Oisín and Stephen couldn't help staring, along with everybody else. Deirdre of the Sorrows kept on stirring at her well, in the same kind of trance Cassandra had been in. Oisín felt his stomach churn as he watched what was happening on the waterfall. Stephen's sword had broken and Stephen was on the floor, fires swirling around him. Standing over him in the smoke was Oisín, holding a small book up towards the sky. The image kept repeating as if on a loop: Stephen falling, Oisín holding up the book, Stephen falling. Oisín saw with a terrible start that it wasn't just Stephen who was falling, but Sorcha as well, and Antimony and Tom and Caoimhe and Lysander Quicksilver.

'Stop!'

There was a flash of fire and silver. The picture burst into flames and cleared. Stephen waded over and retrieved An Freagarach, which he had flung across like a dart. Oisín could see that he was trying to be calm, but his hands shook as he picked up the sword and his face looked very red and confused.

'Oh, my child –' Deirdre of the Sorrows began, but Stephen cut her off.

'I'm done with this, thanks,' he said.

Oisín couldn't look at him as he stormed by. The words from Cassandra's prophecy swirled in his head. *Brother will fight brother, siblings sunder.* Mrs Fitzfeather hadn't believed it, though. And what did Deirdre of the Sorrows know about anything?

She seemed to know about water at least, for, as Stephen left, she scooped one of her watery hands through the pool and picked up a drop that looked identical to the rest.

'Oh, my children,' she said, holding the drop up so that it sparkled in the sunlight. 'That boy has done what none of you has yet. He has produced a real magical tear.'

Chapter 15
The Enchanted Forest

Just when Oisín was ready to have some time away from the Book of Magic, he found himself spending more time with it than ever. Although *Eachtra* veered around the dense Enchanted Forest, the Wrens went through it for a week. It was one of *Eachtra*'s many traditions, ensuring that the Wrens could have their own adventure and the druids could have a bit of peace. The Keeper of Books fussed about the Book of Magic leaving its drawer ('Moonlight shining on it and it won't even be at the right temperature!') but eventually she relented.

Mrs Fitzfeather was equally concerned. 'I can smell trouble,' she said gruffly as Oisín prepared to leave *Eachtra*. 'You might be better just leaving that thing in the forest, boy.'

Oisín wasn't sure what to say, so he gave a polite nod and headed towards the boundary of the Enchanted Forest where the Houlihans were already clambering aboard an oak. The Wrens would travel through the forest on trees, and Tom and Caoimhe were gently encouraging their tree to move its giant roots. Antimony, who had very little interest in Earth Magic, was interpreting Mrs Fitzfeather's comments.

'Of course she wants you to think that she doesn't want the Book,' she said knowingly. 'But think about how suspicious she's been, wearing those shawls as if she's always cold, turning up in the cave right after the Morrígan left. And I know that eyepatch is hiding something.'

Oisín nodded mechanically. By the time their oak tree had started to move, Antimony had already accused half of *Eachtra* of being in league with the Morrígan. Oisín opened the Book of Magic and tried to ignore her various theories, which implicated everybody from Nuala Nugent to the merry-go-round horses.

The Book of Magic snuggled into his hands, breathing in the deep magic of the forest. Swirls of green and woodland creatures were already appearing in the Earth Magic section. They weren't the only addition. Oisín had noticed several small new black lines in the Book, but he'd never seen one form until now. He watched as a spindly black line slowly spread across the page, like a crack in the parchment. Another line joined it, cobwebbing out from the edge. Oisín placed his finger upon it and felt the page crackle.

'Oisín! Put that thing down. We're here.'

Oisín turned to Tom in surprise. Surely he hadn't spent the last two hours just staring at the Book of Magic? It seemed that he had, though, for when he looked out from his branch, the clearing was bright with the afternoon sun. Antimony was still speculating about the Morrígan.

'Antimony, we can't ban people with green eyes from coming on our tree,' Caoimhe said patiently. 'It would exclude most of us for a start.'

'Everything is welcome on our tree,' Tom said, as a red squirrel hopped over. Tom cleared his throat. 'Everything good, anyway.'

Oisín looked up and caught Tom looking at the Book of Magic. Oisín was about to challenge him, but Tom turned around quickly, suddenly absorbed in helping the squirrel crack an acorn.

After a few days, Oisín got used to the rhythm of the forest, which experienced four seasons every day. Each morning, the forest was full of the life of spring. Bluebells popped up, birds cracked out of eggs, leaves curled off the tips of trees. The Wrens did most of their work in the morning, taking care of the trees and harvesting any useful herbs. Cathad, a cheery druid with long white hair that trailed along the forest floor, told them about *dinnseanchas* (the lore of placenames) and how to speak Forest, the sign language that all the animals shared.

Their break arrived with summer every afternoon, which meant the Wrens could lounge in hammocks or play mossball. In the evenings, the Wrens travelled in their trees (except for Stephen, who preferred to walk on his own). The leaves had turned golden by this stage, and it was the perfect time for roasting chestnuts over a fire and telling stories about the Great Elk that Cathad insisted still roamed through the trees.

As night fell, winter crept through the forest. Snow drifted through bare branches, all the animals curled into holes in tree-trunks, and the Wrens bundled up in blankets in their trees.

Though Oisín got used to snow melting every morning, he couldn't quite get the hang of Earth Magic. It should have been easy, since both Tom and Caoimhe were eager to help him with it. Caoimhe knew the names of every herb and Tom could speak fluent Forest and had hands as tough as bark. Earth Magic was all about touch, and Cathad kept telling them that any good druid's palms were full of calluses (his hand reminded Oisín of an Ordnance Survey map). But while Tom could feel a tree's heartbeat just by pressing his palm against it, every time Oisín tried to steer their oak they ended up stuck in shadow-swamp. Part of the problem was the Book of Magic. More and more black lines were appearing on each page, like cracks in tarmac, and Oisín found himself captivated by their progress.

He told himself that it didn't matter whether or not he mastered Earth Magic. After all, Antimony had no time for it and Lysander Quicksilver refused to get his sky-silk shirt dirty with tree-sap. There was a part of Oisín, the part that loved running through trees with his hands in the air, that felt sad that all the green swirls in the Book of Magic were slowly being covered with black lines. This was a small part, though, a tiny voice at the back of Oisín's head, as quiet as snow falling in the night.

By their last afternoon in the forest, the part of Oisín that was suspicious of the Book was smaller than the insects that buzzed around their oak. Oisín was in the crow's nest that Tom had made at the top of their tree, the Book of Magic nuzzled in his hands.

There was a lot happening in the forest below. Nuala and Noreen were bouncing on the moss trampoline (they were experts at falling over), Orion Jones was playing the magical scales in a field of musical toadstools and Yuriko Ada was admiring the Butterfly Tree, which had a different set of bright, fluttering 'leaves' every afternoon. Most of the other Wrens were playing mossball. Magical moss was a bit like green snow, except less cold and a good bit furrier. It was also easier to pick up than normal moss and made a satisfying squelch when it met its target. Even Caoimhe, who had been busy experimenting on daffodils, couldn't help launching several mossballs at the Gambaro twins when they attempted an ambush.

There was only one thing that Oisín wanted to look at, though, and it was already in his hands. He was so absorbed in the Book of Magic that he didn't hear Tom climbing up the ladder behind him.

'Mossball?'

Oisín didn't bother to turn around.

'No, thanks.'

Tom was still standing in the crow's nest.

'Did you see the Garden of Wishes?' he said, pointing down to a small garden below. Oisín wished there was a spell to stop Tom from talking.

'You plant a tree for every wish you have. As long as your wish is alive, so is the tree. Dad brings me here every year to make a wish. My first one was that little chestnut tree over there. Ten years ago and it's still growing.'

'What did you wish for?' Oisín couldn't help asking.

'To be taller.'

Neither Tom nor the tree was particularly tall, but Oisín supposed there was still time. Tom continued pointing out each tree: a flourishing elder when he wished that his mother's vegetables would have a good year, a confused cactus when he hoped his Dad would find the secret spice he was looking for, a shrivelled clump of nettles which seemed as unsuccessful as Tom's wish five years ago that Caoimhe would stop practising magic medicine on him.

'Somebody just made a wish,' Oisín said, pointing to a small bud.

'Me,' Tom said, colouring slightly.

'What did you wish for?'

'I can't say yet.'

Oisín felt the Book of Magic flutter in his hands. He felt a blast of irritation. 'You wished for this, didn't you?'

Tom couldn't have looked more shocked.

Oisín was surprised to find the words coming out so easily. 'Because you don't have your own *croíacht*. You're jealous.'

Tom's face had turned beetroot. 'Not every druid needs a *croíacht* to do magic. There's lots of magic you can do without toys.'

Oisín felt the Book wriggle in his hands. He thought of the nastiest thing he could say to Tom. 'Caoimhe said that's why you couldn't be a Wren last year, even though you were twelve. Because you still hadn't found a *croíacht*. They just took you on this year out of pity.'

Tom looked as if he might hit Oisín or, worse, start to cry. He took a moment before he spoke.

'Be careful of that book. Those black lines can't be a good thing. I think you should spend some time away from it.'

'Yeah,' said Oisín, 'and give it to you? Nice try.'

Before Tom could respond, Oisín pushed past him and climbed down to the branches below. All he wanted was some quiet. Instead he found Antimony in the middle of her conspiracy theories.

'It's easy for you, she's not trying to kill you,' she said to Caoimhe. 'I'm sure she's here. And I'm going to figure out who she's disguised as.'

Caoimhe focused on removing magical moss from her hair. Antimony didn't need an interested audience.

'I bet Deirdre of the Sorrows would love to see us swallowed in shadow-swamp. She feeds on misery.'

'She doesn't even have green eyes,' Caoimhe said, exasperated.

'Not now. But who knows what colour her eyes were when she wasn't made of water? Or Madame Q? We all know how much she wants the Book.'

'She was with us when Sorcha went missing.'

Caoimhe turned her attention to their tree, which was swerving wildly as if it was trying to throw them off.

'She could have transformed easily while we were searching,' Antimony said. 'And her eyes turned green when she held the Book of Magic, as if it was revealing what she really was.'

'Most druids have green eyes,' Caoimhe said in exasperation. 'I have green eyes. Am I a suspect?'

Antimony shrugged, as if she hadn't discounted the possibility. Their tree started to pick up pace, even though Caoimhe was urging it to slow down.

'So everybody who has green eyes is a suspect,' Caoimhe said sarcastically. 'Medb Gaultney, the Keeper of Books, Gael and Gabriela Gambaro, Mrs Fitzfeather –'

Antimony was about to express her feelings on Mrs Fitzfeather when Tom came running down the ladder.

'What's going on? Why are you steering us towards the Forest of Shadows?'

'Probably because I'm the Morrígan,' Caoimhe snapped. 'Why don't you take over? This thing won't listen to me.'

Usually the oak responded as soon as it felt Tom's hand. This time, though, it ignored him, and went on stomping through the forest at a ferocious pace. Oisín peeked out through the branches. They were in a different part of the forest where winter fell a lot sooner. The air was bitterly cold and the bare trees were much thinner and closer together. The oak tree didn't mind, sending branches crashing to the forest floor. When Oisín pulled his head back, Caoimhe and Antimony were almost shouting.

'Or the Quicksilvers,' Antimony said darkly. 'Both of them were hanging around our tree earlier.'

'They have blue eyes!'

'Quints can change the colour of their eyes,' Antimony continued.

'Lysander saved us from the snow-snakes,' Caoimhe said. 'He's hardly trying to kill you.'

'You just like him because of his posh accent,' Antimony said. 'I wouldn't be surprised if you were helping him. I bet you'd love to practise medicine on my bones!'

'I'm not the one who talks to ravens.'

'Stop!' Tom shouted.

Both of his sisters turned to look at him in surprise.

'Don't you see what's happening?' he said, his voice shaking. 'It's the shadows. They'll make you feel bad things. Say things you don't mean.'

Antimony seemed to wake from a dream and looked out at the dark forest ahead of them. Though the trees were bare, shadows clung to their branches like leaves, shifting ominously with the breeze.

'Why did you bring us here?' she asked.

Tom looked over at Oisín.

'It's that thing,' he said slowly. 'It's pulling us in.'

As soon as he said it, Oisín knew it was true. He could feel the Book of Magic pulse in his hands, could feel it pulling them into the Forest of Shadows, an adjacent forest north of the Enchanted Forest, which they definitely weren't supposed to travel through.

'The Book can do that?' Antimony said, suddenly afraid.

'You're the Keeper, make it stop,' Caoimhe said sharply.

'Fine,' Oisín said, standing. 'Stop!'

To his great surprise, that was exactly what the Book did. Their oak pulled to an immediate halt, its roots dangling in mid-air.

'I can see when we're not welcome,' Oisín said, shoving the Book into his hoodie pocket.

'Oisín, wait. You can't get off here! We're by the Forest of Shadows.'

Oisín ignored Tom's voice. He ignored Cathad's warnings about leaving their tree at night. He clambered down their tree and ran into the Forest of Shadows. Within only a few steps, the Houlihans' calls sounded very far away.

There was one other thing that Oisín ignored: the steady stream of insects past his feet, rushing as if to get away from something, scurrying from the very direction that Oisín was walking towards.

Chapter 16
Mysteries in Moonlight

Oisín had been camping in the woods before. The trails had been carefully marked, his parents had packed enough sandwiches to last a month, and their tent had been huge, a home from home. Even in the dark, when Stephen had tried to convince him that every crackling twig was a monster, Oisín had known that the Wicklow mountains were probably more likely to house beetles or badgers than flesh-eating trees or zombie bears.

Walking through the Forest of Shadows at night was a very different experience. Shadows drooped from every branch, shifting slightly as if they could sense an intruder. Hardly any moonlight penetrated the shadowy cover, but Oisín could still make out the shadows of tangled branches on the forest floor. He was also pretty sure he could *feel* them. As he pushed through the maze of twisting branches and gnarly roots, Oisín felt his hand brush through something dark and cold. Remembering the shadow-fish, he shook it off and blundered ahead through the tightly packed trees.

Unlike the rest of the Enchanted Forest, there weren't any trails here and it wasn't long before Oisín was completely lost. He stopped, unable to remember why he had felt the urgent need to leave the Houlihans' tree. He tried to turn back in the direction he had come. The problem with the forest was that soon everything started to look the same. Oisín also had the uncomfortable feeling that the trees themselves were moving. He tried to listen for Tom or Caoimhe's voice but all he heard was the twitch of the night air and the beat of his heart, hammering harder and harder. Oisín suddenly wished that he was camping with his family instead, with access to the thousand things their mother packed for emergencies that never arose. He would have loved a torch or even one of Granny Keane's banana curry sandwiches. The only thing he had was the Book of Magic. He pulled it out of his hoodie, hoping he could get it to illuminate itself. If anything, though, the Book of Magic seemed darker than the rest of the forest, like a black hole, sucking in all the light around it.

Oisín broke into a run. He knew that it wasn't sensible to run in a dark forest, but he couldn't help it. Branches scratched at his face, roots threatened to trip him and the shadows swarmed around him. No matter how fast he ran, he didn't seem to make any progress. There were always more branches to brush through, always more shadows slithering towards him. All he could do was keep running until – THUD!

Oisín slipped over a root and slammed onto the snow. He raised his head to see where he was but realised with a lurch that he couldn't see anything. The dark around him was impenetrable. Oisín was totally disoriented. He reached his hands across the ground but couldn't tell which direction was which any more. He could hear the rustle of roots and branches as they crept closer but he had no idea which way he should run. He felt a swarm of insects crawl over him, desparate to get away from whatever was closing around him.

'Hello?' Oisín called, aware of how small his voice sounded in the complete darkness.

There was no answer, only the frantic scurrying of beetles and the creak of the trees. Oisín reached for the Book of Magic but it had dived out of his hoodie pocket when he fell. Oisín felt something grab hold of his arms and had a terrible moment when he wasn't sure if he was falling or being pulled up. It was as if the shadows were reaching inside of him and pulling out every bright thought until all he could imagine was darkness.

Just as Oisín was sure the shadows were going to do something terrible, he heard a thunderous noise and felt whatever was holding him let go. Now it was the trees' turn to scurry away and the moon appeared in time to let Oisín know he was definitely falling.

He landed with a crash on top of a large animal. Oisín thought that one of *Eachtra*'s horses had got lost until he slid off and saw the size of the creature.

It was the great Irish elk, the animal that Oisín hadn't believed was real. It looked real enough in the moonlight. It was bigger than a car, with huge sharp antlers, a dark sleek coat and intelligent black eyes. It tapped its huge hooves on the ground and rotated its antlers, speaking to Oisín in Forest, the sign-language that Cathad had taught them.

'The Enchanted Forest welcomes Oisín the gentle,' the great beast signed to him. 'You would do well to remember your name.'

Oisín remembered Granny Keane had said the same words as the DART had pulled off: *Remember your name.* He had been named after one of the old heroes of the Fianna, Oisín the gentle, but Oisín wasn't sure what that had to do with anything.

Except, Oisín realised as he looked into the deep eyes of the great elk, he hadn't been very gentle as he pushed past the Houlihans and insulted Tom.

The elk sensed that he didn't fully understand and signed something else: *Be careful who you trust.*

Oisín could trust the elk, he knew that much. There was something so ancient about the goodness in the creature's eyes that Oisín knew he could believe in it. The elk twisted its antlers again and Oisín realised he hadn't fully understood the earlier message. Not be careful who you trust but be careful *what* you trust.

It was the Book of Magic, Oisín realised. That was what had made him be rude to Tom, that was what had dragged him towards the Forest of Shadows. The further north they travelled, the stronger it became. And the harder it became for him to think apart from it. He had to give it up, Oisín realised, not just to save Sorcha, but to save himself.

'Thank you,' Oisín signed.

For the first time in a while, Oisín felt like himself, free from the lure of The Book of Magic. The elk was about to sway its head in acknowledgement but then it pricked its ears and signed something else. It was one of the most commonly used phrases in Forest, something every animal understood instant-ly: *Danger is coming. Beware.*

With a crash of its huge hooves, the great elk bolted off into the depths of the forest. Oisín felt very alone until he saw the figure running out of the Forest of Shadows: Cassandra Quicksilver, looking very flustered about something.

'What are you doing in the Forest of Shadows?' she said to Oisín.

'We could ask you the same thing, sis.'

Oisín turned to see the four male Quints emerge from the other direction, their eyes remarkably silver in the moonlight.

'It's none of your business,' Cassandra said crisply.

Lysander wasn't so easily brushed off.

'Who were you meeting here?' he said, searching the shad-ows for signs of somebody else.

'I was just stargazing,' Cassandra said, blushing. Even Oisín knew that a dark forest was one of the worst places to look at stars.

'Anyway,' Cassandra said, her normal composure returning. 'What are *you* all doing here?'

'We were searching for this little dude,' Brad Washington said, shining a sleek torch around nervously. 'And now that we've found him, maybe we can go. This place seriously creeps me out.'

Lysander stood up from the ground, where he had been examining the elk's tracks.

'What's the matter, Braddy-boy?' he said. 'Scared of the dark?'

'Don't worry, some of us have real *croíacht*s and can get us out of here,' Ben Washington said, pulling out his calculator.

Brad looked like he was about to hit his brother, but Cassandra pushed him aside to hand Ben a thread from her scarf. All it took were a few taps of Ben's calculator and the tiny strand of silver had expanded into a huge cloud, hovering over the ground like a magic carpet.

'Come on, let's go, Pip,' Lysander said, pulling Oisín up.

It was remarkable how quickly you could travel from somewhere extremely dangerous to the safest place in the world. Just a few minutes after he had been surrounded by shadows and menacing trees, Oisín was lying down on a fluffy silver cloud. Ben was steering with his calculator while the other Quints lounged in the folds of the cloud, having a picnic of silver grapes and apples.

Yet Oisín couldn't quite shake off the elk's warning. There were different kinds of danger. There was one kind that he was getting used to, the kind when shadow-fish tried to drown you or snow-snakes tried to strangle you. But there was another kind of danger, something to do with people, that Oisín found much harder to identify. He could feel something in the air, the same kind of heaviness as when his parents pretended to be polite at dinner after an argument. The Quints were offering each other moonmead and silver apples instead of salt and pepper, but there was the same tension, the same danger.

'Drink this,' Cassandra Quicksilver said, handing him a glass of shimmering silver liquid. 'It's moonjuice. It will make you feel better,' she said, seeing him hesitate.

Oisín tipped the liquid to his lips. It was delicious, as if light was pulsing through his body.

'You're lucky we were so close by when we heard you'd gone missing,' Lysander said. 'The moonlight picnic is a Quint tradition. You'll get to travel back to *Eachtra* in style. Moonsmoke?'

'He's only twelve,' Cassandra said as Lysander held out a jar of swirling silver smoke.

Lysander laughed and threw Oisín a silver grape instead. Like the moonjuice, it tasted sweet and fresh, but there was something about it that made Oisín feel slightly sick.

'So what's a moonlight picnic?' Oisín asked.

'A time to contemplate the mysteries of the universe,' Lysander said, sounding as if he was channelling Madame Q.

Lysander stretched back as if he was on a bean bag and made patterns in the moonsmoke with Raqib and Ben. Brad played with some of his gadgets, seemingly uninterested in the mystery of moonlight. Cassandra turned her telescope to the stars, frowning whenever she looked down. Oisín felt as if he had been invited to a party so exclusive that nobody was having any fun. He concentrated on the empty goblets in front of him, which were slowly being filled with clear bright liquid.

'So is that what Quints do? Collect moonlight?'

'Quintessence is much more complicated than that, Pip,' Lysander scoffed. 'It allows geniuses to pursue any idea to its edge.'

He swirled the tumbler of silver smoke he was holding and took a sip.

'Raqib is one of the finest magical chemists in the Himalayas,' Lysander said.

'*The* finest,' Raqib said, adding a tiny silver spice to the large jar of moonsmoke.

Lysander walked over to Cassandra.

'My sister likes to read the stars.'

'Not that anybody listens to me,' Cassandra said softly.

Lysander ignored her and stood between the Washington brothers.

'And then our twins. One who can do things with magical mathematics that would make your head spin. And one who makes the rest of us feel smarter. Nice of your parents to buy you so many toys but shame your *croíacht* doesn't work. What does your baseball actually do? Does it even bounce?'

Brad sprang to his feet and glared at Lysander.

'And what's your speciality? Theft?'

Oisín saw the guilt in Lysander's face. The realisation hit him like cold water. All this time and he hadn't even noticed. Lysander pulled out the Book of Magic, as if the back pocket of his trousers were the most natural place for it to be.

'You're talking about this?' Lysander said innocently. 'It dropped on to the ground. I was just minding it.'

'Then give it back,' Brad said, grabbing Lysander by the scruff of his shirt.

Raqib parted the two before they crashed into his jars of moonsmoke.

'Here you go, Pip,' Lysander said, skidding the Book of Magic across the cloud and glaring at Brad.

Oisín caught it just before it reached the edge of the cloud. He couldn't believe that he had almost left it behind. It might have stayed deep in the shadows if Lysander hadn't picked it up, just as Mrs Fitzfeather had suggested. Would they all be better off without it? Oisín imagined it falling into the depths of the Enchanted Forest below. It would be so easy to make it disappear, covered in snow in seconds.

'We're here,' Ben said, putting away his calculator.

Oisín was startled to find that their cloud had reached the twisting silver tower on *Eachtra*'s stern. Madame Q stood waiting for them in her study at the top, her eyes gleaming in the moonlight.

'I should take this squirt to the library,' Lysander said as they stepped off the cloud and into Madame Q's study. He seemed to be eager to avoid any conversation about what had happened with the Book.

'I can take the kid,' Brad Washington said quickly. 'Come on, little man, want a ride on my skateboard?'

'That won't be necessary,' Madame Q said with a clap of her hands. 'Quints, you have a lot of work to do before the moon wanes. I can look after Mr Keane myself.'

Neither Brad nor Lysander looked very happy about this, but they shuffled out of the study with the rest of the Quints. Oisín was alone with Madame Q for the first time. Her study was full of interesting objects – charts of the planets, whirring telescopes, a strange clock that ticked backwards – but Oisín's attention was directed elsewhere. It was hard not to look at Madame Q as she stared at the Book of Magic, which was sticking out of his hoodie pocket. It was a little difficult to see, as the only light came from a giant skylight in the roof of the study. Even in the moonlight, though, there was no mistaking what happened as Madame Q looked at the Book: a raven landed on the skylight, the temperature dropped several degrees and her silver eyes flashed a shade of green that Oisín had only seen once before.

Chapter 17
M and B

Madame Q caught Oisín looking at her and her eyes returned to their usual colour.

'Is something the matter?' she asked.

Oisín looked up at the skylight. He had been sure a raven had been there but now there was an uninterrupted view of the moon. Had he imagined it?

'I'm just tired,' Oisín said. 'I should get to bed.' *Or get out of here as fast as possible,* he thought. He stepped back to leave but Madame Q's voice stopped him.

'Come now,' she purred. 'No true adventurer could go to bed this early. And you know that magical items are at their most powerful in moonlight'.

'Like a book?' Oisín said innocently.

'Exactly,' Madame Q said.

'I should probably get it back to the library,' Oisín said. 'The Keeper of Books will be worried.'

Madame Q gave an indulgent smile. 'Absolutely right. Although sometimes rules must be bent a little. I haven't had one Quint who hasn't been in trouble with Mrs Fitzfeather at some stage. Genius can't be boxed in.'

'Does Mrs Fitzfeather know I'm here? She was worried about the forest.'

'You don't know the half of it about Mrs Fitzfeather,' Madame Q said irritably, before controlling herself. She smoothed out her dress, even though there wasn't a hint of a wrinkle.

'Let me be clear,' she said after a moment. 'I want to check on the Book of Magic. Make sure it's ready as we approach Lughnasa.'

Madame Q still hadn't told him about her plans for Lughnasa. Oisín wondered if she had told anybody.

'Couldn't you do that in the library?'

'I wanted to see the Book without outside interference. I could have just taken it, you know.'

'But you need me here,' Oisín said shrewdly. 'You need to see what hold I still have over it.'

Madame Q pressed her lips together so tightly that they almost disappeared.

'Here,' Oisín said, handing the Book to her. 'Have a look.'

He felt a tug as Madame Q took it from him. He could sense her restraint, could sense that she had wanted to snatch it. Oisín looked at her carefully. She seemed to have forgotten about him and was opening the pages very gently.

'It's changing, getting stronger,' she said after a moment. 'I'm not sure that you should –'

'It's mine,' Oisín said firmly.

The Book sailed back into his hands. It was the same movement it had made on the first day he'd found it, the same movement as when Stephen had tried to take it from him on the DART. But the Book of Magic felt different now, definitely his. Oisín was no longer sure he wanted it.

'What is all this commotion?'

Oisín turned to find Mrs Fitzfeather bustling in, with Brad Washington behind her.

'I knew that thing was trouble, sending you into the Forest, and on your first trip! If only I'd stopped you from boarding *Eachtra*.'

'And if only Quints knew how to follow orders and Captains knew how to knock on doors,' Madame Q said icily.

'I thought Mrs Fitzfeather should know what was happening,' Brad said.

'I wasn't aware that thinking was your speciality,' Madame Q retorted.

'Brad, take Oisín to the library immediately,' Mrs Fitzfeather said.

Oisín left before Madame Q could say anything. He couldn't wait to leave the Book in its drawer and flop into his hammock.

When they left the study, though, Brad stayed by the door and pressed his ear to the keyhole. Oisín stayed too, torn between tiredness and curiosity. The passion with which Madame Q and Mrs Fitzfeather were speaking meant that it wasn't too hard to hear snatches of their conversation.

'You agreed to stay away from the Book,' Mrs Fitzfeather flared.

'You haven't seen what's happening to it. Or have you?'

'How dare you! You know I want what's best for the Book and for the boy. B, we have to –'

'Don't call me that,' Madame Q hissed.

'You can hide behind all the Qs you want,' Mrs Fitzfeather responded. 'But you can't hide from who you are.'

'Oh, really? Taken off your shawls lately, M?'

The boys heard Mrs Fitzfeather's angry footsteps and they fled, only moments before she came storming out. Brad practically rolled Oisín down the stairs, pushing him through a side door and leading him through the winding corridors to the library without saying a word.

The Keeper of Books was so worried about all the other people who had touched the Book and the black lines that were creeping across it that she forgot to offer Oisín bramble-briar tea, which was some sort of silver lining.

Oisín was very glad to reach his hammock and be away from the Book. Tom was still awake. They spoke in Forest, so they wouldn't wake the others. This also made it easier for Oisín to apologise.

'It doesn't matter,' Tom signed quickly. 'You didn't know what you were saying. It's that book.'

Yes, Oisín thought, feeling the weight of the day catch up with him. It was always the Book. He wanted nothing more than to go to sleep and forget all about it.

Tom, however, was very interested to learn that the Quints had been in the Forest of Shadows.

'Antimony's right,' he signed. 'One of them has to be helping the Morrígan. I wouldn't be surprised if one of the Quicksilvers *was* the Morrígan.'

'I was pretty sure Madame Q was the Morrígan,' Oisín signed, telling Tom about what had happened with the raven and her eyes.

'I *knew* she was suspicious,' Tom shouted, forgetting they were supposed to be quiet.

'Ssssh!' Oisín signed. He was pretty sure that Dimitri and Pádraig were not a threat – unless their snores were fatal – but he thought it was wise to keep the noise down.

'Do you know why Madame Q and Mrs. Fitzfeather would call each other B and M?' Oisín signed.

Tom shook his head.

Oisín lay back in his hammock and tried to get some sleep. His brain hurt from all the mysteries. It was like trying to solve a jigsaw made of mist. Every time he thought he understood something, another piece of the puzzle drifted away. There was Cassandra and her prophecy; Lysander taking the Book of Magic; Brad Washington, whom all the other Quints bullied; the strange names Madame Q and Mrs Fitzfeather called each other; the elk's warning... Before he knew it, the dawn was creeping through the porthole.

'Whoa, look at that!' Dimitri said, leaping up from his hammock.

Oisín followed his gaze, looking through the sliver of clear glass in the porthole. They had arrived at the fire-fields, a grey landscape of craggy rocks that led towards a huge bubbling volcano. It wasn't the volcano that captivated Oisín though, but the hill on the other side, deathly pale in the morning sun.

'Cnoc na gCnámh,' he whispered to himself, surprised at the beauty of a hill made entirely out of bone.

Whoever the Morrígan was disguised as, they didn't have long to figure it out.

★★★

Across the other side of the volcano, many miles away, another child was having trouble sleeping. Sorcha stirred in her sleep on her comfortable bed and thought that Oisín and Stephen would be very jealous if they knew how much chocolate she had been having. And eating it in bed and everything! Sorcha turned over into the pillow.

'It won't be long now, dear,' the nice lady said in her honeyed voice. She'd cast off the shape she shifted to on board *Eachtra* and was her true self. She stroked Sorcha's hair with her long fingernails as Sorcha drifted back to sleep.

'Lughnasa's only one week away, sweetie. And then it will all be over.'

Asleep in her bed, Sorcha couldn't see the gleam in the lady's eyes or the cruel smile that crept across her face.

Chapter 18
Scathach's Challenge

The dragon on Antimony's watch blew out the date in rings of smoke: the twenty-seventh of July. Four more days until the Lughnasa festival. And four more days until she'd have to steal the Book of Magic.

Antimony ignored the nervous feeling in her stomach and vaulted down *Eachtra*'s sock ladder. The other Wrens were already clustered around Scathach, the druid who lived in the volcano and knew all about Fire Magic. Antimony's slingshot flexed in delight. Now that they had finally reached the fire-fields, it could get some real action. Antimony joined Oisín and Tom at the back of the group. Caoimhe was collecting ashgrass, a wispy plant that only grew by volcanoes. Everybody else was captivated by Scathach.

She was the kind of druid that it was difficult not to listen to. For a start, she was made out of smoke. Her red eyes glowed like embers and her long hair blew like strands of smoke in the wind. She had a gravelly, smoky voice and stood very still as she spoke, daring anybody to whisper or divert their eyes. Like all the other druids, Scathach thought her magic was the only kind that mattered.

'This is not about messing with numbers or your feelings. Fire Magic is about survival. Fire Magic is about fighting for your life.'

Scathach's fiery eyes scanned her rapt audience and rested upon Stephen.

'So you're the young thing that has An Freagarach?'

Stephen nodded.

'I've trained every warrior that's ever held that sword,' Scathach said. 'And I can tell by the state of you, you're not even fit to spit on their boots yet.'

Stephen coloured quickly, but he stepped forward and drew An Freagarach.

Scathach smiled and drew a smoking silver sword of her own.

'What's the matter? Don't want to hit a woman?' Scathach said as Stephen hesitated.

Stephen shuffled his feet, wanting a way to prove he was tough but not a breaker of that inviolate code that boys should never hit girls.

'Do you think the Morrígan will wait to ask?' Scathach sneered. 'I should have known you had no hope of saving that sister of –'

Stephen attacked as soon as Sorcha was mentioned. The swords of stone and smoke clashed against each other, sparks flying from An Freagarach. The fight lasted only seconds but it was the fiercest Antimony had ever seen. Stephen had the passion, swinging An Freagarach ferociously. But Scathach had the expertise. In one motion she had leapt over his head and tripped him up. An Freagarach clanged to the ground. Scathach stood over Stephen with her own sword tipped against his chin.

'Anybody can hold the strongest sword,' she said. 'Only a warrior can use it.'

There were a few giggles from the crowd as Stephen walked back to join them.

'Easy to laugh, hard to step up,' Scathach said as the laughter died. 'Anybody else got the fire?'

Antimony heard her own voice carry through the air. 'I do.'

Scathach looked at her curiously. 'I knew your parents. They could have been great warriors.'

'They were great magicians,' Antimony said, reaching into her pouch for her slingshot and some small fire stones.

She sparked the stones against her slingshot and concentrated. Fire Magic was all about the nose. Antimony remembered her mother's voice. *Breathe slowly, find your centre, concentrate.* Antimony looked down and saw that the stones had made a long gleaming sword. She held it above her head and braced herself. This would be easy. All she had to do was lean to the left as she charged and then veer to the right, catching Scathach off guard and sending her sword to the ground. Then she'd release a stone from her slingshot and it would be over.

Two seconds later, she was sitting on the ground, drenched in water.

'Any fool can start a fire,' Scathach said. 'It's knowing how to control a fire that makes you a real fire druid.'

Antimony shook out her hair. Her ribs stung. All she remembered was charging. From the look on the other Wrens' faces, she didn't think she had matched Scathach terribly well.

'If you want to be a true warrior, you'll have to try much harder. This is the first time in years that *Eachtra* has travelled so close to Droichead an Chláimh and not one of you looks like you have a hope of setting foot on it, let alone crossing it.'

Everybody looked at the thin bridge she was talking about, which stretched across the gaping volcano towards Cnoc na gCnámh. It was the most terrifying bridge Antimony had ever seen. Not only did it span a bubbling volcano, but Droichead an Chláimh itself was a long narrow sword. A sharp edge ran along its centre, glinting as though it could cut you just for looking at it. Its surface was wide enough to place a foot on either side of the sharp centre, but both sides sloped down perilously.

'One of the McIntoshes crossed it first,' Conor McIntosh boasted.

'Many a year ago,' Scathach said brusquely. 'No Wren has succeeded in crossing for the last fifty years. Fitzfeather hasn't even bothered to take *Eachtra* here in ten years. Don't think about magical trickery. People have tried to fly across, to ice the lava below or to cover it in grass. None of this will work. The only way to cross Droichead an Chláimh is to be a true warrior. The only thing you need is fire in your belly.'

'And a hole in your head,' Tom whispered.

Antimony ignored him. She had a vision of herself, bravely crossing Droichead an Chláimh, the best Wren on *Eachtra*. That was what her parents would have wanted, wasn't it? Something to be proud of? They'd be proud in a few days. When she had the Book of Magic. Antimony pushed away the thought that maybe they wouldn't be so proud about how she was planning on getting it. Who were her parents to judge?

Whatever they had been mixing had been dangerous enough to get them killed, to send her into exile. Her parents were the last people who could judge her.

'I'm ready,' Antimony said, stepping towards the bridge.

'I'm not into death unless I get the credit,' Scathach said, stepping in front of her. 'You're not ready, nowhere near ready, until you've had some proper training.'

So training was what Antimony did. Her little dragon announced the twenty-eighth of July and Antimony was up with the dawn, running laps around the volcano, practising her balance, shooting fire-apples to improve her concentration. Usually *Eachtra* travelled towards the northwest part of the island so that the Wrens could tackle the Fire dragons that lived in the volcanoes there. This year, *Eachtra* stayed put, parked as close to Cnoc na gCnámh as it could get. Everybody was waiting for the Lughnasa festival. And whatever plan the druids had to battle the Morrígan.

The days whirled by. Antimony's dragon puffed out 29, 30, 31 July: the day before Lughnasa.

Antimony rose with the sun as usual and started her laps of the volcano. The only other people there were Caoimhe, who was collecting more ashgrass, and Stephen, who raced Antimony every morning.

'It's disgraceful,' Caoimhe said as Antimony tried to run by unnoticed. 'This grass should be tended by a team of fire botanists, but Scathach doesn't have even one! Just because it's a bit of work to look after!'

'A bit of work' meant watering the ashgrass with almost boiling water every hour, trimming it carefully so it didn't set itself on fire and giving it the right balance of shadow and sunlight every day so it didn't wilt or bleach out. Caoimhe was sure she would discover some healing properties, even though, so far, ashgrass had proved successful only at singeing her eyebrows.

'Maybe this one will work,' Antimony said, though she was confident that she would find another pile of ash in their cabin that night.

She ran on. She didn't like getting too close to Caoimhe; she didn't like getting too close to anybody. It was better when she was doing laps. Running was great for pushing the thoughts from her head. All Antimony thought about was her route as she leapt over patches of fire and kept one foot in front of another. There was no time to think about the Morrígan or *béal tine* or guilt. Antimony was exhausted; she was happy.

'Move it! Azi Ogoni could lap that volcano in half the time,' Scathach barked as Antimony ran by. Antimony thought of her father beating her best time and found some energy in her calf muscles. Stephen was coming up behind her.

'Naoise would wipe the floor with you,' Scathach shouted after him. 'Fionn Mac Cumhaill would have done a marathon by now.'

Antimony beat Stephen that morning, which made her feel good. They walked over to the small Fire Forest together, where Scathach had already started training the rest of the group. They were aiming darts at fire apples which were perched on top of the bare trees. Medb smiled at Pádraig, wondering if he'd get her an apple.

'That pretty smile might work for you now,' Scathach barked at Medb, 'but if you really want to do great things, you'll have to start fending for yourself.'

For a second, Medb's beautiful face burned with anger. Then, she ripped off the sharp gold necklace she wore and launched it into the air. Everybody gasped as her *torc* struck right through the fire apple. Medb looked annoyed that she had shown her skills and her green eyes flashed with anger.

Antimony vowed to keep a closer eye on Medb. She still hadn't figured out who the Morrígan was in disguise as and she wanted to make sure nobody else got the Book of Magic on Lughnasa before she did. Oisín had filled her in about the moonlight picnic and she was certain that one of the Quints was helping the Morrígan. She wished Cluaiscín was there to help her, but she hadn't seen him for weeks. She was on her own again.

Except for Stephen. If Stephen wasn't running laps beside her, he was sitting opposite her in the library, where Antimony spent all her spare time now. She went there after she left the Fire Forest and headed to the Water Magic section, which was the best place to spy on the Book of Magic and who might be paying it a visit. Sure enough, Stephen was there too, flicking through a stack of dark books as if reading was something to be got through as quickly as possible. Antimony wished he'd go away: she couldn't look at Stephen without thinking about Sorcha.

She opened Deirdre of the Sorrows' autobiography, *Why You Will Never be as Beautiful or Sorrowful as Me – and How to Cry about it*, the one book she was certain wouldn't distract her from spying. She stirred its pages, which were already disintegrating into tears. Her dragon announced that it was six o'clock: Lughnasa was getting closer and closer. Antimony's insides felt like dreadlocks tangling around each other. She had enough *béal tine* left, and she would be able to use the Book of Magic if she stole it. Did she want to, though? There were too many things to consider. There was the power of the Book as it pulled them towards the shadows, a power that even Oisín didn't understand; there was Oisín helping her to swim in the underground caves; Stephen saving her from the Morrígan; Sorcha; her parents. Whenever Antimony remembered her parents, all her insides twisted tight again.

She listened to Nuala and Noreen to distract herself. Neither of them was especially good at Fire Magic so they were stirring a book about underwater ponies instead. Like everybody else aboard *Eachtra*, they were talking about Lughnasa.

'Do you think there'll be a proper Lughnasa feast here?' Nuala asked.

'Oooh, I don't know,' Noreen replied, which, along with giggling, was pretty much her response to everything.

'Because there aren't any real fields or crops,' Nuala continued. 'But maybe we could toast with fire-apples or something?'

'Oooh, I don't know about that.'

'Medb says we're only staying here because of that missing girl and that *Eachtra* usually ends up in a much nicer place.'

'Oooh, that's a shame.' Noreen sighed.

'Do you think the Morrígan's hung up her bones yet?'

'Oooh, I don't know.'

'Medb says that her whole bedroom is made out of bones and that she has a chandelier made out of little girls' … agh! You splashed me!'

Antimony hadn't so much splashed as drenched Nuala Nugent. She couldn't help it. She could see how upset Stephen was getting and she had to do something.

Nuala Nugent stirred her book and sent a shaggy water pony towards Antimony in retaliation. With one vigorous shake, it managed to transfer most of the water from its mane onto Antimony and Stephen. They both stood up, furious, but felt a hand grab them before they could do anything.

'This isn't the lost library of Atlantis,' Lysander Quicksilver said as he pulled them back. 'Can't you children behave?'

'Get off me!' Stephen shouted, pushing him away.

Nuala and Noreen scurried off as Lysander and Stephen glared at each other. Ben and Raqib strolled over, looking at the stack of dark books at Stephen's table.

'What's this? Raqib said. '*Inside The Morrígan's Magic.*'

'What's a Milesian meathead like you doing with dark books?' Lysander asked, suddenly interested.

'None of your business,' Stephen said, gripping An Freagarach meaningfully.

Lysander smirked and strolled over to Antimony.

'Didn't think you needed any help crying, Ogoni,' he said, looking at the book she was stirring.

'You'll be the one crying if you don't get lost,' Antimony snapped. She didn't like how often the Quints ended up in the library, somehow always at the same spot where they could see up to the Book of Magic. None of them ever went to the twelfth floor – that would be too obvious – but she was sure that they were checking up on the Book too.

'Come on, let's go,' Ben said. 'We've got important stuff to do.'

The trio walked over to the glass lift. There was something about the way the three Quints stood – arms folded, noses in the air, smug smiles on their faces – that made Antimony place a fiery paper airplane in her slingshot and Stephen pick up a large book. Together, their missiles had the desired effect. Much to their surprise, all three Quints found themselves flung backwards into the large pool behind them.

Antimony and Stephen couldn't have picked a better book if they'd tried. *Savage Swamps* was not used to many visitors, so the giant mosquitos and snapping swamp-weed that lived in the book were excited to have three teenagers drop in.

'Let me go!' Lysander shouted, but the enthusiastic elephant that had gripped his legs didn't seem to hear. He swung him through the mud like a pendulum, making it rather difficult for Lysander to maintain a superior expression. Meanwhile, an excited alligator was munching on the tails of Ben's blazer and a cluster of vines was having great fun dipping Raqib in and out of the swamp like a yo-yo.

Antimony and Stephen were bumping fists when a stream of mud gushed towards them. The elephant had dropped Lysander and was happily shooting its trunkful of muddy water in every direction. Any of the Wrens who had been trying to read got soaked and found themselves involved in the water fight whether they wanted to be or not.

In only a few seconds, the library floor was chaos. Lysander flicked his tie through the air and sent the entire magical mud section of the library crashing to the floor. Raqib dropped some of his silver spice into the swamp and it gushed up like a geyser, showering everybody with sparkling mud. Antimony leapt on top of the table beside Stephen, helping him to launch mudballs towards the Quints.

'STOP!'

For a seventeen-year-old, Cassandra Quicksilver's voice had a lot of power.

Everybody stopped to look up. Cassandra was leaning over the balcony on the twelfth floor, appalled. She swished her scarf through the air and sent a team of blank books to mop up the mess and herd the inhabitants of the swamp home.

'I cannot believe the lot of you,' Cassandra said, glaring at her fellow Quints when she reached the ground floor. 'You know all the druids are meeting about the plans for Lughnasa. Quints are supposed to guide the younger Wrens, not attack them. Especially when we have important work to do.'

Lysander started to protest but Cassandra was not in a listening mood. She looked at Antimony and Stephen suspiciously.

'And I would think *you* have better things to be doing,' she said to Stephen, before swishing her scarf around her neck and striding back to the glass lift.

Even through the layers of mud on his face, Antimony could see Stephen's blush.

'Don't mind her,' she said, drying herself off with a book about magic towels. 'I don't know why she has to interfere. And what was she doing up on the twelfth floor anyway? All of those Quints are up to something.'

Antimony stopped herself. She had forgotten that she was trying not to be too friendly with Stephen. This was the danger, she warned herself, getting too close to the people she had to betray. It was bad enough becoming friends with Oisín without forming an alliance with his brother too, mudballs or no mudballs.

'I thought you were one of them,' Stephen said after a moment.

'I'm not a Quint,' Antimony snorted.

'But your parents were.'

Antimony caught her breath, seeing the book that lay on the desk in front of Stephen: The *Infamous Ogonis: Traitors or Trailblazers*?

'My parents were Quints,' she said finally. 'And it was probably Quints who killed them. I only care about the kind of magic that burns.'

She turned and walked away. Something was swelling in her eyes and the last thing she wanted was to add to Deirdre of the Sorrows' book.

Antimony went up to her cabin and flopped onto her hammock. So Stephen had found out what most of the other Wrens already knew: Antimony's parents had been among the most powerful practitioners of Quintessence in Nigeria. Stephen would have read all about her story: the potion that her mother was brewing, so secret that nobody else knew its name. The secret society her parents were part of. The day they were branded traitors and decided to run away. That same night, a figure in a shadowy cloak arriving at their house before they could escape. The terrible smell of fire as it burnt away everything that Antimony had ever known …

Antimony wasn't sure the figure in a cloak was a Quint. It had been too dark to see if it had been a man or a woman, or even to tell if it was an adult. There was only one way of finding out for sure, only one way of getting revenge.

Antimony went up to her cabin and got the ingredients for *béal tine* ready. She would have to act soon. Before she knew it, her dragon was puffing out the hours as everybody else went to sleep. Ten…eleven…midnight.

Antimony didn't think about Stephen or Oisín or Sorcha. She thought of her parents, the last time she'd seen them, as fire curled up their house and a shadowy figure ran away.

She crept out of her hammock, picked up her bag with the *béal tine* in it and walked towards the library.

Chapter 19
Lughnasa

Nobody had told the sun that it was going to be a very serious day. It had stretched out early in the morning and beamed across the summer sky with not a single cloud to spoil its mood. Even the grey landscape around the fire-fields looked beautiful in its light. Oisín thought it was odd that the day could be so fine and his stomach could feel so sick. He felt as if he was taking a test but he didn't even know what questions he was supposed to be answering.

Then, as he was going to breakfast, he really felt sick.

'What's wrong?' Tom asked.

Oisín had stopped moving in the middle of the corridor, obstructing the Wrens who were eager for their torched eggs.

'The Book of Magic is gone,' he managed to say.

He wasn't sure how he knew. But he could feel its absence from *Eachtra*, as if an elastic band had connected him to the Book and it had snapped. Since the night in the Forest of Shadows, Oisín had felt distant from the Book, hadn't trusted it entirely. Now that it was gone, Oisín felt horribly abandoned. He turned into the stream of people, setting off for the library. He was sure that the drawer would be empty, but he was equally sure that he had to check. Tom dashed after him, apologising to the Wrens that Oisín ran into.

The library was eerily empty. Caoimhe was checking out *Ashgrass Maintenance for Beginners*, a smouldering volume that looked almost as unpleasant as ashgrass itself. Oisín bolted up the spiral staircase, not stopping until the twelfth floor. It was as quiet as Christmas Eve.

Oisín stopped running and walked slowly to the chestnut drawer which had held the Book of Magic. It was empty. Oisín gripped the cabinet for support. There was a part of him that had to get the Book of Magic back, an ache in his palm where it should fit.

'It's mine,' he whispered to himself. He hoped the Book would come flying back into his hands, but he wasn't surprised when it didn't. It had already gone too far from him.

Oisín stood up and inspected the drawer. The handle had scorch marks around it: somebody had used Fire Magic to open the cabinet. From the look of the burn, it had been several hours ago. Why hadn't he felt a pang as soon as the Book had been taken?

'Dark magic,' Tom said, climbing up the stairs and sensing the shift in the air. 'The Morrígan used very dark magic here.'

'I don't think it was the Morrígan,' Caoimhe said, coming up the stairs behind him.

Tom and Oisín stared at her. Caoimhe hesitated, unsure if she could believe what she was saying herself.

'Antimony didn't sleep in her hammock last night. I can't find her anywhere.'

'No way did Antimony do this,' Tom said, turning to Oisín for support.

But Oisín was looking at the scorch marks on the drawer and thinking about how eager Antimony had been to save the Book from the snow-snakes.

'Come on,' Tom said as he saw Oisín's face. 'Antimony might be a bit of a pain sometimes but she'd never do something like this. She wouldn't even be able to if she wanted.'

'She has *béal tine*,' Caoimhe said quietly. 'I saw it in her bag once. It's the only way she could have taken the Book from its Keeper.'

'You knew Antimony had dark magic and you didn't tell anybody?' Tom spluttered. 'I'm the eldest, you should really –'

'Oh stop,' Caoimhe said. 'I thought she kept it because it reminded her of her parents. I didn't think she'd use it.'

'Where's she gone?' Tom said.

'Cnoc na gCnámh!' Oisín said suddenly. He had no idea why Antimony would want to go there, but he knew that was where the Book was. Perhaps the *béal tine* was fading. He could feel a small connection to the Book, could sense it miles and miles away.

The three children stood in silence. They couldn't believe that Antimony had stolen the Book of Magic and gone to Cnoc na gCnámh. Oisín didn't know what to do: how was he going to rescue Sorcha when he didn't have the Book to bargain with?

A scream from the ground floor broke the silence. The children rushed to the balcony to see Noreen Moriarty below, waving her arms like a windmill.

'Ravens are attacking *Eachtra*!' she squealed, diving into a copy of *Amniotic Aqua* for cover.

Oisín looked out the library's large stained-glass window and saw that she was right. Dark shapes swooped across, heading for *Eachtra*'s deck.

'The Morrígan's creating a diversion,' Oisín said. 'She wants to keep the druids busy here while she gets the Book off Antimony.'

'Maybe Antimony's the Morrígan,' Tom said, as if nothing could surprise him at this stage.

'No, the Morrígan attacked the two of us in the underwater caves,' Oisín said. 'She must have known what Antimony was up to.'

He looked at the ravens streaming by the window. It wouldn't be long before they reached the library. They had to do something.

'We've got to find the Keeper,' Oisín said, searching for the thread of her cardigan.

'She's gone to the Quintessence section,' Caoimhe said. 'I bumped into her this morning. One of the Quints told her that *The Beauty of Black Holes* had gone missing.'

Oisín frowned. It was just like the Keeper of Books to get sidetracked on a wild book chase.

'Which Quint told her that?' he asked. It seemed rather suspicious that one of them would try and get her out of the way like that.

'She didn't say,' Caoimhe responded. 'We could get Mrs Fitzfeather or Madame Q?'

'Do you trust any of the druids here?' Tom said. 'We'll have to do this ourselves. Are you sure Antimony went to Cnoc na gCnámh?'

'I'm certain,' Oisín said, though he couldn't explain why he was so sure.

Tom sighed. 'I wish we still had Mum's air bicycle.'

'There's no way that would make it to Cnoc na gCnámh,' Caoimhe said. 'The druids must know of some secret passage, but I'm not sure how we'll find it in time.'

'There's one other way,' Oisín said slowly, finding the courage to say the words.

'Droichead an Chlaímh.'

Tom and Caoimhe looked at each other.

'You don't have to come,' Oisín said.

Tom took a deep breath, as if he couldn't believe what he was about to say.

'Our sister's there too now. Whatever she's done, we can't leave her to the Morrígan. I'm coming.'

'Me too,' Caoimhe added.

Oisín thought that he should probably tell them not to come, but he felt so happy they were coming that he didn't say anything. It also wasn't the best time to have an argument: several ravens had just made their way into the library and were flying towards them. Luckily, *Ashgrass Maintenance for Beginners* proved to be a useful deterrent. After a couple of ravens had got stinging smoke in their eyes, the others steered clear of the book and the people around it and they managed to make their way onto the deck.

Eachtra's deck was another level of chaos. Ravens were everywhere, pulling and pecking at the sheets and umbrellas. Meanwhile, the wooden wrens had sprung to life to defend *Eachtra*, and Angus Óg had rounded up a flock of swans to help. Scáthach was beside him, swirling her smoking sword and using *Eachtra*'s frying pans to launch fireballs into the sky. Oisín thought he saw Mrs Fitzfeather pulling her shawls around her and running away from the fray, but he was too busy making his way through the chaos to worry about where she was going.

Once they had reached Droichead an Chláimh, Oisín didn't have time to think about anything else. He took a step towards the slender sword-bridge. It was even more terrifying up close.

'Well, go on, Tom,' Caoimhe said. 'Age before beauty and all that.'

'I've always said you were very wise for your years,' Tom said nervously.

'It'll be grand,' Oisín said, struggling to sound convincing.

'You're right,' Caoimhe said. 'We'll just do what Scathach says: empty our minds. And don't touch the blade. Or stay still too long – the metal will be hot from the volcano below. And most of all, don't think about looking down.'

Tom peered over the cliff and looked at the lava. Like any fire, it was mesmerising and terrifying at the same time.

'What if it erupts?' he asked.

'Another thing not to think about.'

'Alright, let's go,' Oisín said, taking a breath and raising his foot.

'Wait!'

Stephen was running towards them, An Freagarach at his side. 'Out of the way, kiddies,' he barked, 'I'm going to cross this for real.'

'So are we,' Oisín said, fire flushing to his face.

'Look, Shortsquirt, I'm not going to have you messing up my plan.'

Stephen gripped his sword, making all too clear what his plan was.

'Wait, look,' Oisín said, opening his mouth wide and pointing towards Cnoc na gCnámh.

Stephen craned his neck around. In that second, Oisín had slipped under his arm and clambered onto Droichead an Chláimh. He started to walk before Stephen could stop him.

Oisín blanked out the string of curses Stephen shouted after him, focusing on putting one foot in front of the other. After a few steps, he realised with a shock that Caoimhe had already stepped onto the bridge while they had been arguing. She was walking ahead, going as fast as she could: the metal surface was hot, so the best thing to do was keep moving.

Oisín kept his runners on either side of the sharp middle, holding his arms out for balance. It was surprisingly easy once he got the hang of it. He just imagined he was walking on a slightly sloped wall. He always leapt up on the park wall when he walked home from school, and really this was no different.

Apart from the bubbling volcano below.

As soon as Oisín stopped to look down, he froze. The chasm yawned below him, achingly big. He could feel the steam rising up, smoky fingers waiting to drag him down. He stared at the hypnotic fire, which seemed to reach hungrily towards him.

'Look at *me.*' It was Caoimhe. She had reached the other side and was standing at the bottom of Cnoc na gCnámh. 'Come on, it's not far. Look at me!'

Oisín tried to raise his head to her but his whole body felt dizzy. He could feel his feet slowly slipping.

'Look at me,' Caoimhe repeated.

Oisín met her eyes.

'You can do it.'

Oisín put a foot forward. He felt Droichead an Chlaímh sway under him, felt the steam curling up towards him. He couldn't do it.

Of course you can't, a voice said in his brain. It sounded sweet and sharp at the same time, velvet covering steel. *You can't do anything. You're not as good as your brother. You can only do magic because of the Book. You're nothing.*

'Oisín!'

Oisín started. He pulled his feet from the edge and swivelled around. Tom had stepped onto Droichead an Chlaímh.

'Oisín, keep going,' he called encouragingly, swaying his arms as he stumbled forward. 'I don't think I can stop and I don't want to run into you.'

'Yeah, come on, Oisín, you're nearly there!' Caoimhe called.

Oisín felt a strange surge of hope in his chest. Tom and Caoimhe were so foolish, crossing Droichead an Chlaímh when they didn't have to. Just because they wanted to help. Oisín had a warm feeling in his belly. He turned towards Caoimhe and started to walk towards her, looking her in the eye, putting one foot after the other, pretending it was just an ordinary wall in the park. Step after step after step.

'Thanks,' he gasped as Caoimhe pulled him onto the cold surface of Cnoc na gCnámh. She smiled for a second. Then her face changed.

'Oh, no,' she said, looking back at Droichead an Chlaímh.

The sky was filling with dark shapes.

'Ravens! Hurry!' Caoimhe shouted.

She didn't need to tell them. Tom was halfway across but Stephen had just started. They picked up pace. Tom stumbled and fell, and the blade of the sword-bridge cut into his knee. Blood gushed down to the volcano below.

'Careful!' Oisín screamed.

Watching was almost worse than crossing. If anything happened to them …

The ravens sensed their weakness and swooped.

'Away!'

Stephen swiped An Freagarach through the air. It glinted fearsomely in the sunlight, slicing into a raven as it lunged towards Tom. The raven stopped in midflight and dropped down towards the volcano below, like a stone plopping into a pond.

'Go on,' Stephen said, brandishing his sword in the air. He sent a few more ravens to a very hot bath, and the rest of them quickly flew away.

He waited until Tom had got to Cnoc na gCnámh before he followed. He strode across the bridge as if it was a footpath. Oisín looked at the figure covered in soot and dirt, determination in his eyes, his sword an extension of his arm: he looked more like a warrior than his brother.

Stephen was three quarters of the way across the bridge when another figure climbed on.It was Brad Washington, standing on top of his skateboard.

'I'm here to help you guys!' he shouted across.

'The idiot,' Caoimhe gasped. 'He can't use his croíacht to cross.'

'That's not his croíacht,' Oisín said. 'It's just an ordinary skateboard.'

'An ordinary skateboard that's about to smash into Stephen,' Tom said.

It was too late. Brad leapt onto the bridge, keeping his balance as his skateboard whizzed across. He held his arms out and gave a whoop of delight that echoed in the volcano below.

Stephen was far from delighted, though. He tried to break into a run to get to the safety of Cnoc na gCnámh but the bridge was too slippery and the skateboard too fast for him to avoid it.

Oisín watched in agonising slow motion. Brad bowled into Stephen and knocked him forward. Brad's skateboard was thrown backwards, wheels spinning in mid-air. For a moment, everything was suspended in the sky: Stephen, Brad, the skateboard. Then gravity remembered its job and they all started to fall.

Oisín rushed to the edge. All he could see was Brad's silver skateboard, gleaming like a log on a river of fire. It only took a few seconds for it to disintegrate into the hungry lava. Oisín was sure Brad and Stephen had already been swallowed by the fire. But then the two boys appeared. That was the moment when Oisín understood why Madame Q had selected Brad as a Quint. Even as he was falling, he had managed to turn his tie into a rope and lasso himself onto the side of the volcano. He scrambled up onto Cnoc na gCnámh, shocked but alive.

This was also the moment when Oisín understood why Stephen had been the one to pull An Freagarach from the underwater caves. He was inching his way, hanging by his hands, across Droichead an Chláimh, the hilt of An Freagarach in his mouth. His hands were streaming blood as he made his way across, but Stephen didn't let go.

The first thing he did after Caoimhe and Oisín pulled him up was to leap on top of Brad Washington.

'You almost killed me,' he shouted, pushing Brad into the chalky dust of Cnoc na gCnámh.

'Dude, I'm sorry,' Brad said. 'I just wanted to help.'

'Where are the other Quints?' Stephen said, holding out An Freagarach.

'I don't know,' Brad said. 'But I know it can't be good.'

'Well, you can stay here and wait for them,' Stephen said.

'I came to help, not to be pushed around.'

Brad pulled out his baseball *croíacht* from his trousers, as if he was ready for a fight.

Caoimhe stepped between them.

'Let me fix that,' she said, taking Stephen's hands and placing ashgrass in her pen. 'It'll sting a bit,' she said as Stephen winced. 'But it'll burn out the cut.'

Caoimhe was right. Tiny ash stitches made their way across the deep red gashes on Stephen's palms. Apart from a thin scar, his hands were back to normal after a moment. Tom's knee had healed just as quickly. Caoimhe allowed herself a small smile of satisfaction.

'Let's get moving before the ravens come back,' Tom said.

Stephen pulled out his sword.

'I can handle this. You all stay here and wait for help.'

Even with the blade of An Freagarach in front of them, nobody was willing to stay behind. Stephen rolled his eyes at the collection of dusty children and one Quint in front of him.

'All right, not exactly my dream crew, but I guess we're going together.'

Stephen dusted off his jeans and held up An Freagarach. Oisín knew that he was thinking of Sorcha.

'Let's get going. We've got one green-eyed monster to kill.'

Up in the sky, the sun continued to shine stupidly, unaware of what was happening below. It shone over the battle on *Eachtra*'s deck. It shone over Droichead an Chláimh's sharply glinting blade. And it shone over Cnoc na gCnámh, its pale white surface gleaming in the light, daring anybody to approach.

Chapter 20
Cnoc na gCnámh

The children climbed up Cnoc na gCnámh in silence. The smooth surface of bone was hot and slippery in the sun and it took all their concentration to keep moving. Oisín scanned the skies for ravens, but it was eerily calm.

After an hour or so they reached an archway that led into a twisting tunnel. Tom touched the sides of the cave. Slowly, his Earth Magic reached some scraps of moss and they started to glow. Oisín wasn't sure if he wanted to see. The inside of the tunnel was carved from bone, but the walls were lined with real skeletons of animals and humans. Small femurs and tibias spelt out a message on the floor.

'Enter at your peril,' Oisín read with a shiver.

'So friendly. And we forgot to bring chocolates,' Tom murmured.

'Ssssh,' Stephen whispered. 'I read in one of the books that there's a Guardian of the Bones. We don't want to wake whatever that is up.'

'Bookworm,' Oisín muttered.

There was the hint of a smile on Stephen's face. Then he gripped An Freagarach and walked past the message and into the cave. Oisín followed. He could feel it as they walked through the twisting passages deeper into Cnoc na gCnámh: they were getting closer and closer to the Book of Magic.

Finally they reached a huge cavern. Like the rest of Cnoc na gCnámh, it was lined with bones, but the ones on the ceiling were gigantic, as if they belonged to a dinosaur. The patches of moss that Tom had enchanted continued to flicker, so Oisín could just make out some of the terrifying skeletons on the wall. He turned away from the long fish in front of him, deciding he didn't want to imagine how sharp its teeth had been when it was alive.

Stephen pushed against a large cylindrical slab in the centre of the room. It looked like the only doorway but no matter how hard Stephen pushed, it refused to budge.

'It won't move,' Caoimhe said. 'It's enchanted.'

Oisín peered at some lines cut into the surface of the slab.

'It's Ogham,' he said after a moment. 'We did this in school. It's the script that was used in ancient Ireland to mark the names of chieftains on stones. It must be a riddle.'

Angus Óg had told them about Ogham too, all those weeks ago in the snowy mountains. He searched his brain, remembering how he had carved out his own name. He scratched out what he could remember of the Ogham alphabet in the dust. Now that he had a task, he felt calmer. He almost forgot about the others until he heard the fear in Caoimhe's voice.

'Tom, what are you doing?'

Tom was looking at the skeletons on the wall.

'It's not right,' he said.

The glowing moss was very dim, so it took Oisín a second to see what was troubling Tom. He was looking at a picture on the wall: two human skeletons were playing with the skeleton of a fox. A woman was pulling at the fox's tail, while a man yanked the fox's ears. Even as a collection of bones, Oisín could see that the fox was in pain, forever trapped with his mouth open.

'We can't leave him like that,' Tom said.

'Tom, it's just a picture,' Caoimhe said.

'Imagine if it was Giant!' Tom said. 'I couldn't leave him trapped here.'

'No!' Stephen hissed.

It was too late. Tom had eased the fox's tail from the triumphant lady's fingers.

'We shouldn't move anything,' Caoimhe said, panic in her voice.

There was an ominous creaking sound, as if the cavern was waking up.

'Let go of me,' Tom said, going on trying to help the fox.

'Tom, nobody's holding you!'

Tom gulped as he turned around to see three bony fingers gripping onto the back of his T-shirt. The female skeleton from the wall had creaked slowly to life and moved forward. Tom tried to step away but the skeleton gripped him tighter, clattering her bony teeth together in anticipation.

'Leave him alone,' Caoimhe shouted, shooting out pebbles from one of her pen's many compartments.

The skeleton tumbled backwards, but her male friend was also coming to life. He raised a sword of bone in the air. With a quick snarl, the fox leapt up and bit his wrist, sending the sword crashing to the floor. There was another creaking sound. The movement of the skeletons had aroused all the other bones lining the cave and, slowly, terribly, they started to come to life, creaking and twisting their forgotten limbs. There was a bear with a huge snapping jaw, a collection of hands not attached to anything, the long fish with very sharp teeth.

'Don't stop, Slowsnail!' Stephen snarled at Oisín. He swiped his sword at a skeleton-snake without pausing for breath. 'We'll never get out of here if you don't solve that riddle. Move it!'

Oisín turned back to the Ogham, which he had just finished deciphering.

'What you see if you look at this for ever,' he read carefully.

What did that mean? His own reflection? The other side? He racked his brain desperately. It was a little hard to concentrate with the sounds of the skeletons behind him. He could hear a low rumbling sound, as if the whole ceiling was shaking. He looked up and saw with horror what was above them: the long skeleton of a slender dragon. It pulled itself off the roof and stretched. It was very long, with a sharp, twisting tail and a huge mouth. The Guardian of the Bones.

'Now would be a great time to solve the riddle,' Brad said, hitting a clatter of hungry teeth with his baseball.

Oisín looked at the Ogham slab desperately. 'What you see if you look at this for ever,' he repeated to himself, feeling none the wiser. He heard the terrible sound of the dragon coiling down the wall, the swish of An Freagarach as it curved through the air. Then there was an awful boom and the cavern was filled with light and smoke. The Guardian could blow fire.

'We're all OK,' Tom shouted, seeing Oisín turn his head to check. 'Just keep going.'

Oisín heard another creak as the Guardian switched position behind him. They were all going to end up as skeletons. They wouldn't see anything if they stayed here for ever, just *death*.

That was it, Oisín realised, with a terrible chill. The answer to the riddle was death.

Oisín picked up a stone and quickly carved the answer in the bone slab. The boulder creaked open. Inside was a narrow passage leading into a murky body of water. Oisín didn't like the look of the shadowy water but at least it wasn't breathing fire.

'Come on!' he said to the others. The boulder was already starting to close.

They all looked at each other. On one side was an army of skeletons and a dragon who'd had several centuries to work on his rage. On the other was an unknown pool of water and the Morrígan's chamber.

The five children took a deep breath and dived in.

Chapter 21
Betrayal

Antimony was in a different part of Cnoc na gCnámh, one of the oldest parts of the mountain where the magic was so deep it made the air feel heavy. It had been a couple of hours since she'd arrived. Crossing Droichead an Chlaímh had been easy for her, but the riddle had taken her a while to work out.

She felt the Book of Magic flutter in her hands. It wasn't sure about her yet, but it wasn't entirely resistant either. She wasn't sure how long the *béal tine* she had used would work. She had to move fast.

She waded through the dark water into a small side chamber. It was the one she'd read about in the library, the reason she'd come to Cnoc na gCnámh: the old chamber had very deep magic, the kind that could make the darkest of spells work. Antimony climbed up onto the small island of bone in the centre of the chamber and put the Book of Magic down. The room pulsed with a strange green glow, from candles which flickered in a chandelier made out of bones. The chandelier made Antimony shiver, so instead she focused on setting up. There was only a small bit of *béal tine* powder left: she'd used most of it to steal the Book. This was her only chance. The Book of Magic flapped its pages to the Quintessence section, bracing itself.

Are you sure you want to do this?

Antimony ignored the voice in her head and placed a drop of her blood into the jar. She pulled out a fire-beetle and placed it inside. Deep in her bag were the two items she had been saving: her mother's favourite turquoise ring and the special spoon her father used to stir his firecocoa. She added them to the jar and picked up the Book of Magic.

'Are you sure you want to do this?'

The voice wasn't coming from her head but from the cavern. Antimony rubbed a couple of loose shards of bone against her slingshot quickly.

'You don't need a weapon,' the voice said softly.

Antimony scanned the small chamber. There was nothing there except the chandelier, the walls of bone and a pool of clear water.

Antimony sparked the bone shards into a sword. Better to be safe.

'I told you, child, you don't need a weapon. Swords can't hurt me any more.'

Antimony turned around to see the pool of water shifting slowly, until Deirdre of the Sorrows had formed her watery self in its centre.

'I'm busy,' Antimony said, turning back to the Book.

'I know,' Deirdre of the Sorrows said. 'Are you sure you want to do this?'

'It's none of your business.'

'I know the sadness you feel.'

There was something different about Deirdre of the Sorrows' voice, a trace of genuine concern.

'You don't know anything,' Antimony said, turning back to the swirling indigo smoke. She mustn't let her brain become distracted. *Béal tine* could only work with total concentration. And she would only be able to use the Book of Magic if she stayed focused. It stretched on the floor beside her, excited.

'You don't want to help your friends?' Deirdre of the Sorrows asked.

'They're just people I know.'

'I don't think that's true.'

Deirdre of the Sorrows flicked back a watery strand of hair. 'I know how hard it is to make friends. Believe me, no girl wants to be friends with the most beautiful woman in Ireland. It's a terrible trial having eyelashes that everybody else would die for.' She stopped herself and continued in a different tone. 'Good friends are hard to find. They're worth keeping.'

Antimony concentrated on her mother's ring, remembering the first time her mother had let her dress up with her jewels. She had to hurry. The kind of magic she wanted to do could only work on Lughnasa. She remembered the first time her father had spoken of the six lost books of the Tuatha Dé Danann. He had told her of the Book of Magic's power. It has the power to overcome everything, he had said. Even death.

'It won't work the way you want it to,' Deirdre of the Sorrows said. '*Béal tine* never does. The Book of Magic is no different: it tells you what to do, not the other way around.'

Antimony tried to ignore her. *Béal tine* had worked when she wanted the Book to stay on the island, hadn't it? She wasn't going to back down now.

'My child, I know your sadness,' Deirdre of the Sorrows said, her watery cheeks swelling. 'But your parents have moved on to the Land of Shade. It's no use pulling them back.'

'If it's so great there, why don't you go?' Antimony said angrily. The Book of Magic shook in her fingers and she struggled to keep hold of it.

'I often wish I did,' Deirdre of the Sorrows said, gazing sadly at her own reflection. 'Tears can't keep me warm in bed like Naoise could. Many a night I wished I could bring him back by my side. It's too late to save my Naoise. But it's not too late to save another warrior.'

'What do you mean?' Antimony couldn't help asking.

'The Keane brothers have come to Cnoc na gCnámh,' Deirdre of the Sorrows said. 'With one of the Quints and your siblings.'

'The Houlihans aren't my siblings.'

'Your friends, then,' Deirdre of the Sorrows continued. 'They're all swimming towards terrible danger.'

'Stephen has An Freagarach. They'll be fine,' Antimony said.

'My Naoise had An Freagarach too,' Deirdre of the Sorrows said sadly. 'He still died. The boy will too, without the aid of the Book. They all will. It's clear as water.'

'They can look after themselves,' Antimony said, her fingers trembling.

Deirdre of the Sorrows closed her watery eyes as she read the vibrations of the other streams in Cnoc na gCnámh.

'There is great danger coming for the brothers. Betrayal is ahead.'

'I've already betrayed them, haven't I?'

'Not yet, my dear.'

Antimony looked down at her father's teaspoon. She couldn't change her mind now.

'Why don't you go and stop the Morrígan then? I'm just a Wren.'

'A Wren who's holding the most powerful book in our world.'

The Book of Magic moved its pages slowly. Antimony stared at the words that were forming in silver writing so small it was almost invisible. The Book of Magic knew what she wanted. All she had to do was use the *béal tine* to make sure it happened.

'She'll get the Book if you do this, you know,' Deirdre of the Sorrows said. 'She'll come for it soon.'

Then I'll have to be fast, Antimony thought. She tried to ignore the sounds of Deirdre of the Sorrows, but her ears couldn't help listening.

'Our world tilts on a knife edge. What you decide today will shape the years to come. If you do this kind of deep magic, you'll change the Book of Magic for ever. The Morrígan will win.'

The silver words gleamed in the bright light. Antimony stared at the sentence that could bring her parents back from the dead.

'Child, you must choose,' Deirdre of the Sorrows said urgently. 'Think about what your parents would want.'

Antimony struggled to hold the Book in her hands. That was the problem: how could she know what her parents would want? Wouldn't they want to be with her? Wouldn't they want her not to be alone?

'You can bring back your parents from the shade,' Deirdre of the Sorrows said, 'or you can save your friends. You must choose: the living or the dead.'

A magical tear rolled down Antimony's cheek and sloshed onto the parchment. It spread across the small silver words, slowly dissolving them. Indigo smoke swirled in the jar beside her. If she wanted to do it, it had to be now. Antimony looked at Deirdre of the Sorrows' watery eyes and knew she shouldn't have. Images flashed across Deirdre of the Sorrows' clear body: Antimony's mother in her laboratory, grinning as lime green dust fizzed in a beaker. Her father teaching her his grand-mother's recipe for firecocoa. Her parents together, watching her win her first game of fireball when she was six. Another tear dropped down. Without needing to look, Antimony knew it was spreading across the parchment. The sentence would be invisible in seconds.

Just as she was about to turn to the *béal tine*, another set of images flashed across Deirdre of the Sorrows. Tom showing her the best tree to climb in the Houlihans' forest. Caoimhe tending her ashgrass. Sorcha hopping onto the beach when the DART landed. Oisín helping her to swim in the underwater caves. Stephen handing her a mudball to throw at the Quints. Tears trickled down her cheeks, a stream now. Antimony closed the Book of Magic and leant her head against the wall. She felt as if somebody had carved open her chest and there was nothing left any more.

Deirdre of the Sorrows glided over to her. She had absorbed some of Antimony's tears, so she was even fuller than usual.

'You don't need to bring them back, my dear. They'll always live on in you.'

Antimony found some anger somewhere in her empty chest. She was tired of people telling her about her parents.

'What do you know? You didn't know them. You don't know what they'd want.'

'I knew your father when he was a Quint here and he was always very kind to me.' Deirdre of the Sorrows' expression changed as she recalled Antimony's mother. 'I met your mother at the wedding. Of course I couldn't help crying about how my Naoise and I could never have a ceremony like that, per-fectly natural. Maybe I did make the wedding cake *slightly* soggy and I suppose it was not *ideal* that your mother had to float down the aisle, but even so, I still don't think she had to shoot so much fire at me when I cried for the thirtieth time!

Even though she put it out, some of my beautiful braids are still charred.'

Something different stirred in Antimony's chest, something warm and ticklish. She felt her mouth curving into a smile. She remembered the photo of her parents' wedding: her mother in an emerald green dress, her father's dreadlocks tied back in a ponytail. She could picture the two of them flashing fire towards Deirdre of the Sorrows' floods of tears one moment and helping her the next. Antimony found her feet and stood up shakily. For the first time, she thought she knew what her parents would want. She picked up the Book of Magic.

'Can you take me to them?'

Deirdre of the Sorrows nodded and merged back into the water. Antimony followed her, wading down the twisting corridors of bone, trying to ignore the skeletons that served as decoration. Finally they reached an ornate door made of bone. The Book of Magic pulsed in Antimony's hands, as if it knew what was inside. Antimony wasn't sure what it wanted now. She had been about to use very deep magic and had stopped just when the Book of Magic could show how powerful it was. It twisted in her hands. She couldn't tell whether it was excited to see its Keeper or the Morrígan.

'I can't go in,' Deirdre of the Sorrows said. 'There are too many shadow-fish in this water.'

Antimony nodded. She felt both very alone and full of fire. She pulled out her slingshot and turned the cold white doorknob very slowly. As Deirdre of the Sorrows floated off, Antimony peered through a crack in the doorway.

The room was huge, the size of a football field. At its centre was an enormous pyramid of skulls and bones, protected by a moat of shadow-fish and a circle of curtains that hung from the ceiling, the thread so thin that it was almost invisible. A magnificent throne of bone sat on top of the pyramid of skulls. Antimony shuddered: she'd arrived at the Morrígan's chamber.

It wasn't the Morrígan standing there, though, but a handsome boy, his blazer slung over the back of the throne and his tie whipping through the air like a weapon.

Lysander Quicksilver looked over at Antimony in surprise.

'Stay out of this, Ogoni,' he said.

Antimony saw who he was fighting: Brad Washington, who was using his own tie as a weapon in defence. The two Quints circled each other, their ties snapping against each other like swords. Brad tripped on the skulls and tumbled over.

'Help me,' he shouted to Antimony as Lysander towered over him.

Antimony raced through the shallow moat of shadow-fish and ducked through a gap in the curtain. She picked up a shard of bone, placed it in her slingshot and aimed for Lysander's chest.

'No!' Lysander shouted as the bone knocked him over.

Brad leapt to his feet. His tie caught Lysander just as he tried to scramble away and Lysander was thrown into the curtain. He stayed there, like a fly stuck in a web. He *was* stuck in a web, Antimony realised with a lurch. The thread was so fine because it wasn't a curtain but a cobweb.

'What do you think you're doing?'

Antimony gasped as somebody grabbed her from behind. It was Raqib Paro.

'Stop messing and give me the Book like a good little Wren,' he said.

Raqib might have been the finest chemist in the Himalayas but he certainly wasn't the finest fighter. Antimony gave him a quick dig in the chest, pushed him away and kicked him into the cobweb-curtain.

Antimony looked up and saw that Ben Washington had attacked Brad at the same time. Brad had managed to push him into the cobweb-curtain, though. The three Quints struggled uselessly against the fine thread, which had bound its way across their mouths so they couldn't talk. Antimony shivered. This felt quite different from throwing mudballs.

'Thanks, dude,' Brad said, pocketing his brother's calculator *croíacht* and gingerly making his way down the pyramid.

'Where are the others?' Antimony asked, scanning the chamber for any sign of her friends.

The cobweb curtain stretched around the perimeter of the pyramid of skulls. Antimony thought she saw some movement behind the throne, but couldn't make out what it was.

'Man, we all got separated,' Brad said. 'The shadow-water was real deep. You should have seen it! I wish I'd had my skateboard – I could have surfed out of there.'

Antimony ignored him. She craned her neck to get a better view of what was behind the throne.

Brad stepped in front of her.

'Lucky you came, man. Those guys would have killed me otherwise. They got here through the passage in the Quintessence section of the library. You'd already taken the Book though, hadn't you?'

Brad gave her his biggest grin.

'Think I could take a look?'

'I'm giving it to Oisín,' Antimony said.

Brad's grin widened.

'I think he's a little tied up at the moment.'

Antimony gasped as she realised what was behind the throne of skulls: Tom, Caoimhe and Oisín were stuck in the cobweb-curtain, their mouths bound as tightly shut as the Quints'. Lysander Quicksilver's blazer was on the floor in front of them – he must have taken it off to fight Brad.

Which meant that the blazer on the Morrígan's throne could only belong to one person, the smiling teenager in front of her.

Brad gripped Antimony's arm before she could reach for her slingshot.

'Now, why don't you give me the Book of Magic?' he said, his usual goofy grin turning into something much more sinister.

Antimony stared at him in surprise.

'What's the matter?' Brad said with a sneer. 'Didn't think the stupid skater-boy had it in him? Neither did your friends. Made it a lot easier to tie them up once we got here. Shame the other Milesian swam into a different room. I almost knocked

175

him off the bridge this morning, though, so he shouldn't be any trouble.'

Antimony did the only thing she could think of: she spat in his face.

Brad's smile hardened and he pulled out his baseball *crofacht* from his pocket.

'That's not going to make me do anything,' Antimony scoffed.

'Maybe not,' Brad said. 'But I think *this* might.'

He tapped the side of his baseball. A small silver blade shot out, glinting in the eerie light of the chamber.

Brad was right. There was nothing like a blade to win an argument and Antimony let him prise the Book of Magic out of her hands. Before she could do anything, he'd shoved her into the cobweb-curtain and a fine thread had looped across her mouth. She cursed herself for being so stupid. The other Quints hadn't been trying to get the Book; they had been trying to stop Brad from getting it.

Everybody looked at Brad now as he strode up the pyramid and sat on the throne, stretching his long legs on top of a skull. He flicked through the Book as if it was the best gadget he could hope to ever get.

'I think you'll have to give it to me officially,' he said to Oisín. 'Otherwise it won't work.'

Brad tapped his fingers against the throne and the threads holding Oisín snapped.

Antimony hoped Oisín might charge at Brad but he just stood there, dazed.

'You can't be the Morrígan,' he said to Brad. 'You don't have green eyes.'

'*I* do, though.'

Everybody turned to see who had just entered the chamber. Antimony twisted her head to see the Morrígan standing at the foot of the pyramid. She looked different to the last time they'd seen her. She wasn't a stingray or the most beautiful woman in Ireland. Instead, she was disguised in the shape she'd been using aboard *Eachtra*, the shape that had fooled all of them.

Brad Washington shot up as if he had been sitting on a fire-ball.

'Your Greatness,' he said, removing his blazer quickly from her throne.

'I'll deal with you later,' the Morrígan said in an icy tone. 'But first I want to welcome our main guest.'

She looked past Antimony and turned to Oisín.

His own green eyes widened in shock as he realised who the Morrígan had been disguised as all along.

Chapter 22
Green-eyed Monsters

The clues had been there all the time. The green eyes that had seemed so kind but were now glittering coldly. The chill in the air whenever he was around her. The one druid aboard *Eachtra* that Oisín had trusted. The Morrígan had been disguised as the Keeper of Books.

'Surprised, dear?' she asked in her fluttery voice, looking strangely out of place in her woollen cardigan.

Oisín couldn't speak, even if he had wanted to. All the time he had been going to the library to check in on the Book, he had been getting closer and closer to the Morrígan. A lot of small details started to make sense. The floor of the library that the Keeper occupied wasn't cold to protect the rare books. It was kept cool to hide the chill of the Morrígan. The Keeper was always making tea for the same reason: so the warmth of the tea would distract from the cold around her. And the huge glasses she wore took attention away from the hard green eyes behind them.

'Figuring it out, are you?' the Morrígan said with a chilly smile. 'I always said you were sharp. Not too sharp, though. All I had to do was appear a little bit like that dotty grandmother of yours and the rest was simple. I knew you'd never suspect a doddering little old lady who cared about books.'

She had been right. There had been something so warm and cosy about the Keeper that Oisín had never suspected that her resemblance to Granny Keane could be a disguise.

The disguise wasn't the only lie. Brad had told him to be careful of Lysander so he wouldn't suspect Brad himself. The Keeper had told Caoimhe that a Quint had sent her in search of a book that morning, but of course the only book she was after was the Book of Magic. The puzzle was slowly becoming more solid. The problem was that Oisín didn't like the picture it was making.

'*You* made the black lines in the Book,' he said. 'You were just pretending to be concerned about them. All the time the Book was in its drawer, you were working dark magic on it.'

The Morrígan's eyes were twinkling.

'You're doing very well. It's a shame you're so late at figuring it out. It has been nice getting to know you. I've been waiting to meet you for years, sitting up in that lonely library with only books to talk to. But I knew you'd come eventually, the prophecies never lie.'

Oisín had to keep her talking. There was still a chance that Stephen could free Sorcha. He'd swum in a different direction when they'd dived into the water, so he had a plan of his own. And he had An Freagarach. There was still some hope.

'How come none of the druids ever found you out?' Oisín asked, stalling for time.

'I put a forget-me-not charm around my floor of the library so none of the druids would ever visit it.'

'They'll come here, though,' Oisín said. 'Madame Q and Mrs Fitzfeather have a plan.'

'You think M and B will come here and rescue you?' the Morrígan asked in a silky voice. 'They never were as brave as I was. I don't think they'll be coming here.'

Oisín struggled to fit this piece together. M and B were the names that Mrs. Fitzfeather and Madame Q had used for each other, but what did they mean?

'Didn't they tell you that we're all sisters?' The Morrígan said with a smile. 'Madame Q and Mrs Fitzfeather! Not quite as elegant as Badb and Macha.'

Oisín remembered the story that Granny Keane had told about the Morrígan. She was one of a trio of goddesses. Macha and Badb were the other two. M and B. That was why Mrs Fitzfeather accused Madame Q of hiding behind a new name. It was also why Madame Q's eyes flashed the exact same shade of green as the Morrígan's when she got excited. Oisín felt a ripple of shock pass through the room. It was clear from the other Quints' faces that none of them had suspected Madame Q of being related to the Morrígan.

The Morrígan pulled her woolly cardigan around her, enjoying the show.

'You see why M and B can't come and visit. It rather brings out the witch in them. Speaking of *which*.'

The Morrígan laughed at her joke and slowly started to transform. The person Oisín had known as the Keeper of Books changed in front of his eyes. Layers of wrinkles smoothed. Her woollen cardigan changed into a black feathered cloak. Her white hair twisted into sleek black strands. All that remained were the same green eyes, gleaming terribly without her glasses.

'Now, perhaps we can get to business,' she said, walking over to Brad, who was pointing Ben's calculator at the Book of Magic. Silver sparks fizzled out of the calculator, but nothing was happening to the Book.

'Who's been a greedy little boy?' she said in a scarily sweet voice, running her hand through Brad's floppy hair.

'I was just testing the Book's powers, O Great One,' Brad stammered.

Her long fingernail pressed into Brad's cheek until it drew blood. Brad winced.

'You've been a useful assistant,' she said. 'I knew an ambitious Quint would be a good spy. But I fear your usefulness is waning.'

She prised the Book from Brad's fingers and pushed him to the ground as if he were no more important than the discarded skulls he had landed on. Oisín felt a pang as the Morrígan opened The Book of Magic.

The whole chamber seemed to sense her increase in power. The shadow-fish pulsed excitedly in the moat. Ravens swooped in, settling on the Morrígan's throne. The skulls and bones shifted as if preparing for battle. And then the sound of tiny, scuttling feet reverberated around the chamber.

Oisín should have expected a room with a cobweb to have spiders, but the kind that lived in Cnoc na gCnámh still came as a surprise. They were the ugliest spiders he had ever seen: their white bodies were as pale as bone and their tiny green eyes gleamed horribly in the dim chamber. They were coming from every direction: crawling down the thin cobweb curtains and creeping up through cracks in the pyramid of skulls. The skulls moved to help them, shifting to reveal a deep well near the bottom of the pyramid, from which hundreds of pale spiders scuttled out. Oisín jumped as a couple scurried across his runners. He really hoped that Stephen had found Sorcha.

He wasn't the only one who was scared. Brad Washington scrambled backwards up the pyramid as a horde of spiders crawled towards him.

'O Great One, could you help me?' Brad said nervously as the spiders swarmed up his legs.

The Morrígan didn't look up from the Book.

'They always eat Quints first,' she said in her silky voice, bored. 'They're attracted to power. Though I'm not sure why they're bothering *you*.'

The insult spurred Brad into action.

'I do have power,' he said, standing. He snapped his tie against the spiders and pulled out his brother's calculator *croíacht*.

The Morrígan was suddenly interested.

'Your brother's the only one who can use that thing,' the Morrígan goaded him. 'He's always been the smart one.'

'Anything Ben can do, I can do better,' Brad said, punching the keys on the calculator and pointing it at the spider in front of him.

'And bigger,' he added as the spider expanded to the size of a bear, its pale white legs as tall as any of the Quints.

The giant spider found its footing on the uneven skulls. For a moment it turned towards Oisín. Oisín took a step back, terrified of its huge pincers and hungry green eyes.

Brad Washington had other ideas, though, whipping the spider's side with his tie as if it was his horse. He didn't seem to be scared anymore.

'That way, buddy,' Brad said, directing the spider towards his brother.

'That's it,' the Morrígan said encouragingly. 'You show the Quints who's really powerful.'

'No!' Oisín shouted as the spiders started to scuttle towards Ben, who was still trapped in the cobweb-curtain. Whatever advanced Quintessence skills Ben had possessed deserted him now. He looked like any sixteen-year-old boy about to be eaten by a giant spider: very frightened.

The spider seemed to be waiting for Brad's instruction.

'Do it,' the Morrígan said softly.

'Don't listen to her,' Oisín shouted. 'She doesn't care about you. She just wants skulls for her chamber.'

Brad snapped his tie. The spider raised its pincers and lunged. Ben arched forward, gasping. 'I do have power,' Brad said, folding his arms in satisfaction.

'So much power that you want more,' The Morrígan said, looking at Brad curiously. She held out the Book of Magic tantalisingly by her side.

'No!' Oisín shouted, seeing what Brad was about to do.

It was too late. Brad had already extended the blade in his baseball and launched himself towards the Book of Magic.

'It's mine,' he shouted, knocking the Book out of the Morrígan's hands.

He gasped as it tumbled down the pyramid and dropped into the well from which the spiders had come.

'No!' Brad screamed desperately, diving after it.

Oisín raced to the edge. Both Brad and the Book of Magic were caught on a giant cobweb that stretched across the well, several feet below its rim. Pale spiders scurried up, excited at the prospect of an early dinner. They weren't the only ones: all the spiders left Ben and scuttled over towards his brother, who promised to be a juicier meal.

Oisín bent over the side and tried to reach Brad's hand. Whatever Brad had done, he was only sixteen; Oisín had to help.

'Throw me your baseball,' Oisín shouted, thinking quickly. 'I'll cut through the thread.'

'No,' Brad said, clutching onto his *croíacht*. His other hand grasped at the Book of Magic, inches away on the cobweb. He twisted his body desperately, oblivious to the spiders crawling towards him, looking only at the Book of Magic.

'I do have power,' he whispered to himself, as his fingers reached the Book's leather spine.

This was also the moment that the giant spider reached the cobweb.

'Dude, I created you,' Brad said, his blue eyes suddenly scared.

The spiders of Cnoc na gCnámh were not known for their loyalty, however, so the giant spider had no hesitation in rolling Brad up in thread.

'I do have power!' Brad screamed as the other spiders gripped onto him and pulled him down. His hand reached for the Book of Magic but the spiders were strong and he disappeared into the dark in seconds. There were some terrible crunching sounds and then two expensive black leather shoes were thrown up from the bottom, as if the spiders hadn't found them terribly appetising.

The Book of Magic remained on the cobweb, perfectly serene.

Oisín felt a chill as the Morrígan walked over to the edge of the well and stood beside him. He turned to her, horrified.

'You knew what would happen. You wanted him to die.'

The Morrígan just smiled and stared at the Book.

'It's mine,' Oisín said before she could do anything.

He wasn't sure if it would still work. He was still its Keeper, though, so the Book shook off the thread and sailed into his hands.

The Morrígan suppressed a scream and twisted her face into a grimace.

'We're alike, you know,' she said. 'We're the only people who understand the Book.'

Oisín felt a chill down his spine watching the Morrígan smile as if they were the best of friends. Even scarier was the warm feeling as the Book snuggled in his palm. Even after everything that had happened, after he had seen Brad Washington die for it, he still felt a connection to the Book.

'Its power will be even greater if you give it to me,' the Morrígan said silkily. 'I'd still let you use it. We're friends, after all.'

'I saw what happened to your last friend,' Oisín said.

'Poor Brad,' the Morrígan said. 'It's not my fault if siblings treat each other terribly. Somebody's always left out. It makes them very easy to convince. Your sister was one of the quickest friends I've made.'

Oisín felt sick. 'Where is she?' he shouted.

He knew from the Morrígan's smile that Stephen hadn't freed her. Oisín looked around the cavern and shouted as loudly as he could.

'Sorcha! Sorcha!'

A sad echo reverberating off bone was the only answer.

'You really think you've come to rescue her?' the Morrígan said.

'Yes,' Oisín said, standing as tall as he could.

'But you don't need to rescue her. She can leave any time.'

It wasn't just the sickly honey tone of her voice that troubled Oisín – it was the sight of the girl who came walking into the chamber.

'There you are, sweetie,' the Morrígan said, making her way over to the little girl and stroking her hair.

'Sorcha?' Oisín said.

'Look at my new toy,' Sorcha said, swinging a sword.

Oisín caught his breath. She was holding An Freagarach. It was far too big for her and glinted dangerously in the gloom of the cave.

'Sorcha, come over here,' Oisín said.

There was something strange about her. She seemed healthy but her eyes were vacant. Her ankle scar had grown deeper.

'I told you they'd try and ruin your fun,' the Morrígan said, stroking Sorcha's hair. The sight of her touching Sorcha made Oisín bristle with anger.

'Let go of her!' he shouted.

'Can I have the Book?' Sorcha said, eyeing the Book of Magic greedily.

'Of course, sweetie,' the Morrígan said, still stroking her hair. 'Once I'm its Keeper, I'll let you use the Book whenever you want. But first your brother has to release the Book to me.'

A cold smile returned to the Morrígan's face.

'It's just a little name,' she said. 'Just a little detail.'

The Book of Magic flapped its pages until it reached the inscription which proclaimed Oisín its Keeper. The creature drawn on the page stretched out its tongue until it became a small pen.

Oisín looked down at the words in front of him, the words that had changed his life: *To Oisín Keane, the Keeper of the Book of Magic.* Could he really give it away?

'Just a little name, that's all it is.'

A memory lurched in the back of Oisín's brain. 'Remember your name,' Granny Keane had said, just before the DART had left Pearse station. The great elk had said the same thing in the Forest of Shadows. What did his name mean?

'Oisín, my little deer,' Granny Keane used to say when he was a baby, stroking his curls fondly. 'My little deer, Oisín the gentle.' Was he supposed to turn into a deer? Could he grow antlers? Was he supposed to be gentle?

The Morrígan tapped her fingernails against her cloak.

'Not feeling so generous?' she said.

With one motion of her hand, a different set of spiders appeared, carrying a large item wrapped tightly in their silken thread. It was Stephen. He was wrapped tight as a mummy, but still breathing.

'The finest warrior in Ireland!' The Morrígan laughed nastily. She bent down to Sorcha as if they were the best of friends. 'Remember what we talked about, sweetie?'

A strange expression passed across Sorcha's face and she nodded.

'No!' Oisín cried as Sorcha held up her heavy sword.

He picked up the pen. He could feel the Book fluttering in his palms.

'Don't give it to her,' Stephen yelled, looking at the sword held above him and not flinching.

'They don't believe you. They don't think you're strong enough, but I know you are.'

185

Oisín tried to catch Sorcha's eyes, but they were somewhere far away. The sword hung heavy in her hands. Oisín felt the weight of the Book of Magic in his own hands, its black lines pulsing in anticipation. He didn't have any choice.

'Don't do it,' Stephen repeated.

Oisín could barely hear him. Words were whirling in his head. *Remember your name. Oisín the little deer, Oisín the gentle.* Granny Keane's voice mixed in with Cassandra Quicksilver's. *The dearest of the deer will be lost. What would be kept must be given away.*

Oisín picked up the pen and started to write. The inscription he had read in Granny Keane's study started to disappear as the Book got a new Keeper. The Morrígan's eyes gleamed in triumph. She held out her palm. The Book of Magic floated to her, a child running over to its mother. The Morrígan clasped it in her pale hands and almost purred with satisfaction. She turned to Sorcha.

'Now, sweetie, why don't we do what we talked about?'

'I gave you the Book,' Oisín shouted, desperate.

'Do it,' the Morrígan commanded.

Stephen looked into Oisín's eyes before his own closed. Sorcha raised the sword high in the air and drove down An Freagarach with all of her strength.

Chapter 23
Into the Book

Oisín turned away as Sorcha raised the sword. He couldn't bear to watch. Instead, he found himself gazing into the Morrígan's triumphant green eyes. She had the Book of Magic. She had twisted Sorcha's mind. She had won.

Then the terrible smile on her face switched. Her beautiful face made more sense when she was angry – it finally matched her eyes. Oisín allowed himself to turn around and saw what had made her furious: instead of killing Stephen, Sorcha had freed him. She held up An Freagarach proudly, threads of sliced cobweb dangling from its blade.

Sorcha turned to the Morrígan and said in a steely voice, 'I knew my brothers would come. Sweetie.'

The Morrígan didn't just look furious, she looked suddenly lonely. She grasped the Book and flicked to the inscription.

'You dare to resist the Keeper of the Book of Magic?'

It happened again, the same twist that turned her cruel smile into something worse. Where the inscription had once read: *For Oisín Keane, the Keeper of the Book of Magic*, it now read: *For everyone, the Keepers of the Book of Magic*.

The Morrígan stared at the Book, horrified. She didn't notice Stephen moving stealthily around the room, cutting the cobwebs that bound the other children. She didn't notice Caoimhe running over to Ben Washington and pressing ashgrass into his chest. She had eyes only for the Book.

'The Book has been with me too long,' she said grimly, plucking a feather from her cloak. 'It will do what I want.'

She pressed her quill into the Book and Oisín saw a familiar thin black line cobwebbing across a page. From the corner of his eye, Oisín could see Stephen edging closer with An Freagarach, Antimony loading her slingshot, Lysander coiling his tie. He ignored them all and faced the Morrígan.

'You're wrong,' he said. 'The Book isn't good or evil. It's how you read it that matters.'

'Or how you write it,' she said with a smile, stabbing her feather into the parchment.

Oisín couldn't help recoiling as the Book of Magic shook. He still felt attached to it, as if an invisible string ran between them. The Morrígan was right. If she continued to write on the Book, she would be able to control it.

At the moment, though, it wasn't the Morrígan who was controlling the Book of Magic. Silver sparks shot out of a calculator on the ground and the small book slowly increased in size. It must have dropped out of Brad's pocket when he had attacked the Morrígan. Oisín picked it up and realised what had happened. Brad had been pointing the calculator at the Book earlier, trying to increase its size. It hadn't worked because Oisín had been the book's Keeper. Now that *everybody* was the Book's Keeper, the calculator's magic was taking hold and the Book was growing as surely as the tiny spider had.

Soon the small book was the size of Granny Keane's volume of Shakespeare. Moments later it was too large for the Morrígan to hold. The Book kept growing, stretching across the chamber of skulls until each letter was almost as large as Oisín. Oisín scrambled on top of its pages, before he was buried underneath.

Stephen gripped An Freagarach, irritated.

'I almost had her,' he grumbled.

In the chaos, the Morrígan had run off into a different part of the Book. Oisín surveyed the landscape. It wasn't only the dimensions of the Book that had changed, but those of the whole chamber, as if Cnoc na gCnámh had been waiting for this moment. Oisín felt as if he had been suddenly transported to the ocean. All he could see for miles was the same scenery: gleaming walls of bone and a floor of creamy parchment.

'The idiot didn't know what he was doing,' Raqib said. 'You can't mess with magical mathematics in a space like this. It wasn't even his *croíacht*, who knows what's going to happen. Ben, do something!'

'He's barely breathing,' Caoimhe said, continuing to push ashgrass onto Ben's wound.

'It's OK,' Lysander said. 'I don't think the magic can last that long, not without anybody controlling it. And it might actually help us.'

He pulled out his own *croíacht*, a silver watch, and addressed it grandly.

'*Stylus.*'

The many hands of Lysander's watch started to lengthen, branching off in several directions. Lysander picked one off and hurled it to Oisín.

'*Eloquentia sagitta,*' Lysander said with a smile. 'Or, as you might say, the pen is mightier than the sword.'

Oisín looked at the bottom of the watch hand and saw that it had a nib. Lysander picked up his own pen and pressed it into the parchment. Thin silver writing curled across the pages.

Oisín turned to the others. 'He's right. All of us are Keepers now. We have to write good magic to stop the Morrígan. The Book of Magic isn't good or evil – it's just the way you write it.'

He guided the pen across the pages as if it were a rake. '*Fás,*' he said hopefully, picking the first Earth Magic enchantment that he remembered.

The grass shot up in a sudden burst, peeking out through the pages and stretching to the edges of the Book. The others looked over in amazement. It was the magnifying power of Cnoc na gCnámh: any magic was much bigger than usual. Lysander hurled several large pens, as if they were spears, to the other Wrens.

'Come on, write,' Oisín cried.

He could hear a rumbling in the distance. The Morrígan wasn't far away.

Tom was the first to start, writing Earth Magic in rich green ink. Caoimhe smudged some of the ashgrass into her own *croíacht* pen and rubbed it across the paper. Grey grass started to grow, sprouting beautiful fire flowers.

'That's it!' Oisín said, smiling as the Book of Magic was being transformed under his feet. Antimony drew dragons in sparkling orange ink. Raqib wrote the formulas for some of his chemical experiments in tiny red writing. Even Sorcha was writing, dancing across the Book with her pen and using it to cross out the black cracks the Morrígan had made.

'Watch out!' Oisín cried as one of the cracks started to widen.

Sorcha pirouetted out of the way just in time. It was as if an earthquake was rumbling through the Book. The black lines the Morrígan made stretched towards them terribly, disappearing deep into the crevices of the Book.

That wasn't all the Morrígan had been doing. Oisín turned in horror as he saw the advancing army. It wasn't the ravens in the sky that bothered him. It was the horde of enormous albino spiders, scurrying towards them and stabbing the Book with their legs as they went. They had expanded along with the Book and each of their legs had the same venom as the Morrígan's quill, leaving a spindly black trail on the Book as they shuffled across.

'Oisín!'

Sorcha grabbed Oisín's hoodie as another large crack opened in the parchment. Oisín was surprised how strong she was. She'd grown up in the month they'd been apart. He supposed that Cnoc na gCnámh could do that to you.

'Nice work, Sorcha,' Stephen said, patting her on the shoulder. 'Look after Shortskittles, will you? I've got a job to do.'

Before Oisín could respond, the page they were standing on started to rise as if it was being blown by the wind. Stephen slashed a hole in the parchment and jumped through to the next page. Oisín felt a pang at the Book of Magic being ripped apart. Another page rose and Stephen cut another hole into the Book.

'She's moving the pages,' Oisín said, starting to understand. 'She's trying to get to the inscription. She still wants to re-write it.'

And she still can, Oisín thought with horror. If he had made everybody the Book's Keeper, did that mean that anybody could change it? He grabbed Sorcha's hand and rushed after Stephen, ducking through the tear in the paper as another page furled down. The other Wrens followed them so as not to get squashed under the falling pages, Lysander and Raqib carrying Ben. Before long, they had reached the first page, the one with the inscription on it.

The Morrígan faced them in the distance. Surrounded by her army of ravens and spiders, she had never looked more terrifying.

Oisín struggled to find his feet, feeling sick and dizzy. A tremendous battle was under way. Some of the pictures from the Book had come to life and were fighting the Morrígan's army. Shimmering serpents and bright red birds launched themselves at ravens and spiders. The Morrígan didn't seem to mind when one of her army died. Oisín remembered what Granny Keane had told them: the Morrígan had flown around the old battles of Ireland, cheering both sides on. She didn't care who won or lost so long as she had some bones to bring back to her chamber. Oisín caught sight of Tom befriending some of the spiders and leading them away from the battle. He realised what he had to do.

He ran as quickly as he could. The calculator's magic was wearing off. Slowly, the Book of Magic was returning to its usual size. Oisín leapt across a shrinking crevice and reached the Morrígan. Stephen had just beaten him to it and was duelling the Morrígan with An Freagarach. Even the Morrígan's quill was no match for An Freagarach and it snapped in two. Stephen held out the sword against the Morrígan's neck. She smiled in surprise.

'You'll do what none of the others could do,' the Morrígan said, a strange expression in her eyes. 'Ferdia, Naoise, Fionn. None of them managed to kill me. You would be the greatest warrior in Ireland.'

Stephen held the sword steady. He could do it, he told himself. This was the woman who had kidnapped his sister. This was the woman who believed in everything evil. His was the only sword that could kill her. All it would take was one flick of his wrist and she'd be gone for ever. It was that easy.

'Do it,' the Morrígan said in a soft voice, staring deep into Stephen's eyes.

'No!'

Stephen turned and looked at his little brother.

'It's what she wants,' Oisín said.

He understood the way the Morrígan operated now. She existed to inspire violence in others. That was why she encouraged Brad to attack his brother, why she wanted Sorcha to stab Stephen when she could easily have done it herself.

'All she wants is for people to kill each other,' Oisín said. 'She just wants death. She doesn't even care if it's her own.'

Stephen's sword quavered.

'You're going to listen to him?' the Morrígan said in a hard voice. 'You really think there wouldn't be death if it wasn't for me? All I have to do is whisper in somebody's ear and they'll pick up the knife and plunge it into their parents. That's all I did to Brad Washington. Whispered that he'd never be as good as his brother or the other Quints. Didn't take too long to convince him. All of human life is pain and suffering. I'm the only person who's honest enough to admit it.'

Oisín looked into her eyes without a trace of fear. The words that had been clashing inside of him tumbled out of his mouth.

'You're wrong. All you see in this world is pain and suffering because that's all you know.'

'I know you,' she said. 'You're nothing without the Book.'

'And I know you. You didn't have to *pretend* to be the Keeper of Books on *Eachtra*. The truth is you really are a lonely old woman.'

The words were like a slap in the face to the Morrígan. She stepped back from the sword, her beautiful face as pale as bone.

'I will destroy you,' she said in a voice as cold as any Oisín had ever heard.

Stephen held An Freagarach. Oisín stepped forward. The Morrígan couldn't be beaten with a sword, not really. She'd just shape-shift into a shadow, she'd find another way to spread evil. As long as there were swords being made and people willing to hold them, there would always be ugliness and fighting in the world. Oisín understood: Stephen might kill the Morrígan, but once he had used An Freagarach to kill, he would destroy himself. Oisín took one last step, placed both of his feet in front of the Morrígan and looked up to meet his older brother's stare.

'Get out of my way,' Stephen said.

'No,' Oisín said firmly.

Oisín had never really looked into his brother's eyes. Usually Stephen was trying to push him. Usually Oisín was trying to duck. Standing on the Book of Magic, though, as the pages shrank beneath them and ravens flapped above them, both of them stood firm, looking at the stubborn person in front of them. Oisín couldn't say if it lasted a millisecond or a millennium. Then Stephen moved his arm. Instead of pushing Oisín, he let An Freagarach fall to the ground.

That was when the Morrígan laughed, a sound to curdle all hope.

Oisín felt the pain immediately. As Stephen had dropped An Freagarach its tip brushed against Oisín's side. It was the tiniest of touches, but it was enough: the tip of An Freagarach had stopped many a life before. Oisín looked down and saw blood pooling across his green hoodie. He put his hand to his side and found the gash the sword had made. Stephen's eyes filled with horror.

'I'm fine,' Oisín said, keeping his hands pressed against the seeping wound.

And then everything turned black, the deep black of the bottom of a well, the kind of black that stretched hungrily into for ever.

Chapter 24
Escape

Antimony loaded her slingshot with another skull and aimed at the raven diving towards her.

'Eighteen,' she said as it dropped to the ground.

She was finding the battle strangely exhilarating, a nice break from all the complicated feelings she'd been struggling with. She kicked at the giant spider that tried to ambush her from behind and grabbed another skull to launch at its eye. She waited until it had turned red and released.

'Nineteen,' she said as the spider keeled backwards.

The Book of Magic had shrunk to its normal size but some of the spiders refused to return to their regular form and the battle continued in the Morrígan's chamber. Antimony hadn't seen what had happened to Oisín and Stephen. It was hard to see anything in the swirl of battling bodies.

'Twenty,' she shouted as she managed to knock out another spider with some smoke from her nose.

'Eleven, twelve,' Raqib said as his tie sent two ravens spinning to the ground.

Antimony was keeping score with Lysander and Raqib. Caoimhe was looking after Ben Washington, while Tom was trying to befriend some of the spiders. The Houlihans did not have the right idea about battles, in Antimony's opinion. Even Sorcha was fighting, using her ballet moves to take out some of the smaller spiders.

Raqib dropped some of his spice into the well where the spiders lived and jumped back. There was a huge explosion and a silver cloud mushroomed up, scattering spindly legs across the chamber.

'That has to count for more,' Raqib said.

'Not bad,' Antimony conceded. 'For a Quint.'

'Maybe you'll think before you throw us into a cobweb next time, Ogoni?' Raqib said. 'My side still hurts from where you kicked me.'

'It'll hurt a lot more if you don't pay attention,' Lysander said, flicking his tie at a spider that was about to attack them. 'Fifteen,' he added as it tumbled back into the hole.

Lysander looked at his watch. Its hands were turning rapidly, sensitive to any shift in the magical air.

'Madame Q's here,' he said, looking around the chamber.

Antimony followed his gaze. Two huge ravens had swooped into the chamber. One was sleek and silver, the other was short and black with only one green eye.

'Macha and Badb,' Antimony said, staring at the ravens in awe. The Morrígan hadn't been lying. Madame Q and Mrs Fitzfeather really were shape-shifters. And the Morrígan's sisters.

Lysander wasn't the only one to sense the shift in energy. There was a cry from the far side of the chamber as the Morrígan realised who had entered. She transformed into a large raven in a swirl of feathers. The other two ravens dived towards her, chasing her into a side-chamber.

'We should get everybody back to the library,' Lysander said.

'You can't. The passage is blocked,' another English voice announced.

Antimony was surprised to find that Cassandra Quicksilver had arrived behind them, looking even paler than usual. She must have come with Madame Q and Mrs Fitzfeather.

'Those spiders caused a cave-in,' Cassandra said, knocking out a raven with her scarf. 'It was lucky the wrens got through.'

The wooden wrens from *Eachtra* had also entered the chamber, led by the large statue from *Eachtra*'s prow. Antimony was impressed that the tiny birds could be such fierce fighters.

'We'll get out, though,' Cassandra said, using her telescope to trace a circle on one of the walls. She directed Raqib to sprinkle some of his spice on a skull and handed it to Antimony, who placed it into her slingshot and aimed at the silver circle.

There was another explosion and a blinding burst of daylight. Antimony felt a surge of hope as she saw the sky. It might all be OK.

'We could have used some help earlier,' Lysander said to his sister.

'I've been consulting the prophecy,' Cassandra answered. 'One part keeps coming up: *brother will fight brother.*'

'You might be too late,' Lysander said, looking over at Ben.

'It's not about the Washington brothers,' Cassandra said, looking across the chamber. 'Where's Stephen? And Oisín?'

'They were over there,' Antimony said, feeling her stomach drop as she saw the look on Cassandra's face. 'Stephen has An Freagarach. They'll be OK.'

Cassandra didn't seem to agree and ran in that direction, swishing her scarf at the ravens.

'Come on,' Antimony said, gathering the others. 'We've got to get out of here.'

She raced across the skulls as fast as she could. The pyramid's shape had been disturbed by the Book of Magic's expansion and retraction, so it was like running over a series of uneven hills. On the other side of one of the mounds, Antimony saw why Cassandra was so worried: Stephen was on the ground, crying, holding his brother's body in his arms.

Suddenly the battle didn't seem fun anymore and Antimony didn't care how many spiders she had knocked out. Her stomach plummeted, like an elevator that had forgotten how to stop. She had used *béal tine* to keep the Book on the island. Oisín had saved her in the underwater caves. And now he was dead.

She turned around to face the others.

'Tom, mind Sorcha for a minute. Caoimhe, bring the ash-grass.'

She skidded down the mound, Caoimhe following. It was quieter now that the wrens were battling the ravens. Most of the spiders had followed the Morrígan when she left. It didn't matter though: Oisín's eyes had already glazed over. Caoimhe pressed some ashgrass into his side but Antimony could tell it wasn't working.

Stephen looked up at her, his face red with tears. An Freagarach lay beside him on the ground, a horrible red colour on its tip.

'I didn't mean to,' he sobbed. 'The sword just brushed against him and …'

Tears took over his words and he collapsed on top of his brother, rocking back and forth. Antimony took his hand, tears swelling in her own eyes. She didn't think she had any left but then she thought of Oisín, of how brave he had been against the Morrígan, of how brave everybody was, and down they came, streaking down her cheeks and onto Oisín's chest.

The Keanes would be safely back in Dublin if she'd never used the *béal tine*. She'd destroyed a family by trying to bring back her own, and she hadn't even done that right.

'Wait, something's happening,' Caoimhe said.

Antimony and Stephen looked up.

'His fingers moved,' Caoimhe said.

'Then put on some more ashgrass,' Antimony almost shouted.

'It's not the ashgrass,' Caoimhe said.

'Then what is it?' Stephen asked, looking at Oisín's hand slowly moving.

'Magical tears,' Cassandra answered, suddenly realising. 'Ordinarily, it wouldn't be enough. But in a place with very deep magic, with tears from somebody very close to the person, somebody who felt a lot … it might be enough.'

Another tear rolled down Stephen's cheek and onto Oisín's chest.

The wren pendant on Oisín's chest flickered slightly.

'The wound's closing,' Caoimhe said, kneeling beside them. She extended some aloe vera from her pen and started to rub it across Oisín's chest.

'He's going to be OK?' Stephen said, standing.

'I think so,' Cassandra answered.

Antimony felt a surge of relief. She found her feet uncertainly. Stephen was still shaking, looking like he could use a hug.

It was Cassandra Quicksilver who embraced him, though, wrapping her arms around him tightly.

'*I was so worried*,' she said. 'I was sure the prophecy meant that one of you was going to die.'

'I'm glad you were wrong for once,' Stephen said.

'Well, I suppose he did die for a moment, so the prophecy wasn't technically wrong, but ...'

Cassandra stopped herself, deciding that the prophecy wasn't the most important thing at that moment.

'Oh, Stephen, you were so brave!' she said, wrapping her fingers around his Wren pendant and pulling him towards her.

Antimony stared at them as they started to kiss: they looked very comfortable together, as if it wasn't their first time.

'Er, I'll get the others,' Antimony said, when it became clear that they would be occupied for a while.

Both Tom and Sorcha were very upset to see Oisín's condition and added a good few tears to his wound before Caoimhe convinced them that he would be fine. It took almost as long for Lysander Quicksilver to come to grips with who his sister was dating.

'You've been sneaking off to meet that Milesian muppet?' Lysander said as they clambered through the hole they had made in the wall. '*He*'s who you were meeting in the Forest of Shadows?'

'I hardly think this is the right time to discuss it,' Cassandra said briskly.

She had a point, Antimony thought. The hole led to a narrow ledge on the side of Cnoc na gCnámh. Neither Oisín nor Ben was able to walk, let alone cross Droichead an Chlaímh. Nobody was able to use Ben's calculator *croíacht*, so the Quints weren't able to use magical mathematics to travel. Raqib was doing a good job of holding off the remaining ravens and spiders, but they needed to get off the mountain fast.

In the end, it was Tom who came up with the solution. He convinced some of the spiders he had befriended to weave ropes between two clouds so that they formed a makeshift air-balloon. Raqib did some quick magical chemistry on the bottom cloud so that it would hold their weight and Tom got the wrens to help steer them. It wasn't bad work for somebody who didn't have a *croíacht*.

'Are you sure we can trust those spiders?' Antimony said, as the cloud left the side of Cnoc na gCnámh.

'They're grand,' Tom said, holding the small creatures fondly. 'Just a bit peckish sometimes,' he added as one of them nipped at his arm.

Antimony leant back into the soft cloud. The sun was setting and the fire-fields glowed in the dusk. Caoimhe was looking after Ben Washington and Oisín. Stephen was holding a sleeping Sorcha. Lysander was too busy arguing with Raqib about who had killed more ravens to notice that his sister's arm was looped around Stephen.

Nobody had said anything about Antimony stealing the Book. She supposed Mrs Fitzfeather would, when they got back. She'd probably have to leave *Eachtra*. And the Houli-hans. Nobody would want to be associated with somebody who'd done the kind of dark magic she had.

She stood up. The cloud had drifted off towards the north-west volcanoes, where the fire dragons lived. Tom was helping the wrens steer them back towards *Eachtra*. Caoimhe had come over to suggest a quicker route.

'Can you get them to drop me off here?' Antimony asked, interrupting their argument.

If she had to go it alone, she might as well be somewhere she could use her Fire Magic. And after Scathach's training she was sure she could tackle a dragon or two.

Tom and Caoimhe looked puzzled.

'I can't go back to *Eachtra*,' Antimony said. 'Not after what I did.'

'You took the Book of Magic to bring back your parents, didn't you?' Caoimhe said after a moment.

Antimony nodded. She had definitely cried enough for one day.

'But you gave it back,' Tom said. 'You did the right thing when it mattered.'

He looked at the spiders playing hopscotch along his arm.

'I think everybody has some good in them,' Tom said quietly.

Antimony wasn't sure if she agreed, but she didn't say anything. Their cloud drifted over the volcano, meandering slowly towards the fire-fields. They could just make out *Eachtra* in the distance, a host of strange colours in the middle of the ash. Antimony was surprised at how affectionate she felt towards it.

'Anyway,' Tom said in a brighter voice, 'I need a sibling who doesn't treat me like a petri-dish.'

'Mum and Dad will definitely let you stay,' Caoimhe said. 'And if they don't, I'm sure I can find a potion that can make them.'

'They have to let you stay,' Tom said. 'They didn't kick Caoimhe out after she turned Granda Houlihan's head into a pumpkin when he had a cold.'

'That was only for a day!' Caoimhe protested.

'He *still* turns orange when he sneezes,' Tom countered.

'Yeah, well, remember the time your cute little baby wolf nearly ate me?'

'You were probably talking too much.'

Antimony let the Houlihans argue and settled back down into the cloud. They weren't the worst brother and sister you could hope for. And she could probably let the fire dragons live for another year or two.

Antimony watched the sun set over Cnoc na gCnámh, far in the distance now, and, for the first time in a long while, she fell asleep without a single worry.

Chapter 25
The Last DART

Oisín stood at the top of the Houlihans' treehouse and looked out at the two strange vehicles below. The first was in many ways the stranger. No matter how many times you looked at *Eachtra*, there were always surprises: the way the coloured sails tickled each other when they thought nobody was looking or the one bicycle wheel that liked to change into a triangle when it wasn't moving (or, if it was feeling grumpy, even when it *was* moving).

Eachtra certainly looked a bit out of place in the Houlihans' garden. It had arrived two days ago and the Houlihans had let Mrs Fitzfeather keep it there so they could all celebrate the Lughnasa festival. Technically, it was over a week too late but Madame Q gave a big speech about how time moved in different streams for different people and everybody agreed with that, mostly because Jimmy Houlihan had brewed a big vat of moonmead that nobody wanted to waste.

The festival had been one of the best nights of Oisín's life. All the druids and Wrens from *Eachtra* were there, plus some of the older Wrens who had come back from some of their own summer adventures. Cathleen Houlihan had set up a small oak stage and a band of Wrens had played: Orion Jones on his flute, Billy Lewis with his air guitar and Yuriko Ada on a fine set of toadstool drums. Oisín practised the Bollywood moves that Granny Keane had taught him with Cassandra Quicksilver before Cassandra danced with Stephen in a way that required much closer contact.

Everybody had stayed up until the early hours of the morning, eating platters of Jimmy's seafood stew and sipping cool moonjuice. The band played for several hours and by the end of the night the ground was covered with dozing musical notes. Somebody even claimed to have seen Madame Q's shoes tapping in time to the music.

Oisín could still see some of the fireworks that Graciela Gambaro had enchanted, fizzling on the ground. He couldn't believe that Lughnasa was over and it was time to go home.

The second vehicle outside certainly wasn't as odd as *Eachtra*, but somehow the bright green DART carriage looked stranger to Oisín now. He had spent so long with the Tuatha Dé Danann that he had almost forgotten what a train was. The DART carriage hadn't forgotten about them, though, and it was waiting on the beach where they'd left it, ready to take them back to Dublin.

Oisín clutched the wren pendant around his neck, not exactly sure how he felt about going home.

'Room for an old lady on that branch? Tom said you were still up here.'

Oisín turned around to see Mrs Fitzfeather climbing up the ladder into Tom's bedroom. She walked over to the branch that Oisín was standing on, which gave such a good view.

'Sure,' Oisín said, sitting down beside her.

'Now, boy, I know you're tired,' she said, her gruff voice making a stab at being gentle. 'But I thought it would be good to have a quick chat before you head off.'

They hadn't really spoken since they'd got back from Cnoc na gCnámh. Oisín knew that the Morrígan had escaped, but that Madame Q and Mrs Fitzfeather had rescued the Book of Magic. He sensed that Mrs Fitzfeather didn't really want to talk about what had happened that day, even now.

'Remember I told your parents that you were at the Gaeltacht in the letter I wrote?' she reminded him. 'So you should probably practise some Irish on the train home.'

'Right,' Oisín said. He had learnt some Irish words, but he wasn't sure that knowing how to say 'The Mountain of Wind' or 'The Bridge of the Sword' would be much use in school.

'Your wound is still healing OK?' Mrs Fitzfeather asked.

'Yeah,' Oisín said. 'Caoimhe was great at stitching it up.'

'I heard somebody else didn't do too badly,' Mrs Fitzfeather said in a soft voice.

Oisín blushed. 'I was the one who spent every day having tea with the Morrígan in the first place.'

'And you were the one who was able to break away from her. Only a very strong-hearted person would be able to do that. It took me a long time.'

Mrs Fitzfeather looked out through the branches and when her eyes turned back to Oisín they seemed a lot older.

'I suppose the Morrígan told you about our relationship?'

It came out as a question, but Oisín could tell that Mrs Fitzfeather knew the answer before he nodded his head.

'It's not something I usually tell Wrens about,' Mrs Fitzfeather said, slowly loosening her shawls. 'But I suppose you have earned the truth.'

Very slowly, Mrs Fitzfeather peeled off her shawls until Oisín saw what was underneath: a mass of black feathers where her chest should have been. She lifted up her eyepatch to reveal another green eye – one that belonged unmistakably to a bird.

'A long time ago I did some things that I'm not proud of,' she said, wrapping her shawls back around her and replacing her eyepatch. 'Eventually I saw what should have been clear long before: that, as well as being one of the most powerful witches in the country, my sister was also the most evil. When I left her to found *Eachtra*, this is how she cursed me.'

'And Madame Q went with you?'

'B came later,' Mrs Fitzfeather said, her voice retaining its usual frost when she spoke of Madame Q. 'But I didn't come here to talk about my past.'

She pulled something else out of her shawls and held out the Book of Magic.

'For many, many centuries the Book of Magic has been passed from Keeper to Keeper and up to now nobody has had the courage to give it away. It takes somebody very brave to give up all the power in the world.'

'I nearly didn't,' Oisín admitted, remembering the feeling of the Book in his hands, how he had wanted to keep it for ever.

'You did, though, and that's what matters,' Mrs Fitzfeather said. 'You did the one thing the Morrígan couldn't understand: share.'

She placed the Book on the bed beside Oisín. It was its normal size again, small enough to fit in his palm. It looked very different from the book that had jumped into his hands in Granny Keane's study. Lots of holes marked its pages, the spots where Stephen had slashed through. The writing was even harder to read than before and in a variety of new colours: Caoimhe's smudges with ashgrass, Antimony's orange ink, tiny inscriptions in silver that Lysander had left at the corners. The biggest change, though, was the thin black cracks that stretched across every page. Oisín gazed into their shadowy depths and felt a chill pass through him.

'It's evil now, isn't it?' he said, looking at the cracks in the Book of Magic.

'I wouldn't say that,' Mrs Fitzfeather said carefully. 'It's a bit more damaged, but it's the same as always. It has the potential to do good or evil. It's the Keeper who decides.'

Oisín turned to the front page and saw that the words he had written in were still there: *For everybody, the Keepers of the Book of Magic.*

'I'm not the Keeper any more,' he said, putting the Book down.

'No, my boy, you're not,' Mrs Fitzfeather agreed.

Oisín felt a little strange, as if he had both lost and gained something. He didn't have a *croíacht* any more. Then again, Brad had died trying to get a better *croíacht*. Tom did all right without one. And what would Oisín need a *croíacht* for in Dublin? He returned the Book to Mrs Fitzfeather.

'Are you going to keep the Book?' he asked.

'We've all discussed the matter. And despite what *some* people think...' Mrs Fitzfeather paused and Oisín had the distinct impression that 'some people' meant Madame Q. 'Most of us have decided that the Book belongs in the library. People will still be able to look at it, but a lot of its power has been diluted now. It's no longer dangerous for other people to hold. If you agree, of course. Technically, you're no longer the Keeper of the Book, but it seemed right to check with you.'

Oisín nodded.

'You can still come and visit it from time to time, if you wish.'

Oisín looked back at her in confusion.

'Oh,' she said, 'perhaps the Houlihans' sink is clogged. The message should have gone out a few days ago, but everybody has been understandably busy. In any case, you have been accepted as a Wren again for next summer. It'll be a different adventure, chance to work on your Water Magic, but I'd say that after tackling the Morrígan you'll be ready for it.'

Oisín felt as if his brain was still asleep and struggling to catch up.

'What do you mean? How can I come back? I have to go to school.'

'We'll work it out, boy,' Mrs Fitzfeather said airily. 'The voyage doesn't start until after Bealtaine, in the summer. It'll be over by Lughnasa, so you should still be able to go to your Milesean school.'

Oisín felt a surge of joy and almost leapt across to hug Mrs Fitzfeather. He wouldn't have to leave the island for ever. He could come back and stay with the Houlihans and –

Oisín's heart dropped. Something was still troubling him.

'But …,' he started, struggling to find the words. 'I can't do magic. It was just the Book. I won't be any use on board *Eachtra* without it.'

Mrs Fitzfeather shook her head. 'Anybody can read a book. It's what you do afterwards that matters.'

'But I don't even know what I want to do,' Oisín started, feeling panic ride up his chest. 'Caoimhe knows she wants to be a druid-doctor and Tom knows that he likes Earth Magic, but there's not one thing I'm really good at, or better than the others at. I'm not really good at anything. So what good would I be on *Eachtra*?'

Mrs Fitzfeather squeezed his hand gently.

'Now, boy, don't be daft. Who was it that solved the riddle in Ogham? Or made a snowstorm in the underwater caves? Or thought to turn into the wind to get up Sliabh na Gaoithe?'

'That was the Book of Magic.'

'The Book of Magic is only what you make of it. Everything you did came from your brain, not the Book.'

Mrs Fitzfeather let go of his hand and smiled.

'And as for not knowing what you want to do, I wouldn't worry about that. Plenty of people don't know what they want to do at sixty, so I shouldn't worry too much about it at twelve. I started off thinking I'd do Air Magic and then I got very excited about Fire Magic for a while and it was only much later that I discovered that it was really Earth Magic that worked for me.'

'And Madame Q? Did she always do Quintessence?'

'That is something you would have to ask her,' Mrs Fitzfeather said, standing up and pulling her shawls around her. 'Come along now, we should really get you on that train. And I should look after the horses. I have a feeling that some of them had a little too much moonmead last night.'

Oisín managed to find some room in his whirl of feelings to be amused at the sight of Mrs Fitzfeather squeezing onto the bamboo slide and whizzing down to the Houlihans' garden.

Oisín followed her and walked through the forest to the beach.

'Pip!'

Oisín turned to see Lysander Quicksilver leaning against a tree and biting into a silver apple.

'I see you came prepared,' Oisín said.

'Seaweed stew doesn't agree with my constitution. So old Fitzfeather's Senior letting you come back to *Eachtra*? One day you might make it into Quintessence and actually do something useful.'

'Maybe,' Oisín said, wondering whether or not he wanted to be a Quint.

'What did you write in the Book?' he asked Lysander. 'It was too small for me to read.'

'One day you'll understand.'

'Something about the mysteries of the universe?'

A strange smile passed across Lysander's face.

'Careful, Pipsqueak. You become too smart and I'll have to find you a different name.'

'You could try Oisín.'

Before Lysander could retort, Tom came running up, Giant at his side.

'Come on, Oisín, they're all waiting,' Tom said, eyeing Lysander suspiciously. The boundless sympathy Tom had for all living creatures seemed to stop at Quints.

'See you next year, Pip,' Lysander said as Oisín followed Tom.

Tom had managed to convince his parents to keep some of the pale spiders (Cathleen relented, as the thread was quite useful for some of her inventions), so they had to negotiate a series of webs as they made their way to the beach.

The others were waiting by the DART.

'You're sure you don't want to take some lavender and nettle stew for your parents?' Jimmy said, holding out a large container.

'I don't think it will keep,' Stephen said, hoping that his face looked appropriately regretful.

'Come on, let's get you off before Jimmy gets any other ideas,' Cathleen said.

There was a lot of hugging. Caoimhe gave Oisín a list of Milesian herbs that she wanted him to bring back from Ireland. Antimony apologised to Sorcha for maybe the hundredth time. Cassandra gave Stephen a long hug and told him that she was researching ways that Water Mail could reach Milesian taps. Finally, it was time to go.

After a month aboard *Eachtra*, with its sock-ladders, glass lifts and magic doors, it felt odd to press the red rubber circle that opened the DART. Oisín stepped inside.

Tom, Caoimhe and Antimony watched sadly as the train pulled off, running to the edge of the beach and waving furiously as it disappeared underwater.

Oisín gazed at the strange assortment of fish and seaweed that drifted by the window and remembered how alien it had all seemed several weeks ago.

'Bye, fishies,' Sorcha called, pressing her nose against the window and waving. She flopped back into her seat and sighed contentedly.

'That Mrs Featherfitz lady –'

'Fitzfeather,' Stephen said with a small sigh.

'That feather lady said I was so brave I could probably be a Wren one day,' Sorcha continued. 'But I don't think I'll go next year. They don't have any television on *Eachtra* and there's no way I'm missing another summer of TV.'

She rested her head back against the window and smiled, thinking of all the things she could do when she got home. Stephen was doing the same thing. Oisín remembered how eager Stephen had been to get home the first day they had washed up on the beach. He wasn't so sure how he felt now. Stephen had left his sword with Scathach the night before. Mrs Fitzfeather had talked to him about returning as a Wren too, but he had decided not to. He had an odd expression on his face as the train drifted further and further from the Tuatha Dé Danann, as if, now that he was finally going home, he wasn't sure that he wanted to.

Oisín hadn't talked to him about what had happened inside the Book of Magic when they had both faced the Morrígan. Neither of them had really talked to Sorcha about her time with the Morrígan either. But they all felt a strange current between them, as if the past few weeks had bound them together in a way that was even deeper than blood.

The DART passed through the forest of misty seaweed and started to move upwards. Soon it was tilting back and making its way up the cliff towards Howth Head. Oisín, Stephen and Sorcha leant back as if they were on a rollercoaster but none of them said anything. They knew it would be OK.

Moments later, the DART was pulling into Howth station, as if there was no other place it would rather end up on a drizzly Sunday morning. Oisín wasn't sure what the train attendant was more confused by the sight of a DART carriage without any engine or driver or Granny Keane, standing on the platform in a bright summer dress and fluorescent pink raincoat, her long white hair blowing in the August air. Oisín smiled when he saw her. He wondered how much she knew about the Tuatha Dé Danann and whether she had ever been on the strange DART herself. There were always more questions, he supposed.

'Ready, Sorcha?' Stephen said, standing up and holding a hand out to his sister. Sorcha leapt up and bounded over to the door, pressing her finger against the red circle.

Oisín stayed on the seat for a moment. He felt the way he sometimes did when their car pulled into its destination after a long trip: excited to be somewhere and also so comfortable that he wished they could just keep driving for another five minutes, that the trip wouldn't have to end. Stephen walked over and put his hand on Oisín's shoulder.

'You ready, mate? Oisín?'

Maybe it wasn't the first time that Stephen had called Oisín by his real name instead of 'Peabrain' or 'Dogbreath'. But it was the first time Oisín remembered and it was the first time Oisín felt that he had a friend as well as a brother. He zipped up his hoodie and stood beside Stephen.

'Yeah.' He nodded as the doors slipped open. 'Yeah, I am.'

The three children stepped onto the platform, so happy to be home that they didn't notice the green DART slinking away behind them. The train attendant wondered if he had been doing too much overtime. If somebody had told him that magic was involved he probably would have decided that they'd had a bit too much whiskey and gone back to worrying about how the new ticket machine had got jammed again, which was a real mystery worth considering, in his opinion. He decided not to think about it: ordinary trains didn't move by themselves.

Except sometimes they did, Oisín thought, as he walked past the bewildered man and smiled at Granny Keane, who returned a twinkling grin of her own.

Sometimes the world wasn't ordinary at all, and he quite liked it that way.

Irish words and names

The pronunciations given here are only a rough guide, because Irish (Gaeilge) sounds are not really very like English ones. When *ch* is used here, don't sound it as in 'church,' but as in 'Loch Ness' or 'chutzpah'. Also, *th* is used here to indicate a sound softer than an English *t* but not as soft as an English *th*.

An Freagarach: The Retaliator; pronounce *on fragag-roch*

Badb: pronounce *Bav*

Bealtaine: the Celtic summer festival, 1 May; also the name of the whole month of May; pronounce *Bal-thin-ah*

béal tine: mouth of fire; pronounce *bail thin-ah*

Caoimhe: pronounce *Kweeva*

Cathad: pronounce *Ca-ha*

Cliodhna: pronounce *Clee-unna*

Cluaiscín: pronounce *clue-ish-keen*

Cnoc na gCnámh: Hill of Bones; pronounce *K'nuck na G'nawv*

Croíacht: a magical object; pronounce *cree-ucht*

déan deifir: hurry up; pronounce *dane deffer*

Deirdre of the Sorrows: a famous beauty of Irish legend who was doomed from birth and was the cause of the death of her lover and his warrior brothers; pronounce her name *Dear-dra* or *Dare-dra* (not *Dear-dree*)

dinnseanchas: lore of place, study of placenames; pronouce *din-shan-ach-as*

Droichead an Chláimh: the Bridge of the Sword; pronounce *Drih-had on Chlee-av*

Eachtra: adventure; pronounce *ach-thra*

fás: grow; pronounce *fawce*

Fionn Mac Cumhaill: famous hero of Irish legend; pronounce *Finn Mac Cool*

Gaeltacht: Irish–speaking areas of Ireland; children often go to these places on summer camps, to perfect their Irish; pronounce *gale-thocht* geas (plural geasa): a rule that forbids a person to do something specific; this rule cannot be broken, because it is enforced by magic; pronounce *g'yass* (*g'yassa*)

liathróidí tine: fireballs; pronounce *lee-roady thin-ah*

Linn an Bhróin: Pool of Sadness; pronounce *Lin on Vrone*

Lughnasa: harvest festival, 1 August, also the name of the whole month of August; pronounce *Loo-na-ssa*

Macha: pronounce *Mah-hah*

Medb: pronounce *Mave* (to rhyme with save)

Milesian: pronounce *mile-ee-shun* (This is actually an English word.)

muise: meaningless word, a bit like 'well' in English; pronounce *mush-ah*

Naoise: pronounce *Nee-sha*

Nuala: pronounce *Noo-la*

Ogham: ancient Irish script; pronounce *Ogg-am* or *Oh-am*

Oisín: pronounce *Usheen*

Pádraig: pronounce *Paw-rick* or *Pawd-rig*

rith ar nós na gaoithe: run like the wind; pronounce *rih err noce na gweeha*

scamall: cloud; pronounce *ska-mull*

Scathach: pronounce *Ska-hach*

Sliabh na Gaoithe: Mountain of the Wind; pronounce *Shleeve na Gweeha*

Sorcha: pronounce *Surr'cha*

Spéir. Bogha báistí. An ghriain ag taithneamh: Sky. Rainbow. The sun shining; pronounce *Spare. Boa bawshthy. On green egg tha-niv.*

téigh faoin uisce: go under the water; pronounce *chay* or *thay fween ishka*

Tuatha Dé Danann: people of the goddess Dana; pronounce *thooha day dannan*